MW01712513

Seventh Fire

An Emily Taylor Mystery

Catherine Astolfo

Copyright © 2010 by Catherine Astolfo

All rights reserved. No part of this work covered by the copyrights hereon may be reproduced or used in any form or by any means - graphic, electronic or mechanical, including photocopying, recording, taping or information storage and retrieval systems without the prior written permission of the publisher.

Moe Publications
24 Shenstone Ave.
Brampton, ON
L6Z 2Y8

Canadian Cataloguing in Publication Data
Astolfo, Catherine, 1950-
Seventh Fire
ISBN 978-0-9737273-2-6
1. Fiction. I. Title.
Painting on cover by Helen Duplassie.

Printed and bound in Canada.

This book is a work of fiction. All names, characters, places and incidents either are the product of the author's imagination or are used fictitiously, and any resemblance to actual persons living or dead, events, or locales, is entirely coincidental. Burchill and its inhabitants are fictional. However, if you visit Merrickville - one of the most beautiful towns in Ontario - you'll see the similarities. The sites aroundVancouver, both City and Island, are used fictitiously and some are completely imaginary.

For my best friend, my husband, Vince.

Acknowledgements

I have been extraordinarily blessed in my life, because I have a wealth of family and friends who sustain me. I haven't the space to mention all of them here, but luckily, they know who they are and what they mean to me.

Special thanks to the following:

- My editors: Maire Kearns, Sarah Barkwell, Mary Jo Wiley Dwyer, Kristen Henderson, Frances Daley, Scott Hummel and Vince Astolfo
- Helen Duplassie, *artiste extraordinaire*
- And for making it all possible, for inspiration and unconditional love throughout the writing process, for support, editing and great critiques, my husband, Vince Astolfo, and my children, both by birth and by love.

The legal procedures in the story are based on some research, but please don't take them literally. Langford's case was, after all, fictional.

Chapter One
September, 1980
The Artist

The Artist stood back and admired his masterpiece. At first, he had not felt the rush of inspiration that most often accompanied his best work. Perhaps he had been tired out by all the activity in which he'd indulged before beginning the composition, but a second spurt of energy had surprised him. Flinging the oils against the backdrop, the muse had overtaken him at last. The rush, the thrill of creation, flooded his head, puppetting his hands. Suddenly he was in total control and yet completely out of control. He watched himself as the pattern flourished, the globules became design, the colours burgeoned.

Pinks and yellows and blues blended with the pale background to create a pre-dawn sky that pleased him immensely. The pallet spewed out all over the canvas with wild abandon like an English garden, seemingly disparate pieces and colours coming together in an exquisite array.

Fascinated by the way the liquids combined, he spent a long time watching the paint, mixed with those other fluids, as it seeped slowly downward. As though pulled by an unseen hand, the liquid would bounce back up, leaving just a little bit behind at a time, a bungee cord of ooze.

Finally, he realized that he was exhausted, satiated. Now he could compose himself enough to stand back, to marvel at what he had done. Not only did the composition itself warrant reverence, but his action was also worthy of respect; the moment, the life-changing event, that he alone had put into motion, was beyond his wildest expectations.

With a renewed sense of purpose, he began to pack up his precious brushes and pallet. Only then did he clean up the blood.

Chapter Two
September, 1980

After years of patrolling the infamous Hastings Street and environs, Sergeant Charles Haynes thought that he had seen it all as a police officer in Vancouver, British Columbia. Junkies lying in piss and shit. Women shriveled up into old derelicts, slicing open veins that seemed to leak far more fluid than their bodies could hold. Little kids moaning over a mother – if she could be called that – who had been strangled to death by a 'partner'.

Yet that morning, he was struck by this murder in a way that he had never been affected before. Perhaps it was the incongruously sunny day, a rarity for autumn in this city; or maybe it was the juxtaposition of apparent innocence with a demented touch that drove home the hideousness of the crime. Maybe he simply didn't expect it any more. Most likely, he admitted years later, it was the twisted use of his beloved true calling that awakened an uncontrollable, seething anger.

Charlie had long been generally discontent with his career. Despite the fact that he was good at what he did, he'd spent many years scanning the classifieds to see if he could find another job. He'd never found anything to compare with the stability, the decent pay and benefits, of police work.

Recently, he had acquired a plum assignment by way of seniority and some minor health problems that required his taking it easier. Charlie's territory now exclusively covered the more beautiful, placid areas of the city. Even though the position involved working shifts, Charlie was thrilled that one of his patrols included Granville Island. Surrounded by the water, the mountains shimmering in the distance, Charlie would take his time walking from one end to the other, enjoying the ambience in rain or shine.

By day, the Island was a feast of galleries and boutiques; by night it was a carnival, crammed with pub-crawlers enjoying the fresh air. Over the months, he had gotten to know many of the storeowners, who kept him comfortable with coffee or healthy treats. One of his shifts covered from three in the afternoon until eleven at night, so he enjoyed both the bustle of the shoppers and the enthusiasm of the evening revelers. The other shift, his early morning to afternoon day patrol, gave him the sense of the island as both a shoppers' paradise and a picnic, pleasure font. He felt like an old-fashioned flat foot and enjoyed it immensely.

Slowly, however, Charlie became aware of an underlying depression, similar to the hum of a motor, dismissed as white noise until it begins to misfire. He knew the source of his dissatisfaction immediately, because it was both cause and obsession. Art. Charlie Haynes had only one regret; he had chosen stability over art.

Until now, the regret had been a small, nagging feeling that he rarely allowed himself to consider. He had adored his wife, Joan, from the moment they met in Grade Nine. When, at nineteen years old, she was pregnant, Charlie happily got married. Charlie still considered her his true better half. Policing, at that time, was a career he could enter without post secondary education. Yet it offered both job security and advancement opportunity. Their two daughters and a vigorous yet comfortable life in a nice part of Vancouver were a constant source of delight. The loving partnership with Joan became Charlie's focus.

Lately, with the girls grown, Charlie had begun to regret more fiercely the fact that he hadn't pursued his true calling. When Charlie first began his new assignment, he was as proud of The Emily Carr College of Art and The Three Arts Institute as though he'd been a graduate of both, instead of neither. He spent more hours patrolling past the schools and the studios than perhaps was warranted, thinking that perhaps Fate had led him to the Island. Maybe he was meant to meet an art teacher who would recognize his talent and nurture it. Charlie was well aware that, although he had an innate ability, he needed to learn some techniques. Joan was urging him to consider signing up for courses once he retired. Charlie figured she didn't want him hanging around the house all day, and he tended to agree with that sentiment. In the meantime, he decided to take his hobby more seriously by entering a contest, offered annually by The Three Arts. Losing the contest simply left him more discouraged.

Charlie was, outwardly, a calm, cheerful person, whose personality appeared to fit his occupation just right. He was empathetic, yet could be dispassionate when necessary. He had a quick wit, an uncomplicated smile, and a round cherubic face that had often fooled many suspects. Charlie was very good at interrogations, even when he was cast in the bad cop role. His manner and appearance worked in his favour whenever he was placed on a murder squad, which happened more often than he secretly wished. The irony for Charlie was that every single one of his Captains had singled him out as one of their best. The only complaint ever lodged by his superiors was that Charles Haynes consistently refused any suggestion that he apply for promotions. For Charlie, policing was second choice. He didn't have any ambition to rise above Sergeant.

Charlie was broad shouldered and muscular, though a small paunch had appeared when he turned forty. His knees were his only physical downfall, but ever since he'd undergone surgery, he was able to walk and even run quite well once more. (A fact that he had not broadcast to his superiors, lest they take his Granville patrol away.) With his very blue eyes, his brown wavy hair dusted with grey, and his erect posture, Charlie was an attractive man. The laugh lines around his mouth and eyes only added to his allure.

Many women had found him irresistible, but Charlie had never noticed: he was a one-woman man and Joan never doubted it. Their daughters, born within the first two years of marriage, adored their father and showered him with attention. Last year, they'd both married wonderful young men. He and Joan were now left with the proverbial empty nest.

Charlie had made a lifelong habit of never bringing his home life to work by banning thoughts of his family while on the job. He didn't even mention his wife and children to his partners, for he superstitiously believed that he could prevent them from entering the negative world of crime by not speaking their names or thinking about them in its sphere. When he got the call about the missing girl, however, he did have a brief moment of gratitude that he had never experienced the worry that these parents were obviously feeling.

On the morning of the murder, he patrolled quickly past the cement factory and Micon Industries. The rest of the island was transforming itself at a rapid rate: the craft and music stores, the one-of-a-kind boutiques (including custom-built kayaks), a farmer's market and some pubs had moved in over the last few years. After a dreary, cold wet night, the sun was a welcome change. The air still chilly, Charlie was standing outside one of his favorite new establishments, enjoying a cup of java with frothy cream, when his CB radio squawked.

"Charlie." Officer Stephanie Mills' tone was uncharacteristically cool. She obviously disapproved of this task. "That big shot – I'm sure you've heard of him, his name's Courtnell? He's a friend of Captain Webster and he's throwing a fit over his daughter being AWOL for a few hours. She's only been gone since last night – they *think*, because she doesn't even live with them. She didn't show up for class this morning. She goes to Three Arts. You know we don't usually do this until the standard twenty-four, but Webster says since you're right there..." She paused, as though the young woman realized that Charlie would know the politics of the police force better than she did. "The missing girl is one of the art students and lately she's worked long hours at some studio. Apparently she would never ever skip class." Stephanie's tone dripped with sarcasm. "The only places the family hasn't checked are these studios. No telephones hooked up yet. Apparently the building isn't officially open. It's that old factory they're converting into a fancy market. There're only a couple of artists who've been allowed in early. I've got the manager heading over with a master key. He just happens to be going to a meeting on the Island."

"Why don't they get in touch with the studio owners instead?"

"They're not officially the owners yet and the family doesn't know which professor's studio she might be in. They're teachers at Three Arts and the Courtnell girl has classes with both of them. The roommate wouldn't or couldn't take a guess about where she might be, just told them the girl didn't show up last night or for class this morning. The mom *immediately* called the husband who of course, called the Captain. Probably Webster just wants to get them an answer fast. I don't know, Charlie. I'm sure it's a tempest in a tea cup." She sounded very impatient.

"OK, Steph, I'll head over there." He disconnected, hitched the walky-talky to his belt, and turned toward the long, low building to the east.

While the top of the old factory had been preserved pretty much the way it was designed, the bottom had been scraped and hollowed out. It reminded Charlie of the houses in Florida that stood on stilts in case of flooding. In this case, huge steel girders were exposed and the floor was muddy ground. Awaiting the finishing touches that would transform its bottom storey into stalls for an upscale fruit and vegetable market, it looked as though it might sag, top-heavy, into a Pisa tower position at any time.

The kid was probably off with some guy, Charlie thought, mentally preparing himself to give the daughter a dressing-down when he found her. Or she could be the type of artist who was so obsessed with her work that she didn't even realize how much time had gone by. Now *that* Charlie would have a difficult time criticizing.

The manager was a diminutive, slight man with a shiny bald head, who scurried up to Charlie like a small bird, key in hand. He was obviously far too busy to be bothered with inconsequential matters such as missing art students.

"Frank Jeffries, Officer," he introduced himself, his words staccato, self-important. "I sincerely hope this won't take very long. I've got an appointment shortly."

Charlie was amused at his use of the word shortly, an adverb he thought Frank should avoid. "Oh I'm sure it won't take long," he replied affably. "It's Sergeant Haynes, by the way."

Though Charlie, by choice, had not risen very far in the ranks, he still liked people to know his status. He found it useful when dealing with arrogant men like Jeffries. To his satisfaction, Jeffries gave him a nod of respect.

The stairs were steep and narrow, so Charlie followed Jeffries, their footsteps clanging in the empty space below. At the top was a landing with a closed door, which was unlocked. The two men entered a long, silent hallway.

Frank wanted to explain. "The building isn't really finished yet. I've allowed occupancy in two studios on the second floor to a couple of eager beavers – it's actually completely safe, but the painting, the flooring – well, you know. It's the finishing touches that aren't complete, but these artsy types didn't seem to care about that. They haven't officially signed the tenant agreements and such, but that doesn't seem to bother them either."

Charlie could see for himself that the building was not finished. A chalky cement floor was surrounded by bare drywall. All of the spaces had closed doors, but nothing was painted. Everything smelled incomplete and damp.

"Which studio is the girl supposed to be in, Sergeant? Professor Thompson has the studio at the end, on the right. Professor Hughes has the one directly across." Jeffries pointed to the end of the corridor. "Professor Thompson wanted to take the studio now because he was determined to get the one that looks out onto the Creek."

"Thompson and Hughes?" Charlie worked hard at keeping the surprise out of his voice, ensuring that his tone was inquisitive only.

"Yes. They both teach at the art college. Professor Thompson gives extra classes – tutoring them, I guess. He has a whole bunch of students already. I don't know why you just didn't go and ask the Professor. "

Charlie didn't bother giving the man any information. "And Hughes?" he asked as though he didn't know the answer.

"As far as I know, Professor Hughes just moved in a bunch of stuff. I haven't seen any students there."

"Well, Mr. Jeffries, we don't really know which studio the girl might be at, or even if she's here, so we'll just take a quick look in both of them, since you still technically have the right to enter. That way, we'll find her quickly and not bother her teachers."

Jeffries stopped at the last door. Charlie tried the door; it was locked. He directed Jeffries to insert the key and the door swung open silently. Charlie entered first. The studio had huge windows gracing one wall, affording a magnificent view of False Creek, where boats glittered in the sunlight. Piles of untouched and unfinished canvasses, a few scattered easels, and several tables strewn with paints and brushes made the room look small and cluttered.

But it was the display to their immediate right that sucked the air from the studio, suddenly made it feel claustrophobic, walls close and uncomfortable. The huge windows were closed tight, making the room a vacuum of odour as the sun boosted the temperature to an uncomfortable level. The sickly sweet scent of paint combined with a slight musty smell that signified death and the beginnings of decay.

Behind him, the policeman could hear Frank Jeffries gag and whimper. Under the spell of the grotesque, the mix of beauty with death, Charlie's universe shifted. All the sadness he'd experienced, the deaths of some friends, his brother, his parents, the stillborn baby they even now mourned, rushed up to choke him, forcing tears from his eyes. He could not imagine the mind that had brought this horror, this grief, to such loveliness.

Her small, slight body was splayed in an X across the wall, her arms and legs attached with huge spikes, crucified, through her wrists and ankles. Her lustrous blond hair hung over her shoulders, hiding one side of her bent head. Charlie could still see the straight, youthful contours of her chin, her mouth, her pert nose, the carefully applied make-up and lipstick. She looked like a distorted female Christ, with her head curved in sacrifice, her lips turned down in disappointment. A single tear had been painted on her cheek, freezing the anguish on her lovely skin.

From her neck to her breasts, down her flat childless belly, surrounding her pubic hairs, across her legs and arms, an obviously professional hand had created a stunning landscape. The painter had followed the contours of her body, creating hills and valleys, water and grass. A shimmering pinkish sky was infused with blues and yellows. The pale skin canvas gave the oils a striking texture, little imperfections that brought a reality to the unreal scene. Tiny pore holes had soaked up the paint, imbuing each of the colours with a deeper resonance, an almost burnished quality. The artist had used each of her bumps and freckles and hairs as props for the scenery, incorporating them into the picture. Streams and ponds had been carved into her body and painted blue. The mix of brownish-red from her clotted blood gave them a polluted appearance. Her pale vaginal mound had been transformed into an aqua pool from which carved rivulets flowed down her legs. Only her face was untouched, youthful and beautiful, except for the tear.

Instinctively, Charlie stepped forward and put his finger at her neck, but, as expected, he felt no pulse. Then he unclipped his short wave radio from his belt, surprised that his fingers were steady as he held the device to his lips. He managed to tell Stephanie in short, clipped sentences that they had a homicide on the premises. She obviously heard the horror in his tone, for she asked no questions. He could hear her relay the message along the line.

"Emergency services and back-up on the way," she told him, her voice reassuring. "Hold on, Charlie."

The Sergeant turned to his companion then. Frank had doubled over in a crouch position, his eyes cast downward, away from the body on the wall. Something in his posture led Charlie to believe the man's shock was part recognition.

"Do you know this girl?" Charlie asked quietly, leaning next to Jeffries.

"Yes, yes, her name is Linda Courtnell."

"You're positive?"

"Yes, I can tell by her hair – it's a beautiful shade of blond – and it's cut really stylishly. And her face, of course. She's – she's beautiful, really. She's – her parents are the Courtnells. You know? The big real estate magnate." Jeffries choked out each of the words, gasping as though he had run out of breath at the end of every sentence. "I know her father and I've seen Linda lots of times."

Charlie knew who the Courtnells were; everyone in Vancouver knew who the Courtnells were. This case was going to be complicated, in more ways than one.

"OK, Frank, we're going to back out of here. Just exactly the way we came in. We haven't far to go, then we'll lock the door again until back-up comes. You can wait in the hall, OK?"

The two men had been joined together by their shock, the smaller one accepting the authority of the bigger man without question. They retraced their footsteps carefully. Once the door was shut, Jeffries appeared to rally slightly, his breathing becoming more normal.

"Are the unoccupied suites locked, Frank?" Charlie asked. "Have you got all the keys? I have to make sure there's no one else in the building."

Jeffries nodded, holding up the keys, which he continued to clutch in his hands. "These are the masters."

"Good, excellent. So it's just this one other studio rented out, right?" Charlie gestured across the hall.

"Yes, just these two. They wanted the ends because you can see the Creek, especially from..." He seemed to realize he was automatically degenerating into another sales pitch, so he stopped and simply handed over the keys with trembling fingers. "The others should be locked too. Don't want vagrants, you know..."

"OK. Listen, you stay right here. I'll go look. I'll make it as quick as possible. You yell very loudly if you see anyone at all, OK, pal?"

Jeffries nodded silently, his face pale and shiny with sweat, his eyes still huge with shock. Charlie didn't want him to fall over in a faint, so he eased the man down onto the cement floor. He'd be covered in dust, but that was better than bursting his head open if he passed out.

Quickly, Charlie went into Professor Hughes' studio. Boxes, easels, and tables were strewn about, but the place had an uninhabited air. The other second floor rooms were completely empty, in various stages of readiness, so ascertaining that they were devoid of human presence was relatively easy. When Charlie returned to the hallway for the last time, Frank Jeffries was still slumped on the floor, but he continued to be alert and wide-eyed as he searched the hallway for movement.

Charlie helped him to his feet and they made a vague attempt at dusting him off. "How about the third floor, Frank?"

"It's completely empty. The hall doors should be locked because it's all steel girders and boards. No windows or doors even. A big art store is going in there, taking up the whole floor. We're awaiting the specs from..." Once more, he caught himself in a rant; his lips clamped shut. He pointed to this end of the hallway, where the door to the stairwell was clamped shut with a lock and chain.

"OK, we're gonna let the others search that floor. Is that the only other way in or out of here?" Charlie gestured toward the locked entry.

Frank nodded his head. "Yes. The door at the back also has a big lock and chain on it, just like this one, so I don't think..."

"Great. Wonderful. Let's go outside and wait for the troops then."

When they reached the open underbelly of the factory, both men gulped in the fresh air that wafted from the salt water in the distance. The two men stood motionless and silent for a moment. Charlie sprinted quickly around to the back, checking that the lock was still fastened on the entry door. When he returned, he became aware of the sounds from the city, the island activity, the waterway beyond.

Charlie saw the indifference of the world as a personal insult. By the time the police cars and emergency vehicles squealed up, he was engulfed with rage. All his dissatisfaction and jealousy became focused on the artist who had misused an obvious talent. Charles Haynes knew, as surely as he knew he loved his wife and daughters, that he would catch the animal who had committed this twisted crime.

Chapter Three
December, 2008

Reading through the report was making my heart pound, so I looked up from my desk for relief. Perhaps it was the movement of my head that made my daughter Cate look up too, or more likely, I suspected, she was so in tune with me that she felt my change in attention. We met one another's gaze, her eyes a startling greenish-blue, mine just blue. She smiled, so I did too, even though my thoughts were still sluggish with the residue of my past.

The three of us were sitting in our den, a large room on the second floor lined with bookshelves. Two sets of deep windows overlooked the street where huge maple trees crammed the roadside and peered over the sidewalks. In summertime we looked down onto a bouquet of leaves. In winter, the branches cuddled fluffy pillows of white and in fall, the view was an artists' pallet of red and yellow.

Prominently displayed on one wall of the den was a famous Langford Taylor painting – the original – of a mother and child, sitting near our own little lake, entitled *Daughter*. Though the child was blond, not redheaded, I still thought of that picture as prescient; a foretelling of my astonishing chance at motherhood.

The girls were both doing their homework, while I tackled this long overdue duty of my own. Our little dog, Angel, slept contentedly at Cate's feet. Angel was part collie and part terrier, a medium sized little rectangle of fur with a face that prompted love at first sight. Cate and Angel were the best of friends, spending any free time together, romping in the yard, running along the beach, or curled up in bed. When Cate sat quietly doing one task or another, Angel was there too. My husband Langford and I might have felt somewhat jealous of the little dog's switch in loyalty, except for the look on Cate's face as she caught sight of our pet bounding toward her at the end of a school day.

Catherine and Carly Sanderson are our foster daughters. A tragedy that defied words landed them in our house, our arms, and our hearts. Their mother and oldest brother, and to some extent their father, had been responsible for several deaths. The Church of Leviticus, established with some sense of biblical thought, had been warped into a seat of power and madness by Dorothy and Carl Sanderson. Carly had been terribly burned in a fire that had consumed the country church where their parents and brother had preached, delved into madness, and set the wooden structure ablaze.

Carly's curly red hair had lightened, tinged with white, a result of the ordeal she had endured. Her head was bent over her assignment, back hunched in the wheelchair, mind engrossed in the figures on the page. She continued to have difficulty focusing, but she was a determined soul, a fighter. She argued incessantly over every little thing, but I understood that need: she was exerting control. Her body, her injuries, and especially her past were all events and occurrences that she was not able to influence and with which she still struggled. So she dominated where she could. I not only understood that need; I had been there and, in many ways, I was *still* there. We clashed fairly often, both of us in our desire to assert our will, but we had a deep, unshakable love and respect that always won out.

Cate was very different, more like Langford. He handled our past by becoming introspective, dignified, intense. He had a way of listening, of looking *into* you when he listened, that exemplified the depth of his attention. In dealing with her own troubles, Cate had become creative, insightful and calm in much the same ways. Langford started giving her painting lessons and he was of the opinion that she had great promise. Since he was an artist whose work has been admired by many, that was a terrific compliment. Another promising sign – which tingled through me every time I looked at her – was that Cate had straightened her shoulders to face life more eye-to-eye. She was no longer hunched over like an old woman as she'd been less than a year ago. She was a bough unfurling in the sun.

Though the report I was reading was not about Cate and Carly, they were the reasons for pursuing the next legal step available to us. Langford and I had been named foster parents for the girls. Though orphaned, they were not up for adoption at the moment, but that could change. In all likelihood, given their ages and disabilities, they would get to live with us forever as foster children, but we – and they - wanted our relationship to be legally permanent. None of us could bear the thought that some legal glitch had the potential to break up the loving family we'd become.

However unlikely that scenario might be, we wanted to clear Langford's name so that we could adopt Catherine and Carly Sanderson. With the assistance of our family therapist we'd had long talks about the possibilities, and we'd told them about what had happened to Langford long ago in Vancouver. Both girls made it clear that they wanted to stay with us, even after hearing the story of our past.

We wanted to be the kind of parents theirs had not been. We needed to leave them a legacy of pride and love. The girls were filled with shame and guilt surrounding the crimes and horrors committed by their biological mother and father. Perhaps in time, Cate and Carly would realize that insanity is a type of illness and begin to feel pity instead of hatred. Certainly in the case of their brother, Aaron, who was brainwashed from a young age, there might eventually be room for understanding and forgiveness. Therapy continued to help them cope in their different ways, but Cate and Carly would probably always suffer from the taint that the Sandersons left behind.

The other surviving children were living with May and Alain Reneaux, our best friends, who were in the process of adopting them. Ironically - since this was exactly what my husband and I had done years before - the girls and their other siblings said they might opt for changing their names after the adoptions. In our case, that could only happen if our court appeal went forward successfully.

I smiled at Cate, bent my head to read once more, and found myself gazing out the window. Though it was fairly early in December, lots of snow had already hit us and today was one of those perfect wintry days. This morning Langford, Cate and I had played ball outside with Angel – or rather, she played with us. The sun glinted off the whiteness; icicles dripped in rhythm. Our footsteps were just crunchy enough to keep us gliding over the tops of wavy ridges. Angel would catch the ball in her mouth, shaking her head as though deciding who would be honoured with the prize next, and then she'd come flying at our legs. More often than not, we landed butt up in a snow bank, the ball still in the little dog's possession. Sometimes we made snow figures while we were down there.

Angel often trotted over to Carly, sitting in her wheelchair at the edge of the yard, and handed the ball over freely. Then the little dog chased it vigorously when it was thrown back. Carly actually smiled and clapped, though I knew she still struggled with being unable to participate fully. Maybe next year, the doctors told us.

Our house was my dream come true, even more so now that it was filled. We always had four bedrooms, two of which had stood empty, guest beds pristine without company. Now they swelled with feminine duvets and clothes and toys. Posters of idols plastered the walls. We allowed the girls to decorate any way they wanted; they needed the sense of a space that belonged only to them. At first we would find Cate curled up with her sister in the mornings, but that had been happening less often lately.

On the other side of the house from the den and girls' rooms, from the kitchen, family room, and, above that, the master bedroom, we enjoyed Ogeechee Lake in all its moods and seasons. Our little bay is a tiny cove cut into Ogeechee Lake almost as though it were an afterthought. The narrow section between the shores is not friendly to boats, even the non-motorized kind. Those were the only kind of crafts allowed on the lake, by City Council and Native Council agreement. But not even they ventured into our little area, making our shoreline exceedingly private. When it was iced over, now and then someone passed through on skis or snowshoes, but generally it was quiet, unspoiled, natural.

The beautiful Scarlett O'Hara staircase in the front hall was the only item in the household that did not respond nicely to the changes: the electronic wheelchair lift looked incongruous. Luckily, because the house was built a long time ago, the doorways were already wide enough: they'd once welcomed ladies' crinolines much as now embraced Carly's wheelchair. We hadn't had to make too many structural changes, though we would have gone so far as to leave this dream house if that had been necessary to accommodate Carly.

These first six months post-retirement from Principal of Burchill Public School continued to astound me. For the most part, I spent it close to home, working with the girls to establish their trust and security. I home-schooled Carly, as she was not yet ready for our local school. Maybe next year, when she was outfitted with her artificial limbs. For several weeks after the fire, Carly stayed in a respite residence, where she had full-time nursing care. Her feet had been so badly burned that she'd suffered amputation to the knees. As both her teacher and her foster mother, I used some of our time together to cover the final stages of Grade 5, and now we were tackling the Grade 6 curriculum at home. Carly was a very smart little girl, but the ordeal had taken its toll not only in a physical way. She worked very hard to overcome the tendency to lose her concentration, to be able to commit the ideas and facts to a memory that had also been burned.

As for Cate, she was never at the top of her class, but that quiet introversion was a blessing at school. She listened well, concentrated, and though her work was not inspired, it was steady. The area in which she shone was art; that was where her creativity had an outlet, one that can be accomplished all alone, yet surrounded by colour and imagination. She and Langford spent hours in the little workshop beside our house. Langford set up an area just for Cate, with her own easel, pallet, and brushes, right in the window where she could see the smiling corners of the lake.

My husband continued traveling all over the province and even to the United States, to promote and sell his art. Langford Taylor was now a household name. For the two of us, his fame was an ironic twist. We'd tried so hard in the past to escape notoriety and remain hidden. When he was at home, his relationship with the girls had deepened and strengthened. My love for him had consequently soared. Looking at him and the fatherly tenderness that was obviously innate in Langford, my eyes often stung with joy and grief simultaneously.

Denied the privilege of having our own children because of a terrible twist of fate, I was both shocked and gratified that we could fall in love so easily and completely. We adored these young girls; they were strong and fragile, needy and independent, grumpy and joyful, all the dichotomies of pre-teen angst. They were heroes; they were victims. With the help of experts and friends, we helped to guide them as they progressed through anger, grief, and slowly into acceptance.

Lately, though, I've felt the old stress seeping back in. Anger and fear are addictions that overtake you so easily you can't remember the years without it. In the early fall, we started preliminary steps toward the court case. When I opened that Pandora's filing cabinet, which held all of the transcripts, reports and appeals, I knew the wounds would be reopened, too. But I was frightened at how simple it was for the horrors to reassert themselves. I was anxious, sleepless, scared and suspicious once more. I jumped at the smallest sound; I read double entendres into every person's remarks. Tears always hovered. I assumed that over the years, I had built a hard shell to protect me. Certainly I had played the part: the confident teacher who'd become a principal and had a very successful career. How little it took to plunge me right back to the young, devastated victim that I was in the 1980's. The rapidity of the change caused me to question everything – again. I would think that my mind was unquestionably going, except that the same demons hit my husband too. In the last few months, therapy sessions belonged as much to us as they did to our girls.

May and Alain also held Langford and me together. We all took courage from the astonishing heroism of Cate and Carly and their surviving siblings. Trevor, Benjaman and Meghan were now nine, eight and seven respectively, and were progressing well. Both Carly and Trevor lost their twins, Devon and Tyler; they also lost their sister Jennifer. It was difficult, if not impossible, to accept and understand that their parents and eldest brother had caused the devastation. The girls didn't mourn their loss; they were still angry and confused. Perhaps they always would be.

Whenever possible, Langford and I made certain that we ended each night in one another's arms, always thankful for the ability to touch and make love. We'd learned from Agnes Lake, the village Shaman, that friendship and love would carry us through any ordeal.

"Mem?"

I smiled with pure delight at Carly. She and Cate both had a difficult time with "Emily", because they'd known me as Mrs. Taylor at Burchill Public School for many years. "Mom" was still laced with bad memories, so Mem suited us perfectly.

"I'm just trying to write up this experiment. I don't really like Science much. How come you do?"

I smiled at her. "I didn't really like it when I was your age, either. But then one day, when I was quite a bit older, I had to teach Grade Seven and Eight Science. So I had to learn more about it, experiments, chemicals, things like that, and I started to really like it."

"Maybe I will too, just like you." As she bent once more over the page, my skin goose bumped.

Cate caught my attention next.

"Stuck on something, honey?"

"Not really, but I was wondering. Is May a Métis like Louis Riel was?"

"Nope," I answered, coming to stand beside her as she tackled the project. "Riel's father's mother was a Métis and he spent a lot of time with his extended family. He came to believe that the Métis were being mistreated, so he tried to fight for their rights. May, on the other hand, is full-blooded Canadian Native. Both her parents were Ojibwa natives."

"Like Ms Ogemah?"

"Like Ms Ogemah."

"She says we can call her Indian."

I laughed. That's Renae for you, I said to myself. She was the social worker at Burchill Public School and had been instrumental in saving the girls' lives, both literally and figuratively. "Ms Ogemah is a special person. I think the correct way to speak of May and our other friends' heritage is to say native or First Nation, because their ancestors were here before yours and mine were, so they are native to Canada. But Ms Ogemah tells that story about Indian meaning In Dio – or in god, with god. She means we should respect all people and not judge, even with words."

Cate nodded and scribbled a few notes. "I wish Ms Ogemah could be the social worker at North Grenville," she said wistfully, speaking about the new high school she would attend next year, already worrying about another loss.

"I know, sweetheart. There's no one like Ms Ogemah."

"She saved us," Cate said, her eyes simple and complex at the same time.

"Yes, she did, Cate. She's still saving us in a lot of ways. We'll keep seeing her, no matter what schools she goes to - don't worry. She's coming to the party on Saturday."

"What about Alain's background?" Cate asked, pulling back to her assignment, yet diverting from it as well. "Is he a Métis? Or is he a coureur de bois?"

This time I laughed out loud. "The people in Burchill called him a coureur de bois when they first met him. You know how he's so tall and big shouldered and strong?"

Both girls nodded in agreement.

"Well, when he first came to town, they thought he was from the woods. He never told them anything about his background, so they guessed. They told stories that he was either half native, or a descendent of the coureurs de bois. These were men who traded fur, so they lived their entire lives in the forest. But actually, Alain's descendents were Irish and he never lived in the woods."

Cate and Carly giggled.

"Just imagine," Cate said. "The people in Burchill who thought he lived in the forest must be turning red! Now he's the richest man ever."

"Alain said he was rich before," Carly inserted. "But he didn't have as much money as he has now."

"I think he meant he was rich in other ways," I said. "Like rich in love."

Cate nodded her head wisely. "Alain and May are so much in love, aren't they, Mem? Even though she's a lot older than he is."

This time I laughed very loudly. "Who told you about the difference in their ages?"

"May did. Benjaman was doing a class project about families and for some reason he asked when they were born."

May must have loved that, I thought. Alain was twelve years her junior, not that anyone could tell by looking at them.

"I don't think age matters when you love somebody," I said.

"Like Frances and Edgar. He's a lot older than she is, but they're perfect together," Carly pronounced.

I couldn't believe the insight from my two daughters. "They really are. And now that they have Faith, they're even happier."

"Did they name Faith after Frances and Alain's sister? The one who died?" Cate asked.

"They did. And have you noticed the way her Uncle Alain adores her? It's so cute. They're coming on Saturday too of course."

"I'm so excited about the party I can hardly concentrate," Cate said, sounding very mature. "I'm glad we're having it at our house for a change. Are you excited too, Mem? Are you nervous?"

"I am very nervous, to be honest," I answered.

At the Ceremony of Declaration planned for this weekend, all the people we'd come to love would know of our past. We knew perfectly well that soon afterward, all the people of Burchill and beyond would know the real identity of Langford Taylor.

On Saturday, we spent all afternoon decorating. May, Alain, Meghan, Benjaman and Trevor arrived early to help. They brought May's Aunt Oona in her own wheelchair. The elderly woman had lost many of her faculties, but she was smiling and happy and thrilled with the noise of the children. She kept patting Carly's hand, as though reassuring her that being in a wheelchair was not the end of the world.

Carly and Cate were ecstatic to have their sister and brothers on their turf. Most of the time, we held our celebrations or meetings at the Reneaux domain, not really on purpose, but because their place was so much larger than ours. The Reneaux had built an enormous house on a beautiful plot of land that was once the site of a puppy mill. All of that horror had been erased by the wealth from a quirk of nature.

Oona had inherited land that held a very rare gold streak. Not only rare in our part of the Canadian Shield, but also atypical because the resultant gold mine proved to be worth millions. As Oona's only heir, May was now a very rich woman. The house the Reneaux built was spectacular – they were able to accommodate Oona, the children, and many guests. The barns where so much pain had been suffered were razed and transformed into kennels and animal hospitals, along with acres of flowers and crops. May and Alain shared their largesse with everyone.

We were benefiting, too, because our legal battles were being entirely financed by Bezhig Asin, the company that May owned with Alain and Oona. At first, we'd resisted the charity, but May and Alain convinced us that our collective foster children needed the stability and this lawsuit was one way to ensure that. May reminded me that she had called the company "Bezhig Asin", one rock, because it meant that we would all be steady and solid now and for the future. Bezhig Asin's lawyer, Jacob Finch, was now our lawyer too.

Meghan Sanderson was barely distinguishable as the once mute little girl who literally suffered in silence as her family disintegrated. Her enormous blue eyes now danced with the sparkle and vigour of any eight year old. Her witty, animated personality was captivating as she danced into the house, a wave of energy flowing over everyone she touched. Trevor, still reed thin and climbing taller every month, mostly overcame the slouch he and his older siblings, especially Cate, had adopted in defense. Now he met another person's eyes more often; now he let me give him a hello hug. Still somewhat lonely, still quiet and fearful, Trevor had a long way to go yet. Benjaman, his innate spunkiness and affectionate nature set free, leapt into my arms, his wiry body almost knocking me over. In the circle of May and Alain's love, he had blossomed the most: he was mischievous, inquisitive, and he caused ripples of laughter wherever he went.

At 3 o'clock, the guests began to arrive. Frances, Edgar and baby Faith were the first. Edgar Brennan was not just one of our best friends; he was our Chief Superintendent of Police for the Ontario Provincial Police Department in Burchill. Frances had taken an indefinite leave from her job as a Police Officer. She and Ed wanted two children and, because they were a little older when they began, they wanted to raise a family immediately. I was certain Faith would have a sibling in short order.

I felt guilty about Edgar and Frances. Today they would learn our story, lumped in with the rest of our guests.

Langford and I had lied to them really - by omission. We didn't tell Frances and Edgar who we were, even when they became very close friends, even when we confided in May and Alain. The most compelling reason for not telling the other two, I had to confess, was their profession. Despite all that we went through with them, despite the emotions and the intimacy that developed, we allowed the badge to intervene.

Frankly, I didn't know if we would be telling anyone, ever, if it were not for the impending court proceedings. At least we are being thoroughly honest now; even if it meant that a wedge would be driven between some of our friends and us. When they heard everything, both Langford and I were hoping they would understand - in particular, Frances and Edgar.

Jacob Finch, our lawyer, and his wife Kristen were next, with Jacob's daughter Adrienne and son Jordan. Their nanny Helen Lake rounded out the little family. Although it seemed impossible that Jacob and Kristen could be any more gorgeous than they were physically, their love created an aura of beauty that always filled me with hope and courage.

Jacob Finch had moved to our small town from Toronto. His first wife, deeply depressed, had committed suicide and almost drowned their son Jordan. Jacob had left the city with almost the same alacrity as Langford and I had left Vancouver. Hired as Oona Nabigon's exclusive lawyer, Jacob handled the negotiations with the mining company and the myriad of tasks so much money involved. And now, us.

He was happy in Burchill, content with our community's close-knit atmosphere, ecstatic with the job and May's leadership in the company. Then miraculously, Jacob had found love again – or perhaps, he'd found real love for the first time. He and Kristen, a teacher at Burchill Public, were definite soul mates. They handled Jordan's emotional and mental problems, a result of his near drowning, with intelligence and devotion. Adrienne, who had been almost too mature for her age, blossomed under the touch of two wonderful, natural "mothers".

Helen Lake, our Shaman's niece, was a kind, nurturing caregiver who deeply loved Jacob and his children. The addition of Kristen simply completed the circle. Since the beautiful wedding this August, their relationships had blossomed even further.

Today, Agnes was one of our guests of honour; she had agreed to lead the ceremony of declaration. She arrived with Chief Dan Mahdahbee. Chief Dan was leader of the Sahsejewon Reserve, the First Nations district at the edge of Burchill. With his highly successful, lucrative business acumen, his keen sense of politics and community, this man who stood only five feet tall was a towering presence in our town. He had been a friend and supporter through many crises and was especially tuned into Agnes and her spiritual power. Dressed today in traditional costume, his colourful shirt, his leggings and moccasins, were pure Ojibwa. If you didn't notice the Gucci watch and the sparkling rings, you would assume that he was an ordinary citizen of the reserve. Dan flashed his typical frowning smile, his eyes pools of deep awareness as he embraced me. He knew this was a difficult, yet liberating, day for us. Declarations were important, personal journeys for the native people in Sahsejewon. I had begun to see the wisdom of making this step, though it filled me with a deep-seated fear.

Agnes Lake was the most beautiful person I had ever met. Perhaps not physically; short and stocky, her face was embedded with age lines. But the loveliness of her eyes, her long grey hair, and the delicate touch of her hands added up to the impression of beauty. She was wise, calm, sensitive and strong. In her embrace, I was strengthened and had faith once more in this path of truth.

Several more invitees bustled in the door at different times. Teddy Lavalle, owner and chef of The Burchill Inn, supplied the food. Soon the house was crammed with adults and children, all talking and laughing and helping themselves to delicious treats from Teddy's magical stores.

By the time dinner was over and everything clean again, it was well and truly dark. The sky was a deep cold blue and stars blinked in the brightness of the unclouded half moon. All the children went upstairs to watch a movie, except for Faith. She fell asleep in her baby seat, exhausted by the attention that had buzzed around her throughout the afternoon and evening. The adults gathered in the living room, most of us with liqueurs cradled in our hands. Chief

Dan began with his signature opening: a soft roll of the drum, the beat in sync with our hearts. A silence fell over us; we were drawn into the meditation offered by the traditions that Agnes had taught us.

It suddenly occurred to me that this scene was more than surreal: it was almost unbelievable. All those years ago, I could never have envisioned sitting in my own living room, participating in a native ceremony, having a Shaman introduce my dishonorable, horrific past. Though I'd been taught by my parents to accept people as they were, I'd suffered from the same prejudices as many residents of Vancouver had. Until I came to live in Burchill, I'd never had the opportunity to really get to know a native person. Or perhaps I'd never bothered. I certainly never considered that my best friend, the woman to whom I am closest on this planet, would be a native Canadian whose roots and sensibilities were so much deeper than mine. I was enormously fortunate to have been drawn into this spirituality, a philosophy that intertwined with the earth and united mind with body, thought with feeling.

Soon Agnes's flat, deep voice began to lead our thoughts, to introduce the story that Langford and I had to tell.

"We as a community have suffered so much." Agnes' speech pattern was an amalgam of singsong and monotone, relaxing and mesmerizing. "The Anishinabe would say that we have been through the fires. When the evil of the Church of Leviticus was visited upon us, that fire was real and consuming."

Though I hadn't been there, I imagined Carly's burning feet, the screams of the poor children who died, the suffering of the misguided adults who'd believed they'd found religious guidance and instead, found madness and death. I remembered the smell of smoke on Langford and the odour of his horror and sorrow.

"But there have been many fires for the twin communities of Burchill and Sahsejewon, in the Ojibwa way of thinking. We fought to build our town and our reserve into a cohesive group. In those struggles, many of us here lost our loved ones, our soul mates, our children. We were almost derailed by the evil of animal abuse. Our citizens had to fight those who would have taken money from our land and ravaged it at the same time. We almost lost our faith when people who held themselves up as messengers from god were proven to be false prophets. Murder and death have threatened to bring our community to ruin, to destroy our spirit, our faith, our hope."

She paused for a moment. Dan continued to drum, his large round fingers dancing intimately over the canvas. I thought of my recent bouts of depression, of mistrust, and I felt both ashamed and uplifted. Perhaps I would be strong enough this time not to lose my faith or hope. I had learned so much; I was not the young, self-centred, naïve girl of my past. This time, I would not falter. This time, I would be brave. I straightened my shoulders, touched my husband's strong, artistic hand, snuggled a little closer to May.

"Our people have a prophecy called the Seventh Fire. In this tale, we, the elders, lose our way. We are unable, in our darkness, to give the younger generation our support and guidance. Many of us have died, or lost our light, or are crippled physically and spiritually." She stopped speaking again, and even Oona seemed to understand; her head, shaky and heavy, tried to nod up and down. "But most of you gathered here, you are our younger generation, and our young are strong and resilient. You will not let our own failings be your failings. You will listen to the spirits of our forefathers, speaking to you of the truth of finding our way through hardship, of the rewards that will come to you if only you prevail."

The drumbeat continued softly, echoing in my chest, following the pulse of my heart as I thought of the journey ahead.

"Our dear friends Langford and Emily have a declaration to make. It is a story of tragedy and love, one of despair and hope, with both heroes and humans. It is a confession, a plea for forgiveness. They have prevailed, they have survived, and now they need our support and guidance as they complete the last part of their journey out of the darkness that once surrounded their lives.

"You, my people gathered here and those outside these walls, will have to decide whether to embrace Langford and

Emily or reject them in their plea. We elders cannot help you make this decision of the heart.

"We elders cannot, nor can any of you here, make the journey for Emily and Langford. We have not the knowledge. We have not the advice. They must make their own way. What we can give them is our love and forgiveness.

"Emily and Langford will be journeying through a kind of earthquake. They will be forced to go backwards in order to go forwards. Their whole landscape will be changed. Whether they will be able to traverse this new landscape will depend upon their own inner strength.

"From my own visioning, Emily and Langford, I must tell you that your Seventh Fire looks to be deep and cataclysmic. The experience will change you in some way. But I also foresee a love that will not be defeated."

My heart was beating so loudly in the silence, in the shock of Agnes's prediction that I could scarcely focus. My thoughts leapt to the future, to the faces of our daughters.

"My people, we will all go through our own versions of the Seventh Fire. We can only hope that each of us will discover the next level, the Eighth Fire, in which the world will be shifted, but ultimately, will be a better place. Langford, I believe that you have elected to tell your story."

And in the depth of the silent surprise that emanated from our circle of friends, my past roared out to meet me, crashed into me like a white water wave, a brutal, weighty fist.

Chapter Four
September, 1980

Dawn brought dark grey and drizzle, the clouds sitting petulantly on the mountains, making the city feel trapped. From unseasonably warm, the air turned cold and damp, a clammy mood that caused shivers inside and out.

Emily Taylor laid in the bed under the twisted sheets, fetus-like, the tears flowing from a seemingly endless supply. Earlier, the door had slammed in the apartment and she knew Will had gone. Still, she could not force herself out of the bed in which she'd been lying for over twelve hours now. Emily could not yet grasp his reaction to her news. Yes, they'd agreed, made a promise, but things change, don't they?

She sat up and caught a glimpse of herself in the mirror. The room was tiny, so the dresser almost touched the edge of the bed, affording a perfect view of her rumpled blond hair, swollen eyes and flushed skin. She tried to shake the depression, but it flooded back over her in a fit of fresh tears. How could he have acted that way? Everything that was happening seemed to be completely out of character for both of them. Emily felt as though she were being carried along a current that she couldn't fight and couldn't define. She was inside a paper bag, not able to see the opening so she could get herself back out again. She sank back into the bed, covered her head with the duvet, and thought back over the horrendous events of the night before.

Will worked all day Saturday again with his tutors. After her visit to the clinic, Emily walked to the farmer's market. It was cloudy and windy, but not too cool, and she needed the exercise. On the way back, though, laden down with all the supplies, she gave in and took a taxi. An unforgivable expense on their budget, but she was sure Will would understand.

Emily carefully constructed the dinner: steak marinated and then barbequed to medium rare, just enough red, the way he loved it. Caesar salad with her own, somewhat spicy, dressing, real bacon, crunchy croutons. Twice-baked potatoes, rich with sour cream and green onion; a side plate of asparagus in olive oil. She opened the red wine and the timing had been exactly right: Will mounted the steps and flung open the door just as she poured him a big glass.

His smile was suffused with surprise; he couldn't resist asking, "What's all this?"

She reached up to put her arms around his neck, her short lean figure childlike next to his tall, square stature. "You've been working so hard. I figured you needed a special dinner."

"This looks amazing, Em," he said, really smiling now. "I'll go change into something a little more comfortable."

And he'd given her that grin, the one backlit by the deep brown of his eyes, the one that tingled down through her toes.

She waited until they were finished dinner before she told him. He'd been so engrossed in the delicious food, he hadn't noticed that she had been drinking grape juice instead of wine. Sitting there in the cramped kitchen, the breeze cool and wet from the tiny balcony, the sounds of Vancouver rising from the street below, Emily delivered her news as though she were presenting him with a well-considered gift.

"Will, I'm pregnant."

He stared at her, the wine glass almost to his lips, frozen in action as though participating in a child's game of *Pose*. "What?" He returned the glass to the table. His eyes turned black in the dim light, his mouth curled in shock. Emily could remember seeing that look on his face only once before.

"I confirmed it this morning. At the clinic. I thought I might be, but now it's for sure." In the silence, Emily said peevishly, "So? What do you think?" as though she couldn't tell from his frowning, heated countenance.

"Emily, we said we wouldn't do this. I took out the lease on the studio. I have lined up a bunch of students. I'm studying for my degree or I'll never get full professor. You are only in your third year of teaching. A pregnancy leave would never bring in enough money even if you could get unemployment insurance, which I don't think you can."

He was speaking to her as though lecturing a particularly troublesome student. Standing up and pacing the length of their couch and back – which was about the extent of the living room – his shoulders were stiff and straight, flung back in anger. His voice shook with barely controlled rage.

Emily was having a difficult time listening. The shock of his anger filled her with dread, sent her back to being a child confronted with something she's never before witnessed. A kind of fear chilled her; she was afraid that the life she celebrated with Will would cease to be.

They had met in high school. He was tall and agile, a born basketball player, and he waltzed over the floor with such grace that all the girls in her class suddenly became far more interested in the sport than they'd ever been before. William Edward Thompson was not only tall: his dark brown hair was always slightly messy, falling in an endearing mop over his forehead; his eyes were pools of light and deeply interested in everything another person had to say. Bedroom eyes, Emily's friends commented. He opened the door for the girls; he helped scoop up armfuls of books and carried them to the next class; he would actually compliment a girl on her new hairstyle. His laugh was loud and uninhibited; he was confident but not conceited, sensitive and kind but popular with the guys as well. Smart and talented, too; he worked on scenery for the school plays, won awards in English and Art; played the bass guitar in the band. His father had been a trustee, extremely well respected in the municipality, and when he was killed in a car accident, the entire town came out to grieve.

Emily had not witnessed Bill Thompson's earlier ascendancy from popular elementary student to high school star, or the death of Edward Thompson. Grant Taylor, her own father, an air force commander who was constantly transferred from city to city or province to province as an instructor of newly minted pilots, dragged his children from school to school. Her mother Siobhan, born in Ireland with a penchant for adventure, was more than happy to pack up every year and move on to something different. Even her brother Sean had inherited his parents' free natures, so only Emily longed for stability. When her father's assignment to Langford, British Columbia, was contracted for four years, her entire secondary school education, Emily was ecstatic. She cultivated a huge circle of friends, joined clubs, and went to every dance.

Then as soon as she entered university, her parents began the process of moving to Ireland, where a house awaited them, inherited from Siobhan's family, along with a great deal of money. Combined with Grant's pension, they had more than enough to support them and still finance their children's education here in Canada. Sean and Emily had only to decide what they wanted to do. Their parents, with innate spirits of adventure and global perspectives, felt no compunction about leaving their nearly adult children behind.

There was no hesitation for Emily; she would stay put. Sean decided to remain in Canada a few more years to complete university, too. When he graduated, Sean acquired a great job as an advertising executive, married, and had three children in quick succession, all of which delayed his wanderlust. Years later, after Emily's life had disintegrated and then taken on a kind of dismayed routine, Sean and his family went to live in the newly booming economy of Ireland. Of course they wanted Emily to go with them, but she was not free to leave by then.

The reason for Emily's decision to remain in Canada was Bill Thompson. At one of the various high school dances, in the darkened corner where the "wallflowers" stood, when Emily was in Grade Eleven and William in his last year, Bill stuck out his long, elegant hand and asked Emily to dance. A collective sigh rose and waved along the line of girlfriends whose dreams had just coalesced into Emily Taylor's reality.

Bill was immediately enraptured with Emily's witty intelligence, her natural confidence and independence. At sixteen, she was a classic beauty, blond and blue-eyed with the traditional Irish peaches and cream complexion. Not very tall and certainly not skinny, Emily felt solid and curvaceous in his arms. Though narrow at the waist, she had luscious breasts and Bill had a difficult time curbing his physical reaction to her warmth. He spent the entire night dancing and talking, holding her slightly at arm's length so he could look into her eyes as she talked. She told him all about her travels, living in city after city until she was thirteen. Bill told everyone that he'd fallen in love with Emily at first sight, though she often reminded him that he'd walked by her in the halls for three years before.

After that first night, however, they were constantly together. Picnics at Langford Lake, walking along the shore, paddling under moonlight, were their favourite activities. If anyone had not previously believed in soul mates, they began to believe once they witnessed Emily Taylor and Bill Thompson's relationship. Best friends and eventually lovers, they inspired one another, admired each other's accomplishments, respected each other's independence, yet made their plans and decisions together. The only shadow side to their relationship was that their circle of friends began to shrink, until it was a circle of only two. The real, obvious difficulty they had was with Bill's mother.

Emily had begun calling him Will as an endearment, the name that she used only when they were alone, holding her apart from the crowds who followed him and knew him as Bill. When William invited Emily over to dinner at his mother's one night, shortly after they'd made love for the first time, she was aghast that her gentle, loving boyfriend had been borne by this woman.

Margaret Thompson was nearly as tall as her son, with the same colouring and bone structure, but none of his nature came through her eyes. She held herself stiff and aloof; she could have been a stand-in for the wicked witch in The Wizard of Oz. Emily was stunned and completely uncertain as to how to approach her. When she put out her hand to shake after Bill's introduction, Margaret waved her away impatiently, as though she had no time for such frivolities. Yet it was Bill who cooked the dinner, set the table, and served, while his mother sat imperiously presiding, a huge glass of gin beside her, which her son faithfully kept filled. She grilled Emily throughout the meal, about her family, her marks, her ambitions for the future. But Emily felt more as though she'd been pinned like an insect to an examination board than questioned by someone interested in her as a human being. And when Emily had turned to Bill, asking him a question, and inadvertently used the name *Will*, she'd felt the ferocity of Margaret's glare literally burn her skin.

"Why on earth did you call him that?" the woman had demanded, her tone sarcastic and belittling.

It was the only time Will appeared to notice anything amiss. "Yah, isn't that cool, Ma? Emily calls me by Dad's pet name." But his tone was defensive.

Emily thought she could immediately see the problem. Obviously, William had taken after his father in nature and character; was perhaps close to his Dad in a way that no mother could possibly understand. The jealousy radiating from Margaret was palpable. Emily tried to feel more sympathetic toward the older woman, but her attempt at a smile was squashed.

"His Dad was always way too soft on Bill," Margaret sneered.

Will didn't seem to mind. He began to clear the dishes, refusing Emily's offer of help. "Oh, Ma, you know I turned out right, so don't be so nasty." Yet the words were said lightly, with a chuckle, as though his mother were an amusing tease. He continued to pick up the dishes. "Stay here, Em, and talk to Ma. I'll just clean up a bit and leave the rest for tomorrow so we can visit."

Margaret's next words had made Emily avoid her as much as possible over the following years, even through university, their wedding and the woman's agonizing death from liver cancer. Those words had come back to her last night, as she watched William pacing in front of her, his face flushed with anger.

"You better get to know the real William Thompson, my girl, if you intend to marry him. He's not the nice boy you might think. His temper could squash a little bug like you without a second thought."

Emily struggled out of the covers and went to the bathroom. She was a little over two months pregnant, but other than feeling tired and urinating every ten minutes, she hadn't been sick at all. She felt wonderful, up until now at least. Although she'd tried to explain to Will that she hadn't really done it on purpose, he reminded her that the pill had been around for many years now, and had worked just fine for them all through high school, university, and the first years in their respective jobs. Why should it fail now? Human error, Emily had retorted, but Will had not even heard her. Throughout the night, despite her entreaties to stop, slow down, think, he continued to rant. Even if they could make it through a maternity leave, it would have to be a short one. So who would watch the baby? How could they even afford a good baby-sitter? Where in hell would they even put a baby in this already-cramped little place? Why would she want to give birth when they'd just be forced to have someone else raise it?

Suddenly she couldn't stand the sound of his voice any longer. She'd slammed the bedroom door and, twelve hours later, she was still wrapped in her misery and shock. Will had slept on the couch, she supposed, until the door banged open and shut this morning. She presumed that he'd gone to the studio, the source of his pride and joy, the place upon which he'd staked his ambition.

Emily saw his desire to be a famous artist as an ambition, whereas he saw it as his wellspring, his source of inspiration and motivation. They'd had many pleasant debates about creativity, the process, the need for recognition and appreciation versus the purity of formation. Emily had ambitions too; she knew she had a flare for leadership and envisioned a career in administration as her final goal. But in the meantime she was enjoying the journey; she loved the teaching, the exchange, the beautiful flow of learning with her students. She'd felt that Will had leaned too heavily toward the end-goal lately, ever since he'd received the position of Assistant Professor at The Three Arts Institute. Suddenly, he was addicted to competition, in a way he'd not been since basketball. She had seen that side of him, of course; he competed in the sport throughout high school and university and continued, even now, to belong to a fairly high level league. But Emily had always seen that attribute as a product of the sport, and not the other way around. Lately their debates had become closer to being arguments. Emily had told Will that there was a dangerous light in his eyes; one that used to flare only on the basketball court when his team's score was down. He had laughed, not taking her seriously, but she had meant what she said.

In everything that had happened to them over the years, in the course of growing up, including the loss of his mother in a painful, excruciating way, her parents' move to Ireland, and their entries into the workplace, Emily had always felt completely connected to William. They had journeyed as a unit, talking it all through, laughing or crying together, always able to come home to their little circle of two. The decision to move to Vancouver, embrace city life in place of the quiet, peaceful pace of Langford, had been made carefully – together.

Emily was totally herself with him; confident or devastated, joyful or frightened, and he with her. Late night talks, whispers in bed before passionate reinforcement of their love, had been routine and necessary. As much as they were both independent, able to function entirely well on their own, they were also one another's breath and muse. Though they had some friends, singly as well as in couples, Emily and Will had no need of another confidant. Friendships tended to be somewhat distant.

Real intimacy was something neither of them had ever experienced before, so they learned together, intellectually, spiritually and physically. William had not been a virgin when they met, thanks to one of his parents' friends, who'd been his 'Mrs. Robinson'. She'd been a good teacher, though, so Will was able to ease Emily into lovemaking with tenderness and skill. He had long, gentle fingers, accustomed to translating thought into creative image, so his love for Emily vibrated from his fingertips as he stroked her body. When they had become practiced, it was like a familiar dance, but they added steps as they went along, choreographing just a little bit differently each time. Sometimes ferociously passionate, sometimes slow and tender, they often talked all through and always at the end, making sure the other one was satisfied, though by now they could tell what the shuddering, the trembling or the exclamations meant. Even when they were going through terrible times – or perhaps especially then – their passion sustained them.

Now, as Emily turned in the tiny bathroom to wash her face, and tried to staunch her tears, she reflected that last night had been one of the first to end without being in William's arms. In fact, now that she thought about it, the last few months had been strangely different. It crept up on her slowly; the knowledge that Will had become distant. They'd been so busy this year, each with their burgeoning careers, that she hadn't noticed. Over the summer, they'd both taken courses that forced them to be on completely different schedules for the first time in their relationship. While Emily's classes started earlier in the day and ended in the afternoon, Will's began around 3 p.m. and weren't finished until 9 at night. At first they'd eaten dinner together, but soon figured out that having their meal that late didn't suit either of them, so after a while it was breakfast that they shared most often. When Emily thought back, she pictured the two of them silently reading the paper as they wolfed down a bowl of cereal or some eggs. She suddenly saw clearly a lack of touch, talk, and sharing that she had not experienced before.

Emily washed her face and made the bed, determined to put things right. Perhaps she should have an abortion. The unbidden thought didn't really shock her, though she considered the unborn child as conceived in love and therefore entitled to life. But she had not been raised in any kind of religious atmosphere, so she had some fairly liberal notions. A couple of her friends had had abortions and she had never condemned their decision. She wasn't sure that she could seriously get rid of her own child, though.

Sean was newly married and he and Susan had no children as of yet, so there was no one in her family who could help with childcare. But there were a couple of women in the apartment building who baby-sat; maybe Emily could approach one of them. She went out into the kitchen, a tiny galley-style that led to a very small dining room. They normally ate off TV tables in the living room, because the real dining table was usually piled high with books and paper. Today, however, it was witness to the detritus of a disastrous meal. Emily began to robotically clean up, still thinking through her options.

Linking their bedroom to the living room was a long narrow closet, from which the doors had long since been removed. Perhaps she could make that into a little nursery. Emily stared at the heaps of clothing and other items that filled it, a basketball, rubber boots and raincoats, tennis rackets, big summer hats. If she got rid of some, and stored the rest downstairs in their locker, a crib could easily fit inside. Maybe even one of those change tables. They might come out into the hall a bit, but it could work. Other people managed with a lot less.

She thought of her parents, who were thriving in Dublin. Her father was training young pilots again and her mother's family had left her an astonishing amount of money. Surely they would be thrilled to be grandparents and perhaps, help out while she was on maternity leave. Bolstered by her meanderings, Emily finished cleaning and then looked through her teacher file. The contract with the school board stated that teachers could have six weeks of paid pregnancy leave. After that, they were entitled to ten more weeks on unemployment insurance. Four months, Emily thought, to find a good baby-sitter. It could be done.

Energized now, Emily spent several hours cleaning the apartment and even putting some of the paraphernalia in the cupboard away. The storage space in the basement of the apartment building was fairly large. After a little rearranging, she was able to make room for all the new items. Back upstairs after several trips, she was shocked to see that it was after five o'clock. The day had been such a grey drizzly one that time had been impossible to notice. And still no sign of Will. The enthusiastic high that had carried Emily all day suddenly dissipated. What if he had left her? Feeling more than a little self-pity, she nibbled on some soda crackers and drank a huge glass of milk. Then she crawled back under the duvet and promptly fell into an exhausted sleep.

In the pitch darkness, Emily awoke with a start. Something was wrong. She felt Will's side of the bed and all the wretchedness came flooding back. Slipping out of the covers, realizing she hadn't even bothered to undress, she crept into the living room. Will was fast asleep on the couch, his feet dangling over the end, snoring lightly. Emily couldn't help it; she started to cry and threw herself onto his prone figure.

His long arms immediately reached for her, pulling her on top of him, holding her tightly, gently kissing her face. "Emily, I am so sorry, so sorry. It's okay, honey, it's all going to be okay."

She struggled to speak, gulping back the sobs of fear, gratitude, love. "I figured out some ways that we can do it, Will. I'm sorry it happened now, when we didn't plan, but…"

"It's our baby, though, Em. We love each other so much. I don't know how I could have been so selfish. We will adore our little one, we'll make it work, sweetheart. Don't cry now, the baby will hear you."

They talked a while longer, then Will carried Emily into their bed and made love to her, tenderly, gently, leaving them both sated and at peace. Just before she fell asleep, cradled in his arms, she heard him say, "Everything is going to be wonderful, Em."

If only she'd known how wrong her husband could be.

Chapter Five
September, 1980

The activity at the scene was slowly winding down. Pictures had been snapped; the room had been scoured for fingerprints, paint samples, hair, and fibres. At one point, with blinds pulled and lights out, the crime scene specialists had sprayed the darkened room with Luminol. Instantly, the entire area lit up with a bluish-white glow.

Charlie could hear the coroner and his assistants *tsking* and whispering their way through the scene, but he was having difficulty concentrating. The presence of the girl splayed on the wall made his heart race and his eyes blur.

Eventually, any trace evidence had been bagged. All but four of the police officers left, their immediate part of the task completed. Two crime scene technicians remained. One busily scribbled on a clipboard as he followed the medical examiner around the site. The drapes were pushed back again and the windows opened wide. At least they could breathe again. The room was quiet. Only the sounds from the Creek and the highway reminded the officers that life still pulsed outside these walls.

The four officers were assisting the coroner in removing the nails from the body's hands and feet in preparation for lowering her from the wall, each holding one limb. The concrete nails had been fastened at the mortar lines but were deeply embedded. Suddenly two things happened in rapid sequence: one unsettling, the other horrific.

First, Captain Kenneth Webster appeared at the door, his face uncharacteristically expressive. Captain Webster was a huge man, most often described as beefy. His broad shoulders and equally wide, round face gave him the appearance of a small truck. Opaque eyes, almost hidden by flesh, added to his inscrutable countenance. At this moment, however, he was uncharacteristically pale, the normal splotches of red missing from his cheeks and nose. His eyes were actually wide with horror. When he saw the girl splayed on the wall, he looked as though he might vomit.

The coroner, whose full name was Takumi Sato, had worked with the Captain for several years; he was not timid about asking the obvious. Did the Captain know the victim? Webster nodded slowly.

"Her name is Linda Courtnell," the big man croaked.

The Courtnells must be very good friends indeed, Charlie thought. Webster was known as a cold, heartless bastard and Charlie had never seen anything to contradict the sentiment until just now. The Captain stood silently in the middle of the room, looming over the other officers, a force that made them especially nervous.

What happened next was so unexpected, so appalling, that the trained policemen had a very difficult time keeping their composure, particularly as their boss stood so formidably in the centre.

Just as the last spike was pulled from her small, delicate foot, the girl's legs jerked. A poignant sigh whistled from her mouth, which was pulled in a straight line, lips bluish white in the morning sun. The sound was high-pitched, vibrations of agony, as though Linda railed at the violence of her death. Although the officers still clung to her body, they all jumped, so that she landed somewhat inelegantly on the floor, arms and legs stuck out in their crucified positions. The holes in her wrists and ankles gawped like hideous mouths, red tongues and white bone teeth. A horrified jolt quaked through the room.

Charlie knew he would never forget that sound. He would always picture this beautiful child desecrated and humiliated in death, lying askew on that white sheet. The destruction of this girl's angelic appearance was intermingled with the bastardization of his venerated art. The injustice seeped into Charlie's being and transformed into an anger so fierce that he felt like a balloon ready to burst.

The coroner let out a sound, an OH, but it was tinged with curiosity as he stepped toward the body. Captain Webster also moved closer to her, his face a dreadful shade.

"She can't be..."

"No, no, Captain," Sato said quickly, afraid the man would further embarrass himself. "This happens in extreme cases when death has occurred quickly and the body is placed in extreme positions. Very rare. The gases will escape when it is moved, rattling the vocal cords and jerking the limbs." He spoke rapidly as he knelt beside the dead girl's body, tenderly touching her, trying to restore some dignity. Her arms and legs were stiff, flung out as though she were waiting for a lover.

Charlie turned from the sight of her; the small breasts, the labia, painted and grotesque. The colours were incongruously sharp and bright; the picturesque scenery, the obvious skill of the artist, lent a horror that was particularly demeaning.

Dr. Sato was known as Ted to his friends, Charlie among them. He was the most experienced coroner in the area. In all likelihood, the Captain had insisted on his presence. The medical examiner took her temperature and muttered to himself as he felt along the corpse, his fingers expert at detecting information from the dead. Once in a while, he would sit back on his haunches and scribble in his notebook. The photographer snapped pictures when Ted pointed at spots of interest that only he could see beneath the thick oily paint. They carefully turned her over; the pale bloodless skin where her body had been pressed against the wall was almost a relief.

"She's been dead about twelve hours." As Ted spoke, an officer took rapid short-hand notes, following him around like a pet. "Rigor mortis is complete. We have seen a rare case of cadaveric spasm – she exhibited the death rattle and the body contractions. When the murderer stretched her body onto the wall, she very likely wasn't quite dead, but certainly dying." Dr. Sato directed his findings to the Captain, who was avoiding the sight of the body splayed on the sheet by looking the coroner in the eye. Seemingly oblivious to the officer's distress, Ted glanced at his watch. "That means I'll set the estimated time of death for between 9 p.m. and 9 a.m., when the body was found." He began to speak in a monotone, as though lecturing or rehearsing his courtroom appearance. "Of course, I will have to take into consideration the temperature last night – both inside and outside, since she was affixed to a brick wall and there's no heat source in here. It was cold last night but heated up with the sun today. It's often difficult in these cases when there is such trauma to the body – but I still might be able to set the time of death a little more exactly when the autopsy is done. She shows signs of sexual assault. There are ruptures in the vaginal area, but again, it's hard to see until I get rid of this paint. He could've cut her there, I suppose."

The doctor stood up and stretched his legs before he continued. His droning, formal speech created a vortex around him, giving the dreadful scene a framework upon which to place the remaining officers' attention. "The cause of death isn't terribly clear. I can see some petechial hemorrhaging, so she may have been strangled, but there are no obvious marks on her neck. Hard to see under all that paint, though. The cuts in her skin were performed as she was dying; her heart must have still been pumping, though slowly. Gravity did the rest. However, the murderer certainly did a great job of cleaning it up. Must've used some kind of bleach..."

Ted looked around then, as though he'd just remembered there were other people in the room. "Of course, I will have lots more answers after the autopsy. Speaking of which – ah, Captain, can I talk to you..." The pathologist gestured to the corner, where the two men adjourned and began speaking in low tones.

Charlie could see his boss's shoulders quivering, as though he were bearing an enormous weight. At first, he shook his head violently in answer to whatever Ted was suggesting, but as the coroner continued to talk, Webster obviously became resigned. It was only when Sato turned toward the two crime scene assistants that Charlie realized the enormity of what was going to happen next.

Gently, each of the men perched at one of the girl's sides, while Ted, with ruthless expertise, snapped the hardened muscles in her shoulders, then her hips, in order to lower her arms and legs. The sound in the room was excruciating; the solid crack of the joints echoed in Charlie's head. Now the slim, beautiful blond, a girl barely out of her teens, looked like a monstrous tattooed old woman from a seedy circus, crumpled and misshapen, her image in tatters from the defilement to her body. Charlie felt tears behind his eyelids; he saw his colleagues blink and turn their heads.

Quickly, the aides wrapped Linda in the sheet, positioned the body bag, and covered her in black. Soon the stretcher was heading out the door. Charlie felt relieved and ashamed at the same time.

The coroner gave a short wave and a brief smile to everyone as he gathered up his tools.

Appearing to realize the toll this discovery had taken on the sergeant, Ted placed a hand on Charlie's shoulder before following the body down the hall. "See you later," he murmured.

Captain Webster wasted no time on sentiment. "Haynes, Fairburn," he commanded, inclining his head toward the two officers in that condescending, get-over-here manner his squads so detested.

Charlie had a feeling that he knew exactly what the Captain was going to say.

More times than he wanted, Sgt Haynes had been part of a "Murder Team", squads that were formed to investigate a killing. There were no dedicated Homicide Units in Vancouver in 1980. The Captains of each Region were forced to assemble a group of investigators on site or very shortly afterward. The Captains naturally wanted their best officers on the team. Charlie's interrogation skills made him an excellent choice, plus he was good at keeping the group motivated.

The Captains always needed the crime to be solved yesterday. Not to comfort the families, not to achieve justice for the victims, but mostly, Charlie thought, so they didn't have to face the political backlash if the crime went unsolved. The number of cold cases a jurisdiction filed away was a sign of incompetence, according to the elected officials, who didn't consider the real reasons for the truth being elusive: the people who lived in that area; the conditions under which they struggled, or sometimes, how seasoned the criminals. Perhaps in this case, however, it *would* be about justice for Webster.

For the first time, Charlie had a perfect way out: he could and should declare a conflict of interest. But also for the first time, Charlie was glad that he might be selected to manage this particular hunt. He was hungry for it. He felt confident that he could be objective.

"I want you to lead up the Murder Team, Haynes." Webster waited until the Sergeant gave him the expected nod of subservience. "Fairburn, you're on the squad too."

Tom's eyes actually shone with eagerness. Charlie figured his friend couldn't wait to tell his wife Betty, ambitious Betty, that her husband had been hand picked by the Captain for an inquiry that was guaranteed to be big news.

"I'm going to talk to the girl's family," the Captain continued, trying to sound distanced from the victim but not quite succeeding. "I want you guys to find the man who rents this place – what's his name?"

"Professor Thompson," Charlie supplied. "He's a teacher at Three Arts."

"Find out what he was doing last night. I'll ask the family for names of any boyfriends and then you can chase them down too."

Tom gave Charlie a knowing look. Webster was hot for this one and there would be no rest until the culprit was in custody. As for Charlie, that was fine with him. They were going to catch this bastard.

Charlie and Tom walked out from under the steel girders into fresh, sunlit air. "We might as well head over to Three Arts now," Charlie said, "and notify Thompson. Let's bring him back here to inspect the studio, see if anything's missing."

"You think it was a robbery and she walked in on it or something? Were there some valuable paintings in there? Maybe this Thompson guy is famous and his art sells for big numbers."

Charlie looked over at his friend and partner. Tom Fairburn was a very tall, lanky man, with bright red hair, dotted freckles across his face, and a huge bulbous nose. The combination made him extremely homely in a comical way. Once, on one of the few occasions that he came to visit Charlie and Joan, their daughter Lucy had toddled up to him and asked, "Why you have your funny face on?"

Tom possessed an entertainingly quick wit, but was married to a woman who seemed to have no sense of humour at all, which Joan found incomprehensible as well as ironic. They didn't spend much time together as couples, as a result of Betty's dour personality, but Tom, Ted and Charlie had a beer after work now and then. When Charlie considered his friends, which wasn't often, he counted Ted and Tom among them.

"No, I don't think it was robbery. It doesn't have that feel about it. I don't think Thompson would leave valuable paintings in an unfinished, unsecured suite that he doesn't even own yet."

"Good point."

That was another thing Haynes liked about Tom. He never took offense, even when Charlie was caustic, which happened on a fairly regular basis.

They scanned the walkway as they headed toward the Three Arts building. Despite the presence of police cars and a coroner's vehicle, very few people had gathered at the scene. Perhaps because the building was under construction; perhaps because the students were in school at this hour, Tom suggested, though his Sergeant barely registered the words.

Charlie was thinking about Linda Courtnell's body, the way it had been painted, the fusion of colours, the skill of the artist coming through despite the horror. Although he found it difficult to understand someone using his talent in such a way, Charlie had to admit that the killer must be a real artist. Real in the ways Charlie wasn't: trained, innovative, skilled enough in the mixing of paints that the artist had created original hues. Even with skin as a canvas.

Tom was silent, respecting his partner's need for introspection as a method for processing a scene. The two policemen reached the art institute in contemplative silence. Three Arts had arrived on the island two years before The Emily Carr College. An independent, private school, which tended to attract a richer clientele because of its exorbitant tuition fees, it cultivated various talents: visual arts, journalism, and music. Once The Emily Carr moved to Granville, a fierce competition for the visual arts students began, leading Three Arts to hire super star artists and to lower their fees somewhat.

As he always did, Charlie stared up at the building in awe. A massive red-bricked structure, the Institute had once been a factory, but had been redesigned and enlarged. Its soaring ceilings captured the light and suffused the entrance with warmth. The smell of paint, sweet and salty and oily, redolent with the possibility of magnificence, rocketed through Charlie's being like a drug. He was immediately attentive, energetic, and resolute. The pathos of the girl's death was replaced with the determination of his policeman's training. He gathered his anger and used it like a knife sharpener to perfect his skills and experience.

A small reception desk tidily sat in a corner of the huge entranceway. Seated primly, the secretary was speaking into the telephone, her tones modulated, as though she were trying to smooth over someone's objections. Charlie flashed his badge at her and she nodded, quickly ending the call.

She looked up at him with large brown eyes ringed with mascara. Her young, pale white face was framed by jet black, straight hair; one ponytail sat upright on top of her head. She nervously tapped her long red nails on the desk. "The police?" she asked in a high-pitched voice, making Charlie wonder what she was so uneasy about. He knew the presence of officers in the art school must be unusual, but she appeared to be overly anxious.

"Yes, ma'am," he responded in his best Dragnet style. "We're here to see Professor Thompson."

"Really?" Again, incredulity forced her tone up a few notches. Charlie was about to chastise her, when she blurted out a question that made the hairs stand up on his arms. "It's not about Linda, is it?"

"Why would you ask that?" he countered.

She lowered her eyes, the long lashes skimming up some tears in their wake. "Well, Linda Courtnell's my best friend – my roommate - and she's been missing all night, and Professor Thompson is one of our teachers, and I know her parents called the cops. The police. Because I told them she didn't come home and that she wasn't in class this morning. This is my part-time job." She waved her manicured hand over the desk, as though the latter statement was the most important fact.

"What's your name, Miss?" Charlie asked, his most innocent, sympathetic look planted on his face.

In his peripheral vision, he could see Tom prepare to write in his little notebook.

"Wendy Collins," she answered. "This *is* about Linda, isn't it? Has something happened to her?"

"Wendy, we don't know anything yet," Charlie lied. Truthfully, since Captain Webster had identified the body, they did know exactly what had occurred, but he wasn't about to let that information circulate just yet. "We need to speak with Professor Thompson right now. I promise we'll come back and talk to you once we know something for sure."

"Thank-you," Wendy responded, once again prim and efficient. "I'll be here." She consulted a large appointment book on the desk. "Professor Thompson is in Room 240 right now, teaching an art history class. You just go up the stairs and turn left."

Tom and Charlie mounted the wide expanse of steps. A stunning landscape decorated the walls, leading toward the luminosity of the many skylights in the roof above. Students streamed past them, talking, laughing, hurrying, lugging huge portfolios. Charlie again felt that familiar lump of jealousy, wishing once again that he had followed his heart when he was young and vigorous.

The door to Room 240 was shut. Through the window, they could see the very tall, well-built man at the front of a traditional classroom, furiously scribbling on the chalkboard as he talked. The classroom of students avidly took notes, every face enraptured with whatever the professor was saying. After a moment, a couple of students began to notice the officers' scrutiny and obviously alerted the teacher, for Professor Thompson stopped talking and turned toward them.

Thompson was not only tall and lanky, but also fairly young. In addition, he was classically handsome. High cheek bones, wide brown eyes, hair that fell boyishly over his forehead, a sleek nose and sensuous lips. Most riveting were his eyes – the light, the colour, something about the way he looked into you, not at you.

When Charlie had first laid eyes on William Thompson, he had felt an immediate revulsion. This was a man who could manipulate, lie, seduce. This was a man who could look at a great painting and tell the artist, without compassion or hesitation, that it was a piece of shit. He wondered if Thompson would remember him. Would he have to declare that conflict of interest after all?

When one of the students pulled the door open, Charlie felt the breeze behind him and was conscious of stumbling into the classroom. Tom gave him a quizzical look and Charlie straightened up, shaking off a sensation of being sucked into the presence of evil. He had the feeling that they had just found their killer.

Holding up his badge, he asked the formal question. "Professor Thompson?"

The teacher dropped the chalk onto the ledge, dusted his hands on his pants, and put out his hand. It was clear that the professor didn't recognize Charlie at all, which both relieved and infuriated him.

"Yes, I'm Bill Thompson, Officer. How can I help?"

Charlie ignored the proffered handshake in favour of overly polite words. "Can we speak to you out in the hall, please, sir?"

A shocked hush hovered over the young men and women seated in the desks. Thompson nodded, glancing back at his students. "Please read those pages in the text. I'm sure I'll be right back," he said to them, his tone modulated and calm, registering little surprise or anxiety.

Charlie waited until the door closed and then continued in a low voice. "Do you rent a studio over in the market building, Professor?"

"Why, yes I do." Cultured, educated, confident. This time tinged with some surprise.

"And do you have a student by the name of Linda Courtnell?" Once again, Tom was standing close, pencil moving silently.

"She is a student of mine, yes. She's not in this particular course." He nodded toward the window of his classroom. "But she's in other classes of mine. She was absent this morning, though, come to think of it." A small shadow passed through his eyes and he frowned. "Is something wrong?"

"I'm afraid so." Charlie paused, letting the phrase sink into the man's psyche, watching the teacher's face carefully. "A body has been found in your studio."

"A...body?" This time, Thompson's unusual eyes flared with shock; the word stumbled off his tongue as though it was something foreign. "A *dead* body?"

"Yes. Murdered. We have tentatively identified her as Linda Courtnell." Charlie used his friendliest, most empathetic voice to deliver the brutal statements.

"Linda? In my studio? Murdered?"

The man sagged a little in his shock, his shoulders folding over as though a puppeteer had let go of some strings.

Thompson lowered his head into his hands. Charlie noted that he wasn't trembling; in fact, he appeared to be gathering his emotions, regaining control, setting his face. When he looked up, there was some moisture in his eyes. Almost convincing.

"How could this be?" As though reality wouldn't have allowed such an act.

"Can we go to your office or something? Somewhere private?" Charlie asked.

"Of course."

They watched as he straightened up and reopened the door. "Ladies and gentlemen," he announced. "Class will have to be dismissed for now. Make sure you finish that chapter before next week, please."

A murmur spread through the room as the students reacted in surprise. Thompson ignored the raised hands and verbalized queries as the young men and women gathered up their books. He quickly led the officers to a door at the far end of the hall.

The office, a medium-sized, windowless room, was immaculate. Files were meticulously stacked on a small desk; portfolios were primly arranged in a display bin beside it. Every square foot of wall was covered with exquisite paintings. Country scenes, wild seas, birds, vividly fascinating human faces and towering cityscapes all rushed out at Charlie, bursting with colour, gorgeous imagery, flawless genius.

The professor sat heavily in a chair in front of the desk. Charlie sat in the only other chair, not trusting his legs, sucking in his breath, trying to stop his thoughts from running too far ahead. Tom leaned against the closed door.

"How did this happen?" Thompson asked, making it sound as though they owed him an explanation. "How did Linda get into my studio?"

"That's one of our questions, sir," Charlie answered, rearranging his face, trying not to continue staring at the stunning beauties on the walls. Instead, he feigned a look of benevolence for the teacher. "Did she have a key, by any chance?"

"No, no of course not. None of my students have keys to my studio." Peremptory. As though students were not worthy of the keys to the kingdom.

"I see." Charlie nodded, as though thoughtfully contemplating a vexing puzzle. He let a silence fall, but Professor Thompson said nothing. "Well, obviously she got inside. It appears she died some time last night."

Charlie caught a flicker in those luminous eyes; something like fear, or hesitation. He pounced.

"Where were you last night, Professor Thompson?"

"At home with my wife," the man answered, far too quickly, with a tone that was firm and practiced.

"Where do you live, sir?"

He gave an address on Davie, which provoked some surprise in Charlie. The area was not a classy one; it was predominantly a working class section in addition to being well known as a place where many of the city's homosexual population lived.

"And would your wife be home right now?"

"No. She's a teacher at Bidwell Public School. But I'm sure you could call her. Do you need to verify my whereabouts?"

Charlie gave a silent rebuke. *Of course we have to "verify your whereabouts" you arrogant asshole.* "You can imagine, sir, as the occupant of the place where the crime was committed, you must be eliminated from our investigation." He pronounced *occupant* as though Thompson owned the crime, which Charlie was becoming convinced that he did.

"Of course. That makes sense." Silence. "I'm still so shocked. I can't believe something like this could happen here. I mean, the students are all wonderful people – I can't imagine that one of them is a murderer. Linda is – was – a very talented young woman. She's won a number of prizes and she's still got so many years to...well, she had...such potential."

"What makes you think one of the other students might be the murderer?"

Professor Thompson folded his hands on his desk. Charlie noticed that he did this to control the shaking that had begun to move through him. The teacher cleared his throat. "I...just assumed, I guess. Fellow students would be the likely ones to break into my studio with her."

"The studio was not broken into, Professor."

Bill Thompson looked up at Charlie, his deep brown eyes flooded with confusion. "I don't understand any of this. I still can't believe Linda Courtnell is dead, let alone murdered in my own studio. Do you mean someone got in with a key?"

"Well." Charlie appeared to be considering. "Could you have left the door unlocked by accident?"

"It's very unlikely. But I suppose it's possible."

Jumping too quickly at any explanation, the policeman thought. "Does anyone else have a key?"

"Just the manager, Mr. Jeffries. He's got master keys to all the suites."

Charlie nodded, as though once again considering this option. "Do you get along well with your students, Professor?"

"I like to think so. It's been my life dream to have a studio of my own and to teach other artists. I certainly have the motivation to do a good job. I'm not a full professor, though we use the title. I'm an assistant, working on my degree and tenure."

As though he were being interviewed for a position, Charlie thought, trying to make a good impression. Which, in a way, he was.

"What goes on in your studio?"

"What goes on...? I tutor student artists. I go over techniques they've learned in class, try to correct any errors by giving them one-on-one advice. That kind of thing. That's what goes on."

Intelligent bastard, too; recognizing the bait and returning the underlying, sarcastic tone, but making sure it was light enough to avoid mention.

"Just visual art?"

"Yes. I...I got to be fairly well known as an artist – mostly oil paints - so Three Arts recruited me."

"Are these your paintings, sir?" Charlie waved nonchalantly at the walls.

"Yes. I continue to do my own art, of course. It's expected, plus it's a...well, it's my passion."

Though Thompson looked humble, Charlie saw the pride behind the words. The police officer scanned the paintings once again, his heart pounding with the sheer beauty of them.

"Do you keep any of your paintings at the studio?"

"Yes, but not many. They're either here or at home or in a gallery if I have a showing."

"We want you to come with us to the crime scene, sir," Charlie said. "We'll need you to state whether or not anything is missing."

"Do you think someone tried to rob the place and Linda just happened to be there?" The Professor looked almost hopeful.

"Do you keep anything valuable there?" Charlie countered.

"Not really. It's not exactly secure yet. So I guess it's unlikely to be a robbery..."

The teacher's voice trailed off, but Charlie didn't give him a lifeline. Instead, he abruptly stood up.

"If you can come with me now, sir."

"I should let the Dean know...they'll have to cancel my next class..."

Thompson began to fumble with the telephone, but the Sergeant put his hand on top of the other man's. "No need, Professor. We can walk past the Dean's office on our way out."

Charlie noticed that the teacher's hands had begun to shake again. He reached for a cardigan and flung it over his shoulders, as though cold even in the stifling heat of the office. While he fumbled with the sleeves, Charlie took Tom's notebook out of the officer's hands and wrote, *Go see the wife.* Tom nodded and walked swiftly down the hallway.

"Are you sure you've still got your key to the studio, sir?"

William Thompson nodded, holding up a crammed keychain.

As they came down the sweeping staircase, Wendy Collins stood up at her desk, her face vivid with questions and fear. She hurried up to them, eyes already brimming with tears.

"What happened, Professor? Is Linda all right?" Directing the question to her teacher, as though he alone could shield her from bad news, she placed a hand on his arm.

Charlie spoke before Thompson could utter a sound. "Wendy, we will let you know everything as soon as we can, I promise. How long are you working today?"

She turned toward him, warmed by the sound of concern and friendliness in his voice. "I'm here until five."

"I give you my word that I will be back before then, Wendy. I'll talk to you personally."

Charlie noticed that the Professor touched the girl's elbow, reassuringly. Or was the familiarity something more? Certainly there was more on the girl's part. Her eyes were filled with longing, desire, and a glow that was akin to worship.

Chapter Six
September, 1980

Emily was exhausted. After the efforts of cleaning out the cupboard on Sunday, not to mention the emotional roller coaster she'd been on all weekend, she felt drained. That morning, before the bell rang and the students began pouring into the room, she had sat down heavily behind her desk, trying to write in her daily planner. Instead, she found herself gazing out the window. Since she was in one of the many portables that dotted the pavement, there wasn't much of a view. All she could really see was the red-bricked wall of the school. Her eyes were still swollen with tears from the night before. Staring off into nothing was all she could manage.

After a while, she gave up on the planner and began to write the day's activities on the chalkboard. Luckily, her Grade Five students were enthusiastic and industrious, so she knew she could design some very independent work for them while she was emotionally incapable of being truly with them today.

Emily felt safe and isolated in her little portable, especially when surrounded by the students. They chattered obliviously along through their morning routines, completely unaware of their teacher's emotional state, and for that innocence, Emily was extremely grateful. The only child to pick up on her aura was Justin, whose radar seemed to be enhanced by his autism. His little face was pinched into a worried frown. Every time she looked around, he was plastered to Emily's side, looking up at her with his expressive brown eyes, his intense scrutiny off-centre as he carefully avoided direct contact. Once or twice that morning, she gently took his chin in her hand and directed him to look straight at her so she could smile and try to convince him that she was all right.

Laura and Fiona, one pure blonde with blue eyes, the other a brown-eyed mix of Oriental and Caucasian, both straight-haired, almost always wearing ponytails, were mother hens to Justin. They soon began to zoom in on his tension and immediately connected it to the unusual lack of energy from their teacher. They were among Emily's absolute favorites. Kind, thoughtful and enthusiastic learners, they were mature little people, perhaps a bit too grown up, but a teacher's dream nevertheless. Emily hoped they wouldn't give in to pre-teen angst as so many girls did in the sixth grade.

"Miss Taylor, are you okay?" Laura whispered at one point, her voice so grown-up and solicitous.

Laura's parents had saddled their daughter with three names plus a surname, all of which the little girl unfailingly used as her signature. Since Emily had retained her maiden name even when she started teaching, she now wondered if she'd hyphenate it for their child. Would they call the baby Something Taylor Thompson? Would their daughter be blond and sweet like Laura Ann Barnett Cahill?

"I'm not feeling too well, to be honest, Laura," she said, putting her hand gently on the girl's shoulder. "But don't worry, I'll be okay. We just have to convince Justin of that, don't we?"

Laura nodded with precocious gravity. "Fiona and I will take care of him, so you can just sit at your desk, OK?"

Emily smiled. "I would be ever so grateful," she answered in the same serious tone.

Leaders in the way that mothers often are, the two girls somehow spread their magic throughout the classroom and the morning actually flew by. When the lunch bell rang, Emily remained in the portable nibbling at her sandwich. The children's voices outside flowed around her, as though the portable were a raft in the midst of a pleasant sea. Emily was beginning to feel much better when a knock startled her. The door was shoved open before she could answer.

Elaine Martin was a large-boned redhead who filled the room with her presence. Quick to smile or laugh, she had a deep booming voice and a commanding face. Her eyes were green and lively; she homed in on a person with an intensity that was almost psychic. She taught Grade One, constantly dancing around her classroom with an energy that was almost as vigorous as the six-year-olds'. Emily had become very close to Elaine in the three years since she'd joined the staff, admiring her colleague's ferocious love of children and the art of teaching. Lately, Emily and William had been together for dinner numerous times with Bob and Elaine, and they'd enjoyed each other's company immensely.

The moment Elaine entered the classroom, Emily's mood soared. She hadn't realized how much she needed to share her joy and her doubt with someone else. The Martins had two small children of their own and had struggled financially due to Bob's penchant for changing occupations. Though Emily didn't usually confide in anyone other than Will, if anybody could understand how she felt just now, it was Elaine. Soon the entire story of the weekend had tumbled out, with Elaine's arm around Emily's shoulder, comforting and congratulating in turn.

"Bill is going to be an amazing father," Elaine reassured her friend. "He was already warming to the idea after only a few hours. It took Bob about a month to be happy about Natalie and I still don't think he's adjusted to little Bobby."

Emily laughed. "It's only that Bobby's two. It's a rotten age."

Elaine chuckled. "Yah, I'm sure glad you like kids. The last time you were at our place for dinner, he certainly put on a show."

They were still recalling Bobby's antics when another knock resounded through the portable. Once again, the door swung open without waiting for an answer. Principal Dennis Maloney ushered in with a tall, broad-shouldered man dressed in a Vancouver Police Department uniform. Both Elaine and Emily stood up as they entered, their faces mirroring concern, surprise, and fear. Neither woman could say a thing.

"Emily, this is Officer Fairburn," Dennis said. "I don't want you to worry; he just needs to speak with you."

"Is it one of my students?" Emily asked, sliding to a sitting position in a nearby chair.

The policeman was extremely homely. His red hair stood straight on top of his head; his huge nose made him look clown-like. But there was nothing humorous in his staid, serious gaze. "No, ma'am, it's not one of your students. Do you...want some privacy?"

Emily was startled. A cold shiver ran down her spine, a premonition that something terrible was about to shift her world. "Privacy? I don't think so...Elaine and Dennis are...please, they can stay. Just tell me. What *is* it?"

"Nothing has happened to anyone you know, at least I don't think you do," Fairburn said obscurely. He straightened his shoulders, as though strengthening his resolve, then began again. "I just need to ask you a question. Where was your husband last night?"

The sound of the door shutting, the empty bed, the darkness of the living room, all flashed through Emily's memory. Instinctively, she answered, "We were at home last night. Why would you ask? Is he all right?"

She felt Elaine's eyes shift questioningly toward her, but Emily didn't move. She kept her gaze on the officer's squinty eyes, searching for an answer, terrified of hearing the words, *your husband has been killed in an accident...*

Emily's heart was pounding so loudly that, when he did offer some information, she could barely understand the statement.

"I'm afraid a young woman was killed in your husband's studio some time in the last twenty-four hours," Officer Fairburn announced.

Elaine was the first to react. "Killed? You mean she fell or something?"

"No, ma'am, it wasn't an accident. However, I can't say much more than that. We are speaking with your husband right now, Mrs. Thompson, and just needed to verify his whereabouts with you." He scribbled a few lines in his tiny blue notebook. "I don't know if my superior will need to ask you any more questions, but we'll be in touch. It's good that we know where to find you."

"Who was the young woman who died?" Emily asked.

"I'm afraid I can't tell you that, at least not until her family has been informed. You understand." With that statement of assumption, the man turned and placed his hand on the doorknob.

"Before you leave, Officer Fairburn, can we have your badge number and full name, please?" Dennis asked politely. Emily was to be forever grateful for this man's attention to protocol: he would be her model in years to come.

"Of course," the policeman answered stiffly, as though the request was an affront. Once again, he scribbled a couple of lines and tore the page from the booklet. Then, as abruptly as the homely giant had entered the portable, he was gone.

Dennis came over to where Emily still sat. "Emily, why don't you go home?" he suggested, his light blue eyes kind and concerned. "I haven't much on my plate this afternoon and I'd love to teach for a change. You need to be with Bill."

Tired, shocked, Emily couldn't stop the tears from streaming down her face. "Thank-you, Dennis, thank-you. I...I didn't do much of a plan, I wasn't feeling that well this morning...but I wrote this outline on the board..."

After much cajoling and assistance from both Elaine and Dennis, not to mention reassurance that Justin would be fine, Emily was in her car, heading for Granville Island just after one o'clock. The sun, which had maintained the unusually high temperature throughout the morning, sat atop one of the lower mountains, blinding Emily's eyes as she carefully steered the car. As always, the sight of the Rockies soaring into the sky, ringing the city with majesty, gave her a sense of hope and wonder. She felt as though her destiny – reaching Will – would have drowned her, overwhelmed her, had she not been able to raise her eyes to those peaks.

At the reception desk, Wendy Collins was red-eyed and weepy. As Emily approached, she leapt from her chair and came to embrace her. Emily almost recoiled; she had instantly disliked this young woman the first time they'd met. There was something sycophantic, an overt flirtatiousness with William, which made Emily feel uncomfortable. Sometimes Emily was filled with guilt that she was capable of a tawdry jealous streak, but Wendy was one of two students that she didn't trust, didn't seem to be able to like, despite knowing them for two years.

"Oh, Mrs. Thompson! The police came. It's something to do with Linda. You know, Linda Courtnell?"

Emily nodded, once again getting the impression that Wendy said things to make her feel like a much older woman, exaggerating the five or six years between them. She gently extricated herself from the girl's embrace.

"Where is my husband now?" she asked, deliberately using the word.

Wendy looked into Emily's eyes, mascara blatantly mashed against her cheeks, highlighting her grief. An art form within itself, Emily thought, ensuring everyone would know just how upset Ms Collins was.

"The police officer took him over to the studio."

"Okay, thanks, Wendy."

"Are you going over there too? Will you make sure you come back and let me know if something has happened to Linda? I just know something horrible has happened. I'm the one who called her parents when she didn't come home last night." Tears rolled down Wendy's cheeks.

Emily instantly felt guilty again. The girl was probably truly distraught over her friend. Emily also realized that no one else knew there was a body in Professor Thompson's studio – a body that was very likely Linda Courtnell's.

"I'll come back, I promise," she told Wendy, as kindly as she could manage. "If I know anything, I'll tell you."

Wendy smiled, a smile that wiped away any empathy Emily had felt for the girl. She looked as though she had just won a prize.

"Thank-you so much, Mrs. Thompson." The girl fairly danced back to her desk, probably relishing the gossip she would soon have to share with everyone else. Savoring, enjoying the drama.

With the sun high overhead, the birds slicing through the sky and squawking above the waterway, Emily walked rapidly toward the building that housed her husband's studio. All around her, life surged and flourished in the unusually clear, warm air. Emily felt as though she alone could see the fog: the mist of uncertainty, the terrible intuition that something was horribly, mockingly, out of kilter. When she saw the yellow tape and the burly, familiar police officer stationed outside the building, she began to run.

Officer Fairburn actually smiled at her as she arrived, out of breath, in front of him. The smile transformed his ugly face into something far more approachable.

"Mrs. Thompson," he greeted her. "I guess you were worried about your husband."

Emily could only nod, feeling suddenly dizzy and nauseous. A blockage had lodged in her stomach and throat; fear and distress clogged her mind.

"He's in the studio with my boss. Just has to see if anything has been stolen." He seemed to notice her pale countenance and pointed to a huge, flat piece of concrete bathed in the gentle sunlight. "Why don't you sit here, Mrs. Thompson? I'm sure they'll be out soon. It's still a crime scene, you know, so I can't let you go up there." Easy, friendly, as though they were discussing something as ordinary as weather.

Emily, gratefully seated on the flat base, simply nodded again. Fairburn pulled something from a pack stashed behind a pole. He handed her a bottle of water, which Emily took and drank with great relish. When she was finished, she was able to speak once more, but the question that came out astonished her.

"Are you married?"

The policeman smiled again. "Yes, I am. Betty and I have been married for ten years. How about you and the Professor?"

"We've been married for five years. Do you have any children?"

"Nope. We've never been blessed with little feet in the house." His eyes, sharp but kind, shone with a look that made him a little less homely. But it seemed to Emily that he was not unhappy about the lack of little feet running about.

For the second time that day, Emily found herself revealing private thoughts. This man was a complete stranger, yet her befuddled, emotional state unlocked her tongue in a way that was not normal for her.

"I'm pregnant," she told him. "We're going to have our baby in April. Well, around April anyway. I haven't been given the exact date yet. The doctor said she'll be able to tell me more next month."

"Congratulations," he said at once. Emily noticed the spark in his eyes had deepened, making the colour a very dark blue. "I'll bet the Professor is so happy!"

"He wasn't at first," Emily admitted. "But he is now. It's just that we're really starting out and we didn't actually plan this pregnancy..."

He was alert now, like a cat sensing movement in the grass. Emily could almost smell his eagerness. She immediately stopped speaking, the sun on her head like a warm hat, a surreal feeling surging through her. She suddenly imagined a dead body in William's studio – beaten?

Bloodied? Raped? She couldn't stop herself. She leaned over and vomited on the ground, the smell and taste filling her with disgust and shame.

Officer Fairburn helped her to her feet when she had finished, moving her smoothly onto a concrete slab in the shade. Then as if he had been expecting this event, he once again reached into his sack. Handing her a small packet of tissue, he kicked dirt over the vomit. An awkward, stifled silence fell between them. Tears flowed silently down Emily's cheeks; she didn't bother to try and staunch them. Tom Fairburn stood with his back to her, respecting her privacy, staring out into the sun.

Just when Emily thought she couldn't stand the wait any longer, the sound of feet on the stairs rang out through the empty building. Emily jumped up as William's lanky figure appeared at the bottom of the steps. She ignored the other man, another male of huge proportions, and ran straight into her husband's arms. Will was obviously startled to see her, even recoiling a little as she embraced him. Emily, in her distraught state, barely registered the reaction. Sergeant Haynes, however, took careful note.

"Emily, what are you doing here?" Will asked quietly, his body stiff and almost embarrassed.

"When Officer Fairburn told us what happened, Dennis let me go home. Since I had the car this morning, I came to get you."

Emily knew it was an odd comment. Will always took the city bus and the Aqua Bus to work and back; Emily always took their old car. But her husband nodded as though she'd said something normal, although his demeanor continued to be stiff and distant. Emily drew back a little and looked at the other policeman.

He was also quite tall, though he didn't quite reach the six-foot-two that both William and Officer Fairburn did. A round-faced, burly man, the startling adjective that came to Emily was cuddly. He gave her a friendly, crinkled smile, and Emily added handsome to the descriptor.

Charlie held out his hand. "Mrs. Thompson, I'm Sergeant Charles Haynes." As they shook, he directed his deep blue eyes straight into hers, warmth and support emanating from his gaze. "I'm sorry you had to be dragged into this terrible tragedy."

Emily was shaken once again. She slipped her arm through William's. "What happened? Is it Linda Courtnell?"

Charlie tilted his head, surprised. "Why do you ask that?" He glanced suspiciously at Tom.

"Wendy Collins mentioned that Linda has been missing since last night and when Officer Fairburn told me a body had been found in the studio...I just assumed..."

"Well, I'm afraid you are correct, Mrs. Thompson. Linda Courtnell was found murdered in your husband's studio." He pronounced each syllable slowly, as though for effect, or else to cushion the shock, Emily wasn't sure which. "Of course we had to get your husband to check if anything was missing."

"But nothing is," Will inserted quickly, shock and bewilderment tingeing his voice.

"I don't understand it," Emily said. "How could this have happened? You were there earlier yesterday. And Linda wasn't around then. How did she get in?"

The silence should have told Emily that her chatter was not only naive, but was being scrutinized, evaluated. Looking back years later, the older, wiser woman that she became could barely recognize the immature, inexperienced girl that she had been. Innocence can appear to be stupidity, like a person who can barely speak your language may falsely appear to be simple.

"Actually, she *was* here yesterday, Em," Will said quietly, reluctantly. "As I told Sergeant Haynes, Linda dropped by while I was working last evening. I was doing the painting of our island in Langford. Linda saw the light, I guess, and came in for a chat. She was out in one of the restaurants with some friends. She didn't stay very long."

Over-explaining, Emily thought, a chill running through her. He hadn't mentioned Linda being in the studio. But then, they had barely spoken...She thought about lying, saying oh yes of course I'd forgotten you mentioned her, but the puzzlement had already crossed her face – and she knew that both officers had noticed.

"But how did she get back in after you left?" Emily asked. In the silence, she wished she could have bitten back the words.

Sergeant Haynes answered in a cool, patient tone. "That's something we're investigating, Mrs. Thompson. The door could have been left unlocked or perhaps Linda stole a spare key. We'll find out."

Emily took comfort in his last sentence. She thought of it as a promise that the truth would be discovered quickly.

"Can I leave now?" Bill asked. His submissive tone startled his wife.

Sergeant Haynes patted him heartily on the back. "Of course, Professor. I know this has been a shock to you. We've got your address should anything come up. I will have to get you to sign a statement that the studio wasn't robbed, and that you were home last night, but we can do that tomorrow if you like."

Will hesitated. "Tomorrow…could I come down this afternoon instead?"

The big policeman smiled, as though he were pleased at an ingenious suggestion. "Absolutely! I'm sure you don't want to miss any more classes."

"That's what I was thinking," Will answered. He turned to Emily. "Do you want me to take you home first, honey?"

"I'm on my way home right now," Officer Fairburn offered. "I'll drop your wife off and then you'll have your own car. Plus, if you don't mind, we do have a couple of questions for you, too, Mrs. Thompson."

Hesitating, her heart skipping in her chest and echoing in her ears, Emily looked to Will for direction. He gave her a slight nod, his eyes pleading, and she thought she understood. She allowed Officer Fairburn to fold her into his vehicle, thinking incongruously that she had never had a ride in a police car.

"Mrs. Thompson," the tall man said quietly, as he expertly guided the car over the bridge, the cool sun sparkling on the Creek below them. "We have to ask these questions, you understand. I mean, the murder did take place in your husband's studio, so unfortunately you are both drawn into the tragedy. It happens sometimes to the best of people."

Emily knew that bad things happen to good people, as the saying went. She was having trouble adjusting to the enormity of this event: a murder among her husband's tranquil, colour-filled artistry. She said nothing, simply watched the buildings flip past, thinking how odd that everything looked completely normal.

"You told me that your husband was home with you last night. But just now, you mentioned that he was at the studio earlier in the day. What time did your husband get home?"

Emily remembered the heat of their lovemaking in the middle of the cool, dark night. Words had not seemed important. Details such as time had not been important. Now the lack of specifics appeared to be a huge chasm, something vital that she had missed. She tried to concentrate, to remember the steps she'd taken when she got up in the darkness of their little apartment. Had she looked at the bedside clock?

"It was around ten o'clock," she answered finally. "I looked at our alarm clock, because I'd fallen asleep and I was wondering why it was so dark."

"I see. Well, thanks for that, I'm sure the information will be helpful to our investigation." He gave his crooked, wide-mouthed smile that made his ugly face look less threatening, and insisted on walking her to the door.

Emily collapsed on the couch, shocked and weepy. Had she actually looked at the clock last night? Where had ten o'clock come from? Her actual memory or a time that she thought would somehow fit? Would her story and Bill's match? She had a hollow, sickening feeling that she had just made a terrible mistake.

When William still had not returned home hours after the affable Tom Fairburn escorted Emily to the apartment, his kindness and consideration looked more like manipulation. For most of that long afternoon, Emily slept fitfully, exhausted and physically ill. Her usual energy, the determination and gusto for which she was known, had completely deserted her.

Several calls to the police station resulted in assurances that her husband was continuing to "co-operate with the investigation". Emily was frozen, completely lost, unable to consider a next move. It was the early news on the local television station that finally caused her to leap to her feet, every fibre of her being taut and alive with tension. She was like a cat that has caught the scent of danger, her skin, muscles, brain, all rushed with adrenaline to face the fight.

"Earlier today, the daughter of well-known, highly respected businessman Randall Courtnell and his wife Paula, was found brutally murdered in an artist's studio," intoned the porcelain-skinned reporter. "No official confirmation has been made of the artist's name, but a student has claimed the studio belongs to a Professor William Thompson. We go live to the scene with Mariko Toyama."

The impossibly beautiful Japanese Canadian reporter stood in the waning sunshine outside Three Arts next to Wendy Collins. Wendy's tear-stained face gave her an innocent, grief-stricken visage that was endearing and sympathetic.

"Tell us what you experienced earlier today, Miss Collins," Mariko coaxed the girl gently.

"Linda never showed up this morning at home or in class," Wendy simpered. "She's my best friend and roommate, and she never stays away like that, without telling me. So I called her parents and they called the police. When the police checked Professor Thompson's studio, they found her..." Wendy burst into tears.

Mariko put her arm around the girl's shoulders and turned to the camera, empathetic and professional at the same time. "We have confirmed that Professor Thompson is now at police headquarters. We have been told that he is cooperating with the investigation." Same words that Emily had heard, spoken with a tinge of sarcasm that provided a wealth of suspicion and doubt to the listening audience.

At that moment, the door opened and her husband literally fell into the apartment. His shoulders hunched, he collapsed in a spasm of weeping, his heart broken by the obliteration of a young life, by the horrific hurt of even being *suspected* of the kind of madness that could engineer such destruction.

As Emily curled herself around him, while he sobbed prostrate on their little sofa, she knew they had somehow, contrary to their own volition, turned a corner that was leading to a very dark place. A condition, a situation, that they could not control nor predict, where they had no map to follow, no light to guide their movements.

Chapter Seven
September, 1980

As Charlie worded it for Ted and Tom at the pub that Friday evening, he was never so royally pissed off.

"The bastard just sat there like a huge truck with its engine running. I was completely off my game. Couldn't interview that son of a bitch at all." He took a huge gulp of his beer, his face red with alcohol and embarrassment.

The "bastard" was Captain Webster, who had sat in on the questioning of William Thompson on Monday. It was an experience that had never before been Charlie's to endure. His description of the moment when the Mountain Moved had his colleagues wide-eyed in astonishment.

Most of the time, the Professor sat with his head in his hands, propped on his long, folded legs, almost doubled over. Sweat dripped from the bridge of his nose onto the floor; he constantly tried to clear his throat. Charlie had to admit that the air was constrictive, dry and hot, especially with the literal elephant in the room.

"I am not the person you are looking for," Thompson kept telling them over and over. "I would never have murdered someone. I could not have hurt Linda. She was a great kid, really talented and energetic. I can't imagine anyone wanting to hurt her. She had a great future in front of her."

"Were you jealous of her, Professor? Do you think of yourself as THE Artist? Was this upstart little girl going to surpass you?"

"I kept telling him, 'Bill, you found out your wife was pregnant'." Charlie mimicked the monotone quality his voice had adopted during the interview. "With Webster staring at me the whole time, I just repeated the same stuff and I know I sounded bored with it, because I was. I could do nothing creative. I hammered over and over, 'You had to get rid of your girlfriend. She wouldn't let go, so you killed her. Maybe you didn't mean to choke her to death. Or maybe you raped her when she wouldn't consent to some break-up sex, then you figured you had to kill her. But once she was dead, you thought you'd stage the scene as though she'd been raped and crucified by a madman'. Or maybe you killed her because you are THE Artist and she was taking your spot in the limelight."

"Smart," Ted said enthusiastically. "What did he say to that?"

"She wasn't my girlfriend. I keep telling you that."

"Perhaps she was a spoiled little brat who was going to show up her teacher with her brilliance, eh?"

"Of course not. Every artist is different. There can be lots of different kinds of success..." The Professor suddenly looked up as a thought occurred to him. "If I were the murderer, why would I do it in my own studio? Wouldn't that make you suspicious right away?"

"That's exactly why you did it. You're a brilliant man, Bill. You figured we wouldn't suspect you because who would be stupid enough to foul his own nest?"

"Then all of a sudden, Thompson was crushed," Charlie told his friends dramatically. "I had him. But then he looks over at Webster and for some reason, he gets a second breath. He starts to almost whine. 'It doesn't matter what I say. You think I'm guilty. I guess I better get a lawyer in here' he says."

Ted and Tom waited expectantly for the punch line.

"So what does Webster do then?" Charlie said rhetorically, stretching it out. "He gets to his feet, just unfolds that big fat ass of his and towers over us."

The huge man moved from his chair in the corner, staring down at William Thompson with a puffy, anger-smeared face, his eyes bulging in fury.

"I'm Captain Webster, Professor. I was told by Sergeant Haynes that you would be co-operative." His voice was loud and deep, resonating in the small room. He sounded accusatory, as though both Bill and Charlie had lied to him. "Start telling the truth, or so help me God, I'll beat it out of you."

Ted actually gasped out loud. "No shit!"

"No shit," Charlie returned. "And that was the end of it. Even if Thompson hadn't reacted the way he did, I would've had to stop the interview anyway. But of course the Professor suddenly sits up all smart ass once again and this time formally demands a lawyer or we let him go."

"Fuck," Tom muttered.

Charlie nodded his head, morosely taking another swig. "Naturally I went into my best friend mode. I had to smooth it over, practically kiss that pervert's hand, then send him on his way. Good thing the evidence is starting to move our way or we'd have no case left. I couldn't even speak to Webster. I was lucky we were out on the case most of the week, because I think I might've said something I'd be sorry for."

The other men shook their heads in sympathy.

"But the case is looking good, eh?" Ted asked, his Canadian accent tinged with his Japanese inheritance lending a staccato rapidity to his words.

They always sat in a large booth at the back of Flip's Bar. Separated by a long counter stacked with coffee cups and other supplies, it was distanced from the rest of the customers. Pictures of Marilyn Monroe were strung all across the wall behind them. Incongruously, Charlie sat under her most famous photo with the skirt swirling around her slim legs from the subway draft. Despite its cheesy atmosphere, the booth was an area in which they could not be overhead, where they could speak frankly and debate the merits of their cases without censor. It was their unofficial brainstorming conference, each of them bringing their ideas, skills and experience to generate theories.

"We've got a few things going our way," Charlie said circumspectly, gazing into his beer. He could feel the tension in his shoulders and his gut. A thread of hope zinging through him, he held up his fingers and counted the facts. "One, the Professor really has no alibi. He told us he was home with the wife when the girl was murdered, but Tom here just proved he's lying about that one."

Tom beamed under the rare praise. "I had a feeling the wife's friend knew something when I went to her school that first day. Yesterday afternoon, she spilled." He glanced at his notebook. "Her name's Elaine Martin. She teaches with the missus. Seems like the Professor and the wife had a fight that night and he stormed off. Mrs. Thompson really has no idea what time he got home, even though she told us it was ten o'clock. Martin will make a good witness if the wife continues to stick to her story. And even if she doesn't, Martin can establish that he has no real alibi."

"As long as they accept it. Could be hearsay," Ted inserted.

"You a lawyer or a coroner?" Charlie asked sarcastically; then continued as though the man hadn't spoken. "Two, he's got a motive. Tom's also the one who got little wifey to tell him she's pregnant and that the professor wasn't exactly thrilled."

"The pregnancy is the reason the professor stormed off," Tom explained. "He was pissed because they hadn't planned on having kids yet. His career comes first, obviously, even over his wife and potential kids." Tom stated this fact as though his wife weren't a future candidate for the mayor's job and adamant that they would remain childless.

"Third," Charlie said, "we have not one, but two, eyewitnesses."

"Seriously? Who?" Ted leaned far over the table in his eagerness.

"Remember the homeless woman who hangs around the market area?"

Ted shook his head.

"She's an alcoholic. Rumour is that she used to have a good job until she got addicted, then moved onto Granville. We pretty much leave her alone; she doesn't cause any ruckus."

"Doesn't sound too promising as a witness."

"No, but she swears she saw a man coming down the steps with an artist kit slung over his shoulder around 10:30 that night. Her description sounds exactly like Thompson. She keeps her eyes open and knows everything there is to know about the Island. I think if we clean her up, she'll make a pretty good witness."

"Her statement fits with the time of death, too, eh, Ted?" Tom asked.

"The stomach contents might be helpful," the doctor replied thoughtfully. "Her last meal was consumed just before 8 p.m., according to her friends, and the food was barely digested. But of course, some pathologists believe that trauma can stop the digestion process, so…"

Charlie cut him off, as though what other researchers said was unimportant. "You did say the time of death was between 9 p.m. and 9 a.m. originally."

"True," Ted admitted. "But you know it's not an exact science, eh?"

Once again, Charlie ignored him. "The 9 p.m. timeframe fits. The Professor actually admits to seeing Linda then. He says it was just before he left for home at 9 or slightly after. She was at the local bar with some friends, had dinner with them and left around 8. According to Thompson, she saw his lights and just popped in to say hello. Then she was supposed to be heading back to her friends, but they told us she never showed up again. They assumed she stayed at the studio. Apparently she's been doing that a lot lately."

"I wonder what she's been doing at the studio all hours," Tom snickered.

"Are there any other suspects? What about the other artist? The guy with the studio across the hall. What about the boyfriend?" Ted had an amazing capacity to listen to the facts and then question every one of them. Usually Charlie appreciated this skill, but in this case he found it irritating.

"The other artist's a queer," Tom answered, making his voice go up at the end. "Can't be a contender for this one."

Charlie winced. He disliked Tom's deep prejudices. Tom had no idea how unbiased Charlie was and how much he loved the spirit currently energizing Vancouver. Music, art, and every other creative enterprise had benefited from the surge of freedom and acceptance, in Charlie's opinion. To his delight, Joan enjoyed and appreciated this cultural and progressive atmosphere just as much as he did. Greg Hughes was one of the people whom Charlie had befriended, even though they probably appear to be direct opposites if they walked down the street together. Greg was lively, kind, and talented, in both art and music, but unlike Charlie, he was open, flamboyant, unafraid to declare who he was.

Sergeant Haynes was Charlie's public persona. He couldn't reveal the artistic, gentle, dreamy nature of the real Charles Haynes to the people with whom he worked. His closer allies accepted that he dabbled in painting; it was his hobby; his relaxation. Akin to their hobbies of watching hockey or playing a game of poker. Only Charlie knew it was far more than that; it was a part of him, like the need for food or water. A need that he was forced to submerge, except when he was in the company of people like Greg.

The police officer in him, however, often took advantage of the prejudices of others in order to achieve justice. Such as right at this moment.

"His name's Greg Hughes. I know him from the art school. And you're right, Tom, he's not a suspect. The boyfriend has an alibi. He was at the pub with their friends that night. He went home with his roommate, figuring Linda had gotten caught up in her art once again. Thompson is the guilty one. I *know* it. I *feel* it."

And Charlie did. It was a hard certainty that had lodged itself in his chest ever since he'd gazed upon that poor girl, humiliated in death, art twisted into a tool for torture and shame. The certainty had solidified when he'd realized that the privileged bastard who owned the self-important 'studio overlooking the Creek' was none other than the smug, judgmental William Thompson. Handsome, arrogant, incompetent adjudicator of art contests. Thompson was exactly the kind of man who could not only be a cold, merciless killer, but who could also violate the sanctity of art in such a manner.

"She *was* raped, wasn't she, Ted?" Charlie asked.

"Definitely. There were ruptures and bruising in the vaginal area consistent with rape. But he was a careful bastard. Must've used a condom. I found a small amount of seminal fluid. Could've leaked through, maybe because he was so rough, or could've been left from someone else. It might not be of any use as a sample. We're testing it now."

The men fell silent, each in their own form of consternation: the lack of evidence, the awful violation perpetrated on this young woman, Charlie's certainty and Ted's hesitation.

"The reporters are sure going wild about this case," Tom inserted to remove some of the tension from the air.

"Holy shit, yah," Ted agreed. "I know Vancouver is still a small city, but you'd think it was some princess or celebrity who died. I've never seen them go crazy over a murder the way they've glommed onto this one."

Charlie shook his head. "It's her father. He's Randall Courtnell, after all! He owns half the fucking city."

"He got his money from banking and then good investments." Ted was again a fountain of information.

"Bought up a ton of real estate in the early '70's that's now worth a fortune."

"And he's made himself some good friends in very high places. Did you know that Linda Courtnell was Webster's goddaughter?"

"You've gotta be kidding," Tom responded. "I can't even picture that sour puss in church, let alone holding some howling baby over a christening bowl."

The three of them guffawed at the image.

"He was obviously very fond of her, though. You should've seen his face when he saw her body. Then when she did that..."

"...cadaveric spasm," Ted supplied.

"Yah, that...he was actually hoping she was still alive. Speaking of that, you're saying strangulation was the COD, eh, Ted?"

The coroner nodded his head and paused before he spoke, as though gathering his thoughts. "It was weird, though. She was brought very close to death by one of those arm locks – you know, the kind you guys use to subdue people."

"Did he grab her from behind?" Tom asked.

"I'd say so."

"The carotid hold," Charlie supplied. "You block the arteries with your elbow. You go too far and it's game over."

"Well, either he held her in the grip a bit too long and killed her by accident, or he wanted her to feel what he did to her. She was probably unconscious from the lack of oxygen though – at least I hope she was. He didn't break the cartilage or the hyoid. She had the little red dots in the whites of her eyes, petechial hemorrhages, so she was on her way out, but the cutting happened while she was technically still breathing. She bled quite a lot, so her heart had to be pumping, even though it would've been slow and slowing until it stopped. Probably the shock from the cuts put too much extra stress on the heart. Not that she could've been revived at that point most likely, but still..."

"What did he cut her with?"

"You won't believe it, but I think it was with one of those tattoo needles."

Charlie and Tom stared at him, fascinated.

"So Thompson had to have planned it," Tom said. "There wasn't any tattoo equipment in that studio."

Charlie was thoughtful. "It's a similar skill, though, you know. Painting the body I mean. The tattoo artist and the painter, they use some of the same colouring techniques. They do an outline, then colour it in. I wonder if Thompson ever did tattoos in his younger years. Something to look up, Tommy boy."

He signaled for another round of beers. They were taking a cab home. They'd been working very long hours all week under loads of pressure, so they'd decided to make a blowout evening of it.

"So, Ted, you figure time of death fits with what the eye witnesses are saying, right? Around nine? Say between nine and nine fifteen?"

Ted nodded slowly. "Yah, I guess so, Charlie..."

"Good. Another thing I noticed," Charlie went on hurriedly, as though afraid his colleague would change his mind. "I studied some of the Professor's work. He uses a lot of pinks and blues in his landscapes. Very similar to the body art on Linda Courtnell. I bet the Crown could get an expert to say it was most likely Thompson's work."

"Sure is great that you're an artist, Charlie," Tom said. "You know stuff that the others don't."

Tom meant this as a compliment, but Charlie still cringed. Both men each had one of their friend's paintings prominently displayed at home. Only because he'd given them as gifts, Charlie had always thought. Naturally, they had professed to like it. He still flushed when he remembered the humiliation of the judgement handed down by the Three Arts Amateur Artist competitions. He'd been asked if he wanted a critique, but had regretted agreeing to it when he read their opinions. The loss and the terrible criticism had diminished any small amount of confidence he'd had in his art. The only reason he'd put any paint to canvas since then had been Greg's encouragement. But he certainly wasn't about to make the mistake of showing it to his colleagues ever again.

"Who's the other witness, by the way?" Ted asked. "You said there are two."

Ted was still ambivalent, Charlie could tell, but he knew the second witness would go a long way to convincing him of Thompson's guilt. "Now *this* is a great one," he said. "The guy just walked right into the station yesterday."

"We were both there, too," Tom added, "stopping by to get some of the paperwork done before we went back out."

"He works at Micon Industries," Charlie continued, his tone one of clear satisfaction. "An extremely good witness, squeaky clean, middle-aged guy. He says he saw Professor Thompson in his studio some time after 10 p.m. He glanced up at the windows and there was the man himself, just pulling a window shut."

"How did he know it was the Professor?" Ted remained in his get-all-the-details mode.

"He's been in the studio before. His wife likes Thompson's paintings; he actually bought one for her. He swears he recognized him in the window."

"But you haven't arrested Thompson yet." It was not a question, but Ted's voice was inquisitive. Charlie felt a surge of irritation toward his friend that he had to choke off. *The idiot has no idea how tenuous this case is; a twisted, cunning killer might go free to prey on some other innocent girl.*

Instead, Charlie said, "Webster wanted us to arrest him the first day. But the Crown wants this case to be airtight. They want to be able to win it from the start. There's huge public pressure to catch this bastard, to make sure he's punished, so Wilson is even more determined than usual to make sure it's right."

Crown Counsel Robert Sedgwick-Wilson was a highly respected lawyer whose work with the Criminal Justice Branch of the Assistant Deputy Attorney General's Office had been exemplary. He played the impartial card well: he was professional, efficient, and demanded a high level of certainty before he proceeded with criminal charges, especially in murder cases. Thus he had a very high proportion of wins.

"Time of death is going to be crucial, Ted." Charlie leaned over his beer, a suddenly overwhelming presence, his conviction almost palpable. "This guy did it. He had to have done it. He had the motive. He's the only one on the scene at the time. But that timing needs to be precise to satisfy the

Crown and make sure justice is done. What do the stomach contents tell you, Dr. Sato?"

"Well, if I look at the stomach contents as though it was a normal digestion..."

"It *was* a normal digestion, Ted. Think about it. The guy was her teacher, her lover. She never expected anything to happen to her. He probably didn't really plan it all out. His sick genius kicked in afterward. Linda Courtnell, a young impressionable girl with a crush on her teacher, just happened by that night, the night his wife confessed her pregnancy, the night they had a huge fight. And the opportunity presented itself. Maybe he did try to end the affair because his wife was pregnant. Maybe she argued. She had to have been angry and hurt. Maybe she threatened to tell little Wifey."

"So he grabbed her from behind in a fit of anger and..." Ted nodded thoughtfully, picturing the scenario.

Tom watched his friend and superior closely as the tale took shape and suddenly became reality. Charlie's face was red from alcohol and passion as it bobbed up and down under the skirt of Marilyn Monroe. Tom had an unsettled feeling. He worshipped Charlie; thought that his mentor was a genius at interrogations. But at this moment, Charlie was crossing a line, and Tom knew it.

A couple of hours later, when Ted took one cab and Charlie and Tom hopped into another, his suspicion was confirmed.

"Do you want me to visit a tattoo parlor first thing tomorrow, Charlie?"

"Nah." Charlie gave his partner a friendly, victorious punch on the shoulder. "We won't need to mention the tattoo stuff. We got the time of death."

Chapter Eight
September, 1980

A gathering of a similar nature was taking place on the other side of the city from Flip's Bar.

Emily and William sat at their small dining table, across from Patricia and Gary White. The detritus of a simple meal was strewn in front of them: chicken bones, salad leftovers, and several mounds of cooked vegetables congealing in the cooling butter. Two bottles of red wine and one still half full explained the heightened conversation and atypical disclosures. Emily's glass looked the same as the others', but was actually filled with grape juice.

Gary White was a short, rotund man whose Italian ancestry had provided him with a butterscotch skin colouring that contradicted his last name. At the end of this fairly warm and certainly sunny summer, he was deeply tanned. His large brown eyes blinked owlishly from behind the black-framed glasses; he always appeared to be analyzing everything his dinner companions had to say. Although not yet thirty, his receding hairline gave his round face greater maturity.

His wife, whom her friends had all known as Patsy, began insisting she be addressed by her full name when she passed the bar. Patricia was an exceptionally tiny woman whose waist William could probably have surrounded with his two hands. She wore her dark hair long in a perpetual braid that lay on her back like a horse's tail. With her pinched chin and severe black eyes, she reminded Emily of a pigeon. The owl and the pigeon. Yet both Emily and Will genuinely liked this unusual couple.

Six of the Langford group of friends had crossed over to Vancouver to stay: the Thompsons, the Whites, and the Lams. Although they didn't see one another often, they kept in touch as a result of shared interests and roots. Emily had called these friends at the last minute, giving in to a longing for support and advice, but only the Whites had been able to come.

Intelligent, driven, with a wide knowledge about a huge number of topics, Gary and Patricia were enormously interesting conversationalists. Tonight their discussions had been strictly focused on Linda Courtnell's death and the impact on William and Emily.

The week had been horrific. William's studio was still closed, despite being released by the police department two days ago. Will was unable to face going there. The image of Linda's body crucified to his wall had burned itself into the whole province's consciousness. The idea that she'd been tortured and murdered in his own space was far too raw for him to set aside. Not to mention the fact that the media had parked itself outside the old factory on a twenty-four-hour basis. They had not yet discovered where the Professor and his wife lived, thanks to the fact that everything was in Emily's name. All week, reporters had followed Will's movements to and from Three Arts. He'd literally ducked down side streets or jumped into several cabs to avoid being followed home. It was, as they'd told the Whites, like being in a typical movie plot.

Every single day, the televisions and radios had blared facts and photos about the murder and the victim. A sweet, innocent picture of her as a cute six-year-old with a pixyish smile had flashed on the news constantly. If not that image, then the one of her as an award winner, a beautiful blond with a stereotypical bombshell figure, standing next to the painting that had proven she was also a talented artist. Every fact about her father's real estate prowess, his financial successes, his political savvy, had been printed, preached and memorized by the public.

Linda was the exquisite only daughter of a dynasty that had been crowned Vancouver royalty by virtue of an appalling death. Up until recently, Randall Courtnell had been viewed with suspicion fueled by jealousy; suddenly he was the grieving head of a picture perfect family. They appeared on television, poised and upright, even as tears flowed, asking for anyone with information to please come forward. To please respect their privacy, contrary to the fact that they held daily television interviews.

Randall II and Harrison, the two sons, always stood behind their parents, staring solemnly into the cameras. Their faces were inscrutable masks, slightly quizzical, like animals in a zoo uncertain about why everyone's attention is suddenly focused in their direction. In appearance eerily similar to their sister, they had no identity of their own as far as the media were concerned. They were, from now on, strictly Linda Courtnell's younger brothers.

Facts began to emerge about the "crucifixion", the painting of the body, and even the cadaveric spasm. The police department was forced to admit that there was a leak. No one ever revealed the source. Captain Webster appeared in several television interviews with and without the Courtnells. Ostensibly, he was trying to curtail the gossip, but his regular appearances only heightened interest. Soon everyone knew he was the victim's godfather and that his passion for finding her killer had reached obsessive proportions. The media were in a frenzy.

Yesterday, however, the Captain had suddenly become quiet. Patricia White had expressed the opinion that the Crown had told him to bring it down a notch.

So far this evening, the conversation had mostly been a debate about whether or not William really was a suspect. In response to Will's frantic call on Monday, Gary had secured his boss's promise to represent William if necessary. Phillip Shaw was lead counsel in the highly regarded firm. Experienced in criminal law and several high profile homicide cases, he was considered an excellent choice. Their only hesitation in engaging Phillip Shaw as their potential advocate had been financial, until Emily's very difficult, but rewarding call to her parents.

"Darling, naturally we'll help in any way possible," Siobhan had reassured her daughter, the lilt in her voice more pronounced since she'd returned to Ireland. "We've been so lucky here as you know. We won't let you down. But I'll pray that it'll not come to that, Emily."

Both her mother and father were of the opinion that William could not possibly be charged with any crime, let alone a murder. It was the same faith that Gary and Patricia continued to express all evening. Unaware of the case building around him, William still remained the most adamant that he was their prime, and perhaps only, suspect.

"You didn't see their faces during that interview," he told them. "Both Captain Webster and Sergeant Haynes looked at me as if a rat had crawled up their sleeves. They were begging me to say I'd killed her and when I wouldn't, they looked mad enough to kill *me* instead."

Emily felt her stomach lurch at his words. Her hand went instinctively to her still-flat belly, thinking, *poor darling, I haven't even told your grandparents or uncle or any friends about you. What kind of a world are you going to come into?*

Chapter Nine
September, 1980

At 7:30 on Monday morning, Emily and Will were just about to leave for work when a heavy pounding resounded through the apartment. Will's face went still. He threw the door open and stood as though bracing himself for a hurricane. The ferocious wind entered their lives in the forms of Sergeant Haynes, Officer Fairburn and several other unknown faces, each one of them towering and grim.

"William Thompson, you are under arrest for the murder of Linda Courtnell," Haynes announced, unable to completely cover a hint of triumph. "Do you understand?"

Both William and Emily simply stared, frozen in dread and shock.

"Do you understand?" Haynes repeated. "Please answer yes or no."

"Yes," uttered William.

"You have the right to retain and instruct counsel without delay. We will provide you with a toll-free telephone lawyer service, if you do not have your own lawyer. Anything you say can be used in court as evidence. Do you understand?"

"Yes. Emily, call Gary, okay?" Will's voice was quiet and tender as he gazed down at her pale face.

She raised her eyes, already filled with tears of grief and anger, to stare at him, drinking in his presence, afraid to let go of his hand. "Okay," she answered.

Taking a deep breath, she turned to look at Haynes and Fairburn, as though they were friends who had utterly disappointed and betrayed them.

"Where will my husband be taken? We have a lawyer and I want to tell him where to go."

"He will be held in the City jail until the court hearing. His lawyer can visit him there," the Sergeant answered formally, as though still reciting Will's rights.

Will bent down to kiss her, gently holding her head against his chest. For a moment, their eyes held onto one another, the energy between them alive and connecting, as though they could keep touching even as they were being torn apart. Then the police officer bent his arms back, snapped the handcuffs together, and led him out the door.

Emily couldn't bear to watch. Her hands shaking so badly she had trouble holding onto the receiver, she dialed Gary's office number from the card he'd given her. She got through the reception, and the secretary, but when she heard his voice, she dissolved into tears.

Gary waited patiently, talking to her all the while, until she was able to answer him and give him the information he needed. "I'm going into Phillip's office right now, Emily. He's put Bill's case down as a priority. I might even be part of the preliminary stuff, on the team. Let's hope we can get some bail going. You said your parents would help?"

"Yes."

"OK, I don't know what time it is in Ireland, but whatever, you need to wake them up. There isn't much else to do besides sit and wait until you hear from me. They won't let you come with me."

Emily didn't plan what she said next, but her response, at that moment, seemed to make sense. "After I call them, Gary, I'll just go into work. It's a bit late to get a substitute and besides, I don't think I can stand being here on my own."

"Okay, don't worry. He'll likely be back for dinner."

Emily hung up and dialed her mother once more, dreading putting into words their worst fears. As she talked to her parents, her father joining in on the extension, she felt as though she were reading lines from a script. Someone else's life. A fictional account that couldn't have anything to do with a couple from a small town in Canada. Siobhan and Grant Taylor were equally dismayed, but they were loving and supportive of their daughter and son-in-law. They had already been in touch with their banker and were ready to transfer the funds as necessary.

When the conversation was over, Emily sat heavily on the sofa. The silence was a live thing, ringing in her ears, pressing down on her shoulders. She took several deep breaths and leaned back, hand on her womb, talking to the baby.

"I'm going to be strong because of you, Baby," she said. "Your Daddy will be home soon, don't worry. We'll get him back. We must."

Once again, Emily found herself floating among her students, not fully present. This time, she forced herself to act as though she were fine: smiling, nodding, putting enthusiasm into a voice that was nearly choked with fear. She had alerted the secretary, Adeline, to buzz her through the P.A. immediately should any calls come through, but by recess, there had been no such call. Fortunately, Emily was on yard duty, so she had very little time to worry. She walked through the yard accompanied by Justin, Fiona and Laura. The girls chattered away happily, while Justin clung to Emily's hand.

Elaine flew by the portable a few times to check on her, but Emily couldn't bring herself to let her friend know what had happened. It had been difficult enough to acknowledge the reality to her parents.

Emily continued to imagine what Will was going through. Was he at the courthouse? She'd only seen the building from the outside, sitting placid and self-righteous downtown with its drab, blank windows staring sightlessly at the world. Was he in a courtroom, everyone staring at him, shackled hands behind his back? She imagined Gary at Will's side, speaking for him, telling the black robed judge that they had made a terrible mistake. Or was he sitting in a squalid jail with the kind of criminals they'd only seen on television?

Just before lunch, the P.A. box in the portable squawked loudly. Emily had been reading a story to the class and they all jumped as the buzzing tore into the quiet. Justin yelled out and covered his ears.

Emily's voice shook as she asked, "Yes?"

Adeline's voice was hollow and strident. "Ms Taylor, that call you were asking about has come through. Mr. Maloney is on his way to look after your class while you take it."

"Thank-you," Emily answered.

She looked at her students' young, puzzled faces and felt a surge of affection. As she assured them that she would be back in a few minutes, Emily could not have known that she would never see any of them again.

Chapter Ten
September, 1980
The Artist

He was very displeased. Ever since The Professor and His Wife had entered his sphere, he had not experienced the joy, that pure wonderful adrenaline rush, from any of his creative activities. Once or twice, he almost wished he were back on Hastings Street, making the rounds of the tattoo parlours. Almost.

Those who can, do, those who can't, teach, he mumbled to himself over and over. The Professor and His Wife thought they were superior to everyone. So superior in fact, that they truly believed they could *teach* people how to create, how to learn, by standing in front of them in a classroom and spouting platitudes, curricula, talk talk talking. What arrogance.

He, on the other hand, was a doer. He created on a daily basis. His pictures had evolved from simple ink designs to paintings that rivaled the masters. In fact, he had discovered that he could copy anyone's watercolour or acrylic print, ink drawing, charcoal, anything really. He had a deft hand and a photographic eye that, working in partnership, could mimic the lines, the colouring and shading, the very inspiration of the original artist. Long ago, he had mastered the Professor's extraordinarily simple creations and landscapes. Easy peasy. This was the man who had judged The Artist's entries and found them wanting! What a crock.

Three times he had entered their contests, waiting for them to acknowledge his brilliance, his genius. But did they? No. Each time, they returned his offerings, saying they were "not what they were looking for". Sometimes they'd even give him some feeble encouragement or advice. They had no fucking idea what was great and what wasn't. He'd done some research and found out that one Professor William Thompson was Chair of the Adjudicator Committee.

But he was a fair man. Maybe the Professor really did have something to offer. Maybe he did know something The Artist did not. Once or twice he'd sat in on the Professor's lectures, pretending to consider signing up for a course. But he'd been barely able to contain himself for the full hour: such drivel, such absolute nonsense as the man droned on about the "creative process". What the hell did that idiot know about true creativity?

Somewhere in his past, he'd made a decision to take his artistic experiments a little further, and that had made all the difference. He learned that he had a powerful technique for teaching people about vision, inspiration, and most of all, the high that comes from going to the summit of your most vivid imaginings. He discovered that it was pain that awakened someone to the limitless genius of genuine mastery.

He gave his students an experience that literally defined their lives. He didn't talk or spout. He did things to them that brought them to a creative, explosive, and significant death. Thus his pupils experienced the heights of beauty mixed with the depths of pain, which allowed them to see, to understand, everything. Those moments just before they died were a gift, because without the pain, there could be no true awakening. His precious pupils slowly, eventually, came to the realization that nothing beautiful can be created without pain. Just like birth, death rolls out in waves of agony. Their anguish released them from their restrictive earthly bodies, allowing them to be exquisite. He took them there and made them one with Art.

By the time he met The Professor, he was extremely skilled at his own form of teaching. The human body was an exceptional tool for creative expression. He had worked exclusively on prostitutes and other derelicts, sometimes already half dead junkies or drunks. He'd delighted in the cornucopia of skin colours on which to practice the paint combinations that worked best. Then he had branched out to the canvas, discovering that his techniques were well honed and his pictures were quirky, yet mesmerizing. He knew that he could sell them for huge amounts of money, but he had to make a name for himself before any galleries would take him. Hence, the Three Arts Institute, the contests, and The Professor. He had attended each of the presentations of the prize that he coveted, waiting with shallow breath as they announced third, then second, then first place winner. At the initial reception, itself a gilded phony affair, he had actually shouted aloud when the announcements came, his breath punching through the air before he could control it. Everyone had turned to look at him. After that, he was far more careful.

But at the first ceremony, he did make a discovery that he found quite useful – Mrs. William Thompson. She was standing in the hallway outside the auditorium, the florescent lights suffusing her blond hair with gold. Short – at least in comparison to her lanky husband – she was trim, blue-eyed, and frankly, gorgeous. When the Lord and Master came down the stairs, walking blithely past the mural that he ignored each and every day, The Wife gave her husband such a look of adoration that The Artist wanted to puke. Surrounded by his sycophantic and panting students, who didn't just want art lessons from the look of them, The Professor made it very clear through his gestures and endearing glances that he only had eyes for The Wife. The Artist watched her with prurient interest, found out that she was a teacher, even followed her for a time. She didn't attend the second contest, but she was there at the third. Perhaps she would like to experience pure creativity?

But then he saw the winner of that third contest and he forgot about The Wife. Linda Courtnell, Princess of the City, Daughter of the Devil himself. The Professor and his judges had seen fit to present her with the prize – a debut at the Gallery in Gastown, the very thing she didn't need, the very thing he wanted most. The GiG – the Gig – his gig, his launching pad, his beginning. She needed none of that. She had a name, money, a daddy to take her any place she wanted to go. She could have at least allowed The Artist to win the Seattle International Art Fest; she had nothing to lose. But the stupid bitch simply could not let it rest.

He remembered precisely the minute the plan buzzed in his head. Courtnell had the effrontery to confront him with what she knew, to threaten exposure. All the pieces had suddenly come together – he knew exactly how to gain satisfaction all round. He didn't know why he chose the Crucifixion. After all, he wasn't a religious man. But it was fucking brilliant. He *had* allowed her to slip into unconsciousness a bit too quickly; however, he enjoyed the rest of it thoroughly. He'd never raped one of his pupils before and he knew she would not be his last. The explosion of sperm into the condom thrust deep inside the girl had added a dimension to his Artistry that he had never thought possible. After that, the tattooing and the painting had almost been too much, until he'd gotten his second wind.

What fun it had been hanging around the crime scene! Being helpful, professional, sad. The satisfaction that the trail led so deviously to The Professor was deep and exhilarating. He had done it! The perfect crime and the perfect patsy. Two stupid, arrogant, judgmental people dispatched with a show that had all the shock and wonder of a fireworks display.

In the beginning, there was a flurry of activity that kept him keyed up and elated. The media went into overdrive, thrusting microphones into the face of anyone who would talk to them, milling about, careening in their cars to the scenes. The newspapers, radios, magazines and television were jam-packed with stories about the Courtnells and the horrible death scene. He loved it.

Then out of the blue he was hit with a depression that he could not shake. He was upset, disappointed, and unable to think of why. It wasn't as though the excitement about the case had abated – in fact, it was just about to rev up once the arrest made the news. That night, sitting alone in his living room, everyone having gone off somewhere else, staring at the television as some announcer blathered on about the Courtnell Case, he suddenly realized why he was down. Having made such a huge splash – a cannonball of a murder that had sent ripples all over the province, let alone the city – how could he possibly follow up? How could he ever paint a body again?

Sure, none of the others that he'd killed had been found – he'd made sure of that. But how could he regain the heights to which he'd soared as he not only tattooed his victim, but also made her into an artistic masterpiece even as her heart continued to beat, whimper, slow? He'd watched her last breath, felt her breasts sag into sloping hills as her life seeped away. How could it get better than that?

If he painted another one, and it was somehow discovered, they would know The Professor was not guilty. That was a chance he could not take. The Professor must stay in jail for the rest of his worthless life.

The Artist was livid. He had no idea where he could go from here. Back to the tattooing? Back to entering lame contests that he wouldn't win? Back to looking at other people's inferior art hanging on walls that his masterpieces would never grace? At some point in that long agonizing night, he decided there was only one way to diffuse this frustration and anger. He would try something a little different this time, though.

He would kill The Professor's Wife.

Chapter Eleven
September, 1980

Emily was frantic. As she tried to put the key into the ignition, her hand shook so badly that she had to stop and breathe. She was having a difficult time believing what she had just heard.

Adeline had called her down to the office during the lunch break. She spoke quietly, ensuring she wouldn't be overheard. "There's someone on the phone for you who called you Mrs. Thompson, so I figure they don't know you well. I thought it might be a lawyer or a police officer."

"Gary?" She'd picked up the extension in Dennis's office, her anxiety coming through in a shrill bark.

"Mrs. Thompson, it's not Gary." The voice sounded winded and sad, barely able to tell her. "I am calling on his behalf, though. I have some bad news for you."

But Emily already knew. Her heart began to pound, choking off her oxygen, making her eyes blur. A sound, halfway between a sob and a moan, emitted from her clamped lips.

"They've charged your husband. They're holding him over until the preliminary hearing, which will happen in the Provincial Courthouse next week."

"Can I see him?"

"Yes," the man said. "But they have moved him to the Mountain Institution."

"Why would they do that?"

"For his own safety, ma'am. It's a more secure holding centre. It will take you about an hour and three quarters to get there. It's near Agassiz. Just take the Trans Canada to Cemetery Road."

"I can leave immediately. Thank-you."

As soon as Emily hung up, she thought two things: what an apt name for the street that now represented the death of their previous life; and that she had forgotten to ask the name of the man who'd called her.

Emily said very little to her colleagues and they didn't ask. Adeline, Dennis and Elaine were aware of the arrest; they knew she had to leave and they gave their full support without comment. For the second time in a week, Dennis

Maloney took over Emily's class. He hugged her fiercely, nearly lifting her off her feet, as though he could tuck her under his arm and save her from disaster. Her students, tears in many of their eyes, stared uncomprehendingly as she gathered her sweater and tried to reassure them with a wave, telling them she'd be back tomorrow. Adeline gave her a similar bolstering embrace. Elaine popped out of her classroom into the hallway to do the same as Emily hurried by. It took all of her resources not to break down, fling herself into her friends' arms and surrender to the sobs that were forming in her chest.

All of which explained why she was now barely able to insert the damn key and start the car. Emily leaned against the headrest and closed her eyes. She had to regain control. Not only would her despair make things worse for Will, but she also had to think of what the tremours zinging through her nervous system might do to their baby. When the murder charge was proven to be false, Emily did not want to have to worry that this enormous mistake, this terrible travesty, had harmed their unborn child too. Her stomach was knotted and cramped. She could not allow this baby to be affected by her anxiety. The thought gave her strength and cleared her head. She loosened the seat belt along her lap, leaving more room to breathe. Assembling her maps, Emily started the car and headed along Bidwell to Pacific Blvd., trying not to think.

Vancouver had fully divested itself of the unusually warm, sunny weather this week and reverted to its normal autumn drizzle and haze. As Emily steered along the slick pavement, she watched grey clouds race along the sky, chased by flashes of stormy black billows. All across English Bay, the waves were flinging themselves against the rocks and sand, stirring up a thick mist along the shoreline. It was chilly and damp so the parks were deserted.

Emily took Burrard to Davie, knowing she could hurry because she knew this street so well. Winging right past their apartment building, she knew she should take her time, but she too was being chased by storms. She kept her foot steady on the accelerator. She knew the roads beyond the city, too; she and Will had traversed them on numerous occasions. Our "field trips" they called them – tours of the city itself, walks through Stanley Park, a ski trip to Whistler, enjoying the sun on the mountains lining the Sea-to-Sky Highway, excursions farther into the mountains. Emily counted the streets: Mount Pleasant, East Broadway, and all the side roads that she whizzed by. Thankfully, it was the middle of a workday, and the weather deterred "field trips", so traffic was extremely light.

At last she was on Highway One, the Trans Canada, an artery of nearly five thousand miles in length that linked the country west to east. Emily and Will had taken a coach bus tour to Kicking Horse Pass at the Alberta border, the vistas breathtaking and awe-inspiring. It was wonderful when someone else was driving and the weather was sunny. But even though she was traveling a fraction of that trip today, this would be a long, grueling drive; one that Emily knew would take over two hours in the rain.

She stopped twice, her bladder responding to her pregnancy, and ate two power bars from the station kiosks. The drizzle continued unabated, all the way into Abbotsford, making the highway greasy, a misty cloud blocking any vistas. When she emerged past the city, suddenly the mountains were on her left, tall majestic peaks of rock and tree. The rain disappeared, as though too awed to mar the view, and Emily felt bolstered by nature's heights. When she looked up, and up again, she couldn't help but feel that her problems would shrink in this domain. Who could convict an innocent man within sight of this breathtaking splendour? The road began to tighten and wander alongside the mountains. Emily gave driving her rapt attention.

She couldn't remember when the vehicle registered in her rear-view mirror, but suddenly a large green truck, with an enormous front grill, loomed very close to her bumper. Too close, Emily thought. It resembled an army utility vehicle or something that might be used in the mountains. She wondered why he was travelling so close. She slowed right down, hoping he would go around her. After all, there was no traffic. He could easily pass, even in that clunky machine. It stuck to her bumper, hitching a ride.

Pushing the limit of her comfort on the winding road, Emily sped up. As though pulled by a towrope, the truck kept pace. Surprised that the truck could move so fast, she tapped lightly on her breaks, letting the driver know that she was not impressed with his game. Emily was annoyed, but not worried.

When the huge grill struck the rear of her little car, her irritation transformed into horror. Emily was tossed forward, then snapped back against the seat. Her knees began to sting and drip blood; she'd hit the steering column. Involuntarily, she steered the car to the right, where the roadside dipped toward a steep gully. She pulled hard and straightened the shuddering car back onto the pavement. Now absolutely terrified, Emily willed herself onto autopilot: she kept her arms stiff, trying to maintain control of her vehicle.

Suddenly the truck was alongside, hideous and massive, the tinted windows shielding its monstrous driver. Metal howling and screeching, Emily's car was scraped and pushed to the right, heading for the ravine. Emily slammed her foot on the brakes in a fruitless effort to propel the other driver forward and away from her. It was a huge mistake, as her car fishtailed and now pointed straight for the edge of the road. Emily yanked the emergency brake straight upward, hanging onto it as though it was a lifeline.

The truck whipped in behind again, the front grill acting like a shovel as it nearly lifted the car, propelling it forward. Though her tires began to smoke from the effort of going against the brake, the loose gravel of the shoulder quickly allowed the vehicle to pick up speed.

Too petrified to move or think, the world completely slowed down for Emily. She watched the action as though she were at home in front of the television.

The little car was hurtled into the chasm, smashing, grinding, the sound of its demise earsplitting and discordant in the deserted valley. Emily, ripped from the loose lap belt, was tossed upward, backward, and forward in succession, her body a rag doll thrown about violently with the motion. The sudden, crumpling halt as the car hit the bottom of the ditch hurtled her against the windshield in a cloud of dirt and dust.

Before she collided with the ground, however, Emily was gone. She had disappeared into a dark, consuming unconsciousness.

Chapter Twelve
September, 1980

Terry Somers didn't start out that morning planning to become a hero. In fact, he didn't even plan to drive up the Trans Canada. But he was a lumber salesman and times had not been easy lately. A last minute, but potentially lucrative call, led him to an unexpected drive up the mountain highway in the rain.

His little company, which he'd started only last year with a group of close friends, had proffered a bid to provide the Kent Institute, a prison just outside Agassiz, with wood for an inmate furniture business. Terry and his partners figured a deal with Kent could be their real beginning. The Old Mountain Prison was in this area as well, so a deal would be possible there, too. They believed success with the two institutes would lead to more federal contracts. However, their proposal hadn't been chosen initially. Thus they were ecstatic when a last minute cancellation by the winning bidder gave Somers Inc. the chance to meet prison officials face to face. As lead salesman and majority partner, Terry hopped in his car after they'd cobbled their presentation back together again. Amid the fog and pouring rain, he eagerly hightailed it up the mountain.

Despite the miserable weather, Terry was making good time. He was happy when the rain subsided to a sprinkle and the mist began to clear beyond Abbotsford. He was even happier that the roads continued to be deserted. Just as he began to think the mountainside had been evacuated ahead of a bigger storm, he saw a vehicle nearly ricochet out of control as it raced away from the roadside ahead, spewing gravel in its wake, like a guilty rabbit disturbed from plundering someone's garden. As he told the police later, all he really saw were the taillights. It was a dark colour, some kind of utility truck. Its tires were enormous and soon found traction on the road. Within seconds, it had disappeared around a bend. Coupled with the drizzle and cloud, Terry didn't get a good look.

Asshole, he thought, driving like that in this terrain. Terry leaned toward the windshield, as though proximity with it might allow him to see more clearly, when he noticed a column of smoke rising from the ditch where the truck had been stopped. Puzzled, without really analyzing his actions, Terry pulled over to the side. Alighting, he gazed downward and froze in shock. Mangled and sputtering, a car smoldered far below.

Afterward, he couldn't explain how he got the nerve to scramble into the gully. Why he did it was obvious to him at least. There had to be someone in that car and they needed help. Terry Somers was a big man, tall and muscled, extra fat equally distributed over his body. He wasn't in great shape these days, spending far too much time behind a desk, but he wasn't completely sluggish. Crabbing sideways, he dug his feet into the damp earth and inched his way along the steep sides. By the time he reached the bottom, he was covered in mud and bits of clingy weeds.

The car lay turtled on its roof, tires still spinning uselessly. The engine shuddered to its final demise. Terry wiped his mud-soaked hands on his new pants and peered through the shattered driver's window. A woman was wedged in the front, almost standing up, the seat pushed against her legs. Blood poured from her head, which was crushed against the spidered windshield. Terry paused for a few seconds and drew in a deep breath, his head spinning with indecision and shock. Finally, he bashed his hip against the crumpled door, levering it as he would a troublesome jar lid, and at the same time, yanked on the handle. The door almost fell off its hinges, very nearly pushing him backward onto the ground. Instead, he spread-eagled his legs and steadied himself.

Gingerly, afraid of causing more damage to her torn and bloodied body, Terry nudged the seat back, dragging it slowly into a semblance of its original position. The woman was now sitting up, though her head lolled forward and the red gush of her life continued to pulse out with every heartbeat. Her legs looked mangled, but they did not appear to be stuck under the steering wheel. Terrified that the smoke might set the leaking fluids afire, he leaned in and cradled her in his arms. At the same time, he slowly eased her sideways, twisting himself at the hips so he always had her firmly supported. In this ungainly fashion, he eased her outside, dragging her gently along the grass until they were a fair distance away from the now burning vehicle. He removed his suit jacket and laid her tenderly onto the ground. His coat, size XXL, was enough to cover her back to front.

Her face was porcelain white and her skin felt icy. Blood dripped from one arm in addition to her head. He tried clumsily to find a pulse, but he felt nothing; she didn't appear to be breathing. He removed his crisp white shirt and his new, executive-powered dark blue tie, and used them to inexpertly staunch the bleeding. Despite his complete lack of experience with First Aid, Terry was pleased to see that the spurts subsided.

Now he had to find a way to get her up the hill to safety and help. He was afraid to pick her up in his arms, though he had an impulse to carry her as though she were a wounded child. Just as he despaired about what course of action to take, a face appeared on the roadside above him, then another. Several other people had, mercifully, stopped to investigate. He shouted and waved, and kept shouting and waving, even though they clearly had heard him, seen him, and were on their way down.

One of the rescuers, a big husky man in a black raincoat, was evidently on the way to a camping site, for he dragged an army cot slowly down the slope. A young, nimble woman, who traversed the wet ground with the sure-footedness of a mountain goat, wore a sleeping bag like a backpack, which they immediately used to carefully wrap and warm their patient. Someone else produced a first aid kit with supplies to replace the shirt and tie. Bungee cords and luggage straps magically appeared, so gentle hands could strap the injured woman to the cot.

Someone gave Terry a sweater, which he gratefully pulled over his head to stop the shivering. Although he had been unaware that shock had begun to course through his nervous system, the loud chattering of his teeth alerted everyone else.

Slowly, the group began to clamber up the hill with the cot sandwiched between them. Rock by rock, weed over weed, mud squishing under their feet, the little team inched its way along the incline. Luckily, the rain held off.

The group became eagerly invested in the well-being of the silent, wounded bird in their midst. Every one of them drove their RV's, campers, trucks, and cars in a caravan to the hospital. Someone else drove Terry's car while he sat by the injured woman's side in the back of a huge trailer. Though he felt like an invader, he looked in her wallet, and found her license. *Emily Taylor,* he read. Her address was somewhere in Vancouver. She didn't have the usual detritus in her purse, the way his wife did. In fact, it was rather Spartan.

Terry would always remember that pale, perfect face, the battered body and the tiny "mew" she made when they pulled up at the hospital's emergency doors, as though she recognized that she might live. That sound, a brave, willful puff of breath, somehow told him that she wanted to survive, that she might be someone whose life was not supposed to end in a muddy, mountainside ditch.

Chapter Thirteen
November, 1980

Siobhan Taylor ran her hand over her daughter's stiff, dry hair, touched Emily's face tenderly. "I remember when you were born, Emily," she said. "They put the mirror up so I could see. There was so much pain, you know, and then suddenly there you were – all covered in stuff, your little face so intense and red, just bursting into your new world. I never saw anything so amazing in my whole life."

Siobhan would always recall the moments in the darkness, rocking in a chair beside the crib, holding her baby to her breast, the moonlight dancing on the wisps of downy blondness. Emily's hand would always rest gently on her other breast, or curl around her mother's finger, as she stared up into Siobhan's eyes. Even then she was an observer.

Siobhan had always worried about Emily, such a serious little girl born to a couple of wandering gypsies. Intelligent, quiet, thoughtful, her daughter had been friendly and open, but only with a trusted few. Sean, on the other hand, had plowed into life; he was gutsy, pragmatic, and adventurous. Every time they took the children to a new school, Sean leapt out of the car or ran from Siobhan's side with the joy that came from experiencing new things and new people. Emily had always entered an unfamiliar classroom tentatively, observing everything and everyone. Her teachers invariably remarked on her intelligence, but complained in the first few months that she would not participate verbally. By the second term, if the family stayed that long, the teachers were trying to keep Emily quiet.

When they'd finally settled in Langford for a longer period of time than they'd ever known, Emily blossomed. She'd been designed as a homebody, a teacher, a mom, a wife, someone who thrived on stability. Although Siobhan had never worked since she married Grant, she had volunteered for charity organizations and art galleries and hospitals. A free spirit, a gregarious, enthusiastic person, Siobhan enjoyed life by the moment. She embraced her life as a nomad and rejoiced in every new experience. Her female child, however, was nothing like her and did not resemble her father, either. Emily's DNA had been formed in some ancestral cell, Siobhan often thought, a throw-back to the days when people stayed in one geographical location and enjoyed life from that one perspective. Someone who lived in the moment, loving life as it was, not as it would or could be. Siobhan admired that aspect of Emily's character, even wished she had even an ounce of that capacity.

Siobhan had even worried about Emily when she married Bill Thompson. In her opinion, Emily and Bill were too dependent upon one another. They lived in their own little world, which Siobhan had always felt was riskier than having no roots at all. When she entered the hospital and discovered that Emily had retained her maiden name, Siobhan reacted with shock. She realized that her daughter was far more complex than she had given credit for; that in the years of separation by miles, Emily had developed layers of which her mother had been unaware.

Now, as she washed her child's limp, heavy limbs, Siobhan stared down at the wounded young woman, so pale even against the white hospital sheets. The sorrow filled the room, beating relentlessly along with the machines that kept her daughter alive. Poor Emily, her body torn apart by the accident, her heart about to be torn apart as she awakened.

Siobhan had stayed in Abbotsford for the last two and a half months. She'd learned how to wash, turn, and exercise her daughter's coma-induced body. She was there when Emily moaned, when they treated a bedsore, when they lifted her legs in a semblance of walking. She would be there when Emily awoke, brought slowly back to an unforgiving world; a world that wouldn't allow a gentle soul like Emily's to live without hurt. As she whispered into her daughter's ear, Siobhan was filled with both anger and a desire to wrap her child up and whisk her away, spare her the truth.

Siobhan had, at least, been able to snatch the truth away from the reporters and the sensation-seeking public. But only through Emily's act of independence in keeping Taylor. Siobhan filled out every form using that name, boldly told people her daughter was separated – a partial truth – and convinced the lawyers to keep a tent of silence and safety over her daughter.

For Emily, the sensations came in small snippets, old and damaged photos taken through a fuzzy lens. Pain, a pouring of her life from inside, draining her. Cold, hot. A voice. Her mother's tender hand brushing damp hair from her forehead. The darkness that held only echoes and shadows.

The day Emily blinked into consciousness, the light stabbed her eyes and the terrible dryness of her throat sent tremours through her body. Her hand jerked in response and someone shifted toward her.

Siobhan's face appeared, at first hazy and unclear, then laboriously focused. Tears flowing silently, her mother patted Emily's parched lips with a wet cloth, then tenderly held a straw up to her. Emily sipped slowly, some of the luscious liquid seeping down her chin. Her throat expanded with the water and again, the muscles in her arms and legs twitched fitfully.

Several other people began to appear in her peripheral vision. Emily slowly shifted her eyes to take them in. A tall, dark-haired man in a white uniform, the stethoscope signaling that he may be a doctor, smiled down at her. At her left, a stout middle-aged woman with startling red hair adjusted some dials on a tube that was attached to Emily's arm.

The doctor spoke first, in a soft voice tinged with a puzzling triumph. "Emily, I'm Dr. Wayne Singleton. You have been in a deep sleep, a coma, which we induced. It's experimental, something not used too often, and only in extreme cases. I'm telling you this so that you won't be too shocked by the passage of time. Plus because it's new to us, we will be hovering around you a great deal, bringing you through the challenges you still have to face. But I want you to know that you are in the best hands and that all your vitals are looking very good. You have healed amazingly well. Now the test will be getting your muscles and body back to normal."

Emily looked at her mother, who continued to weep silently. She tried to reach out, but felt as though an extremely heavy blanket lay on top of her, preventing her from moving. She pursed her lips and forced questions from her throat, but the sound was a muffled, unintelligible cry. *Will…our baby..*

Siobhan tried at first to staunch the tears, but soon gave up, simply kept a tissue clutched in her fingers.

"It's a very good sign that you are trying to ask questions," the doctor intoned, as though he'd given her the gift of speech in the first place. "But be patient. It will be very difficult at first and I'm sure any of the staff can answer your queries."

Stupid man, Siobhan thought, as he continued to drone on. She considered the doctor a bit of a pompous ass. He was determined that Emily's case would bring him out of the obscurity of a small city hospital into the medical limelight. However, she had to admit that so far, Emily was responding in the ways that he'd predicted. Typically, he assumed "Will" had been the start of a question about his medical prowess. Little did he know, Emily was asking for the one person closest to her, the one person whose hand should be stroking hers right now.

How would Siobhan tell Emily that William Thompson was Vancouver's most notorious convicted killer? After a ridiculously short trial, he now spent every day in solitary confinement in a bleak jail cell, because if he were released into the general population, he would be subjected to the cruel punishment meted out by prison "justice". What would happen when Emily discovered that most people believed her husband was a monster who had desecrated, tortured and murdered the city's Princess? How would she describe the changes in him; how he'd gone from a handsome, gregarious, warm person to a pale, silent shadow of himself?

How was Siobhan going to tell her loving, gentle daughter that their baby had died and that her capacity to birth children had been lost, too?

Ignoring the phalanx of doctors hovering in the background, Siobhan snuggled into the bed next to Emily and took her daughter in her arms.

Chapter Fourteen
December, 2008

Charlie was sitting at his easel in the sunroom when the phone call came. Somehow he wasn't surprised. He just wondered why it had taken so long.

The light that poured in through the screened windows was perfect; spring sunshine, not too bold nor too hot, highlighted the colours but didn't overheat his old bones. It was classic Vancouver weather. Spring came early and was soft and warm. Blossoms dotted the landscape like the colours on Charlie's canvas. The back yard was already green and lush.

Charlie would be eighty years old next month. Though his round face made most people overlook the wrinkles, his life-lined hands showed his age, and the tremor was increasingly annoying. In his retirement, he had indulged his artistic whims with fierce determination, fuelled by a sense of remorse. He had never expected anyone to understand his paintings, but in a world filled with sorrow, yet moved by optimism, his particular viewpoint had touched an amazing number of people. His art business had flourished.

It had been a few years since he'd participated in a show or a sale, but his daughter Grace had taken over the business and had done very well. She knew how to design websites, how to talk to gallery owners, and how to promote her dad's talent. Now that he was too sick to go out much, he'd even become a bit of a mystery man, which had only increased the lure toward his art. Charlie often laughed at the irony.

Joan brought the telephone out to him, along with a cold bottle of beer. She gave him a quick smile and a kiss on the forehead. Still slim and lively at seventy-five, Joan had always supported his artist's ambition. Mostly because his "hobby" kept him from getting in her way, Charlie thought.

"It's Tom," she said and went back to her gardening or cleaning or puttering or whatever it was she did all day.

Tom Fairburn was also retired from the Vancouver Police Department, though more recently. He and his wife Betty had moved to Salt Spring Island this past fall, but Charlie didn't get the impression that Tom was happy living close to the land. Receiving a call from him, however, was fairly unusual. Email was cheaper and faster and the two men had taken to it with alacrity when it was introduced years ago in the department.

"Hey, Tom, how are ya?"

Charlie took a long, grateful sip of the cold beer and looked out past the easel into their pristine, organized back yard. He pictured Tom inside his small log cabin or perhaps stretched out on a chaise lounge in the chaotic garden Betty had cultivated on their property.

"Good, good." Tom sounded somewhat breathless. "I...how are you?" An afterthought, as if recovering his manners, or remembering that his friend was ill.

"I'm fine," Charlie lied. "What's up?"

"Did you hear about the Thompson appeal?"

Charlie sipped his beer, somehow eerily calm now that it was happening. "An appeal?"

"Yah, they're finally taking it to the BC Minister of Justice."

"The appeal they were set to do years ago?"

"The very one. After all these years, they're gonna do it."

Tom's wife had been the Deputy Mayor of Vancouver for a number of years and still had a myriad of connections with the current council.

"What do you think that involves? Do you think they'll ask us to testify or something?"

"I don't know. It depends on the Minister, apparently. Betty says he could treat it like a new appeal or even order a whole new trial. Or he could just declare Thompson innocent."

"I wonder why they left it so long. They're lucky I have a memory left."

Tom laughed. "You have the memory of an elephant, my friend."

They talked a little about other inconsequential things, then rang off. Charlie sat very still, listening to the buzz of insects, feeling a few beads of sweat run down his back. Of course he had never forgotten the Thompson case. Tom was right about his memory, but in the matter of William

Thompson, Charlie Haynes had many reasons for not forgetting.

He could think of only one other person who would be interested in discussing the ramifications of this news. Charlie picked up the telephone again and dialed.

Chapter Fifteen
March, 2009

I fought against the idea for a long time. I argued that our physical presence wasn't necessary to the review. Computers, Skype, cell phones were all at our fingertips – we could use the technology instead. I threw everything I had into the debate: there was nothing we could add or say or do that we hadn't already done or said over the years. Back in British Columbia, the BC Association for the Wrongly Convicted had flicked on the switch that we had disengaged years ago. Thanks to May and Alain's generosity, we had hired a phalanx of lawyers and a renowned private investigator – let the professionals do the work. Cate and Carly couldn't, shouldn't, be without us.

In the end, I gave up or gave in, I can't remember which. Although I don't think I ever fully agreed, I found myself on a private jet to British Columbia just as spring was drying up the land in Ontario. Our little town of Burchill disappeared quickly behind the sun.

Jacob Finch, acting as both lawyer and friend, Will and I, along with a private investigator by the name of Montgomery Cardwell, plunged through skies that had burst into yellow and blue, sailing toward Vancouver. A beautiful, mountain-kissed city, previously beloved, it existed for me only as the site of my agony; the place I'd sworn I would never, ever set eyes on again.

Despite my fears, our friends had gathered around us after the Ceremony of Declaration, offering us support and giving advice when asked. Edgar Brennan scouted information from connections through the Ontario Provincial Police Department whenever we had a question about police procedure. Agnes Lake spent hours with me, listening as I talked through the problem, gentling me toward a decision. Renae Ogemah stepped up her counseling sessions, unafraid to give me honest guidance.

Every single one of our friends thought we should pursue vindication for Langford.

Thus we were about to begin a new journey in a quest for justice. Our lives were about to change - had already changed, in fact. Just by telling our friends about our past, we had opened the gates. Though a close-knit community, neighbors were compelled to tell a friend, who told a friend, and like the ad about some shampoo years ago, the word was soon out there. People spread news like a virus. Even before we left Burchill, a reporter from The Ottawa Citizen had been calling the house.

Like a couple of rash poker players, we were going all in with our chips. William's new identity as Langford Taylor and our sanctuary in this little town were exposed. Soon he would again step into the limelight on the very soil where attention had first been paid. This time, I would be there by his side.

When I was almost killed in the car accident near Vancouver, even the hospital staff had been unaware of my connection to William Thompson. All my identification stated 'Emily Taylor' and my family, wisely, kept it that way. It was unusual in 1980 for a woman to retain her maiden name, but I was proud of my surname. I don't know if my insistence on keeping it had anything to do with Margaret, or knowing the darker side of Edward Thompson, but for some reason, I wanted to retain Taylor for my career. Will, in fact, had encouraged me to do so. That decision proved providential. I was never discovered, never harassed by reporters.

I lost our baby in the accident, along with my capacity to ever have children in the future. My memory of the hours before the crash disappeared. The police could not establish why I was on the road to Agassiz in the first place, and I was unable to give them the answer. On the long journey of recovery, remembering a car accident in the rain on a mountain road seemed insignificant. My rescuer had apparently spied a truck speeding away from the scene, but the police never found the offending vehicle. Compared to the ordeal that Will was going through, I didn't even care about this mystery.

The rumour mill while I languished in the hospital in Abbotsford was free to bubble. Most gossips told the story that Mrs. Thompson had left her husband as soon as the charges were laid. And who could blame her? Who would want to be married to a monster? Even the police officers involved in the case weren't told of my location. They were, in fact, quite thrilled that the only witness to claim that William was home at the time of the murder had disappeared into a coma from which she might never recover. The prosecution was happy to oblige in keeping my name out of the case. Our lawyer watched my progress, knew the coma was induced, but agreed by the time I recovered that my testimony was moot. And as it turned out, my memories were sketchy and unreliable; my story would have easily been torn apart by the Crown attorneys.

The enthusiasm for the ghastly case of Linda Courtnell's murder never abated in Vancouver. Understandably, and even admirably, her parents kept their daughter's memory alive through a variety of charities. Conversely, however, William Thompson suffered under the relentless public reminders.

Despite the Supreme Court review that pronounced Will's case a possible 'miscarriage of justice', he had not been proclaimed innocent. Although Will was released from prison, the Judges did not go the distance. They reported that William Thompson had not proven his 'factual innocence'. We would have to appeal to the Minister of Justice in British Columbia for a review.

Yet another tragedy sent us scurrying away. Instead of appealing, we went into hiding, wounded animals seeking sanctuary. We moved to Burchill, Ontario, in 1999 as Emily and Langford Taylor. We adopted a new life in our small community, living all these years in anonymity.

For a time, we thought we could cope with the obscurity and distance we had to create between our new friends and ourselves. Even before we adopted Cate and Carly, I had struggled under the weight of keeping our secret. Now, we had the children. We had to remove the last vestiges of doubt and disgrace haunting our past. Fortunately, even after our revelations about our past, we had not lost the love and respect of our dearest friends, May, Alain, Frances and Edgar. Their support mattered deeply.

I knew we had very little choice than to forge ahead with the appeal to the BC Minister of Justice. But I was struggling. I hadn't suffered the way William had, but in some ways, my hell had been worse. My identity was squashed and my entire life taken away. When I came out of the coma, I had to learn to walk, to speak, to remember. Most of my memories returned, but then I had to learn how to live without my husband and our baby, or any other future children. I had done it, but only with the love and support of my mother. I was still not sure I would have survived without her. Even after she'd returned to Ireland, she was a constant source of strength over the telephone.

I immersed myself in my career, in the children that I taught, and later took on any leadership role that came my way, until I was appointed Principal. My free time was spent on my husband's case. When William was finally released from prison, we had planned to continue the fight to prove his innocence, but it had not worked out that way.

At May's insistence, we were flying to Vancouver in a private jet. Only in movies had I witnessed such compact decadence: the seats luxurious and wide, our own televisions and telephones, a table between us for our papers, our own steward to serve us drinks. The latter, I must admit, I indulged in quite liberally, to bolster my courage of course. The rest of the amenities, ironically, went untouched: during the five-hour flight, we read and discussed the myriad of reports that outlined William Thompson's case.

For the five hundredth time, I scanned the lines of transcripts and briefs, as though I could wear the words away, make them disappear, force time to go backward and change everything. Like Superman, twist the globe by speeding up time until it reversed itself.

My thoughts slid over to Cate and Carly: if I changed everything, would they be our daughters now? Would the reversal of time eliminate the horrors they experienced at the hands of their parents or would their lives be worse now? While I was at it, why didn't I resolve hunger and hatred in the world? I smiled at myself and shook my head. Maybe the wine that the steward was serving was far too good after all.

At the thought of our girls, I had an urge to call them again. But they would be at school now, Cate at Burchill Public and Carly with her tutor. They were living with May and Alain for the week – or two or three, however long it took – that we were away. Being with the Reneaux and living with their siblings for a while would be really good for them, I had to admit. I was feeling far lonelier than they.

"I'd like to review everything from your initial points of view," Monty suggested and I snapped back to attention.

When I first met Montgomery Cardwell, I was not predisposed to trust him. I thought back over the years, the people we'd hired, worked with, fought against, some with pretty impressive handles to suit their appearances.

The Crown Counsel Robert Sedgwick-Wilson had prosecuted Langford in the first trial. Portly, impeccably dressed, his face was round and soft, his hair nonexistent. He looked like someone's kindly uncle until his light green eyes filled with anger and darkened.

Judge Hajimi Lent, his Japanese roots manifested in a slight accent and a mixed-race visage, presided over that initial court case with a perpetually pinched, quizzical expression. He had decided my husband was guilty from the moment he stepped up on that bench, and struggled, often unsuccessfully, to present an objective, fair-minded façade.

Our own lawyer, Phillip Shaw, whom I got to know far better than I wished, was a tall, thin man with grey hair sporting faultless black streaks. He was a patronizing, arrogant man who perpetuated the lawyer-as-shark stereotype. Yet he had made mistakes that no experienced barrister should ever commit.

The two key police officers in the case were Charles Haynes and Thomas Fairburn. The latter was as tall as Langford, red haired, with a huge bulbous nose, as comical-looking as a clown, although nothing he did or said was at all funny. Sergeant Haynes did not resemble his inner persona either: he had an air of kindness and gentility; he claimed to want justice when all he really wanted was to prove his own theory of events.

Now, as we flew toward Vancouver once more, we were putting our last hope into another stranger's hands: Montgomery Cardwell. Initially, he appeared to fit the stereotype of a private investigator. Handsome, tall, slender, nappy hair cut short, he would have been Denzel Washington's twin, except that his nose was crooked and his lips were fuller. Despite my hesitation, when I looked into his deep brown eyes and his hand shook mine with confidence and warmth, I felt pulled into a circle of hope. Not only did his presence reassure me, but he also came highly recommended by the only man who had garnered my complete confidence in the past, someone I deeply trusted: our old friend, Simon Callas.

Simon was an old friend. My brother, Sean, introduced me to The British Columbia Association for the Wrongfully Convicted, an organization headed by Mr. Callas. Our first appeal had been denied and, even if I'd been able to afford our former lawyer's services, I no longer trusted his competence. Luckily for us, Simon took over our case himself. During the 80's, he spent long hours, days and nights, filing and re-filing appeals.

A short, balding man with piercing blue eyes, Simon was the antithesis of a stereotype. Those new to the courtrooms where he toiled often stared at him openly aghast, as if to say, *this* man is the famous Simon Callas? Disorganized, rambling, with a propensity to be sarcastic and to laugh at his own witticisms, he appeared to win his cases by taking everyone by surprise. He darted from the witness to the jury box to the prosecutor like an angry bee; no one dared take their eyes off him. In a booming voice that belied his small stature, Simon gathered the facts and tossed them outward, and like pieces of a puzzle, they would suddenly land in a clear picture. He had worked tirelessly for people whose lives had been destroyed by grievous error or incompetence.

I'd also gotten to know Eileen Edwards, Simon's wife, who worked alongside him for BCAWC. They'd had no time for children, she told me, so they parented their clients, no matter the difference, or lack of, in age. For the remainder of my life, I would be grateful for her maternal instincts where I was concerned. They lived in a small home in West Vancouver, never amassing a huge fortune, since they took on so many pro-bono cases. Nowadays, they were both retired, but just as parents are parents for life, they'd jumped when we contacted them about the appeal to the Minister of Justice.

"Montgomery Cardwell is the best private investigator in the country," Simon told us. "He's done work for BCAWC for ten years now and I would trust him with my life. He's so good, I'd bet my life savings he'll uncover the stuff that all the others - and I - missed. So when we file the appeal, it's gonna go like a knife through soft butter."

Monty grew up in Seattle, Washington, and immigrated to Canada to marry a girl he'd met on a cruise. "Audrey's a nurse. She wasn't going to leave Vancouver, so he came on up. They're a great couple. He's tall and handsome and she's short and plain. But she's a dynamo."

They had two young children, Simon reported, whom Montgomery adored. "It wasn't easy getting him to go to Ontario. He doesn't like to take many cases personally these days, especially any that are outside of the city; he's moved into managing his company instead. But I somehow convinced him."

In other words, Emily, you better treat this guy well, I had thought, almost resentful at being set up this way. I learned, through Jacob's research on the Internet, that Montgomery had a black belt in Karate and that he was extremely well known, and respected, throughout our country and the U.S.

"He's intelligent and incredibly charismatic," Simon gushed. "He doesn't have to intimidate people, though he certainly can. Most of the time, they spill their guts to him as soon as he opens his mouth."

He'd arrived at the airport in Ottawa, where our partnership began as soon as Will and I picked him up. When the man unfolded his long legs to approach me, spreading his fingers in a steepled greeting, and kept his eyes on mine as he spoke, I was sold. We took him home for two days of quiet discussion, exchange of information, and exploration of our case. Although his questions were often blunt and very personal, we didn't feel awkward or embarrassed. He had a direct, soft way of drawing information from us that we would never have told any other stranger. I very quickly understood exactly what Simon had meant about the power of this man to elicit confession.

"What do you want me to call you, Langford?" was his first question. "I understand your original name was William and that your friends called you Bill. But what are you most comfortable with now?"

My husband gave a rueful chuckle. "For many years I was called Prisoner 465," he said. "Emily calls me Will, but that's hers alone. Most people in Vancouver called me Bill and here they call me Langford. It can get pretty confusing." He was silent for a moment. "How about Langford? I think I've gotten pretty used to that one and it has positive memories."

"Why'd you give up the fight, Langford?" Monty asked next.

At first, neither of us could formulate the words to explain. My mother and father, who'd been our source of strength, optimism, determination and love, had been killed in a car accident in Ireland just as Will was released from prison. How could I describe the depth of the wound, the hurt, the agony at losing them? I decided that I couldn't.

"My parents were killed," I said bluntly. "They had been our source of resilience, our backbones. I was quite literally crushed. I'd survived my accident with the help of my mother and then I lost her in pretty much the same way. We – especially me, I must say – just couldn't face the court case. I felt as though my life had been a series of disasters to that point and all I wanted was peace."

"All *we* wanted," Will said, grabbing my hand. "We had been through two appeals, both of which were denied. No new trial was ordered and I was left in prison. Then Simon made an appeal to the Supreme Court, only to have them throw my case back to the BC Minister of Justice. At least I was paroled then, but I had been in prison for nearly twenty years and was due to be released anyway. Emily and I had been through so much and frankly, I didn't have any faith that the result with the Minister would be any different."

"Ironically, I inherited some money from my parents, which gave us the means to either fight the case or disappear. We chose to disappear. We've been sort of hibernating for a few years," I said with a rueful laugh. "But now we have two little girls and..."

Monty nodded, understanding without explanation, and I remembered what Simon had said about the man's love for his children. His instant rapport with our lawyer was another sign that Montgomery Cardwell was a gift. As I now watched Monty and Jacob Finch sitting across from us in the airplane, I was struck by the phenomenon that sometimes happens when two strangers become instant friends.

Montgomery was explaining what he wanted from us at this stage. Our two days in Burchill had given him time to understand our background and, I realized, to reassure himself that we were trustworthy. Now he wanted details of the ordeal itself.

"Let's use the trial transcript to flesh out the players. I want you to cast your minds back and give me the impressions you had at the very beginning. Before the appeals and the Supreme Court decision, even the option of the Minister's review - all the stuff that came afterward. Emily, I know you weren't at the trial, so this part is mostly up to Langford. But where you knew the participants, I'd like to hear your impressions too."

Mr. Sedgwick-Wilson: Your Honour, I have a witness who can refute the written statement from the defendant's wife stating that he was home at the time of the murder.

Mr. Justice Lent: Is the witness ready to be questioned?

Mr. Sedgwick-Wilson: Yes, Your Honour.

"First, they called this woman, Elaine Martin. She was a friend, right?"

"She was a colleague at work," I said. "Langford and I went over to their place a couple of times for dinner. They had two little kids who were really sweet. She was pretty much the closest friend I had at school."

My friend; my confidante.

"Did she tell the truth?"

"To be honest, we're not sure. I never recovered that memory. But before the accident, I did tell the police I was sure it was around ten o'clock."

"It was more the way that Elaine presented her information that disappointed us," Will said. "She was actually proud to be the friend of a famous killer's wife."

Afterward, when I was able to read the transcript and comb the newspapers, the eagerness with which she confessed to Officer Fairburn, the thrill she got from the notoriety, all combined to wound me deeply and, very nearly, permanently. She'd eagerly embraced the man she called Bill Thompson as guilty, because that made her part in the reality movie a far more coveted role.

"There was disagreement about whether or not Mrs. Martin's testimony was hearsay?" Montgomery framed it as a question, which Jacob answered.

"Despite some vigorous debate, the judge eventually decided in favour of the prosecution. He instructed the jury –

and I quote - that they were to 'consider the evidence as instructive only as to what Mrs. Thompson stated. She was, at the time, competent and able to speak for herself, but her statement is not necessarily proof of what actually occurred'."

"The kind of double speak that drove me to mistrust our justice system," Will said bitterly.

"But the sort of legal point that supports appeals and reviews," Jacob reminded us.

The type of betrayal that led me to surround myself with layers of secrecy, equipped against intimacy and hurt, I thought.

Mr. Sedgwick-Wilson: Mrs. Martin, I understand that you taught with Mr. Thompson's wife.

Mrs. Martin: Yes, we were very close friends.

Mr. Sedgwick-Wilson: Please recount the conversation you had with Mrs. Thompson the day after the murder.

Mrs. Martin: She told me that they'd had a fight over her pregnancy on Saturday and that Bill stormed out. She said he didn't come back until Sunday night.

Mr. Sedgwick-Wilson: And what did she tell you about the timing of his return? Specifically the time that he reappeared on Sunday?

Mrs. Martin: She told me she didn't know what time it was. She said it was very dark and she found him lying on the pull-out…

Mr. Phillip Shaw: Objection!

Mr. Sedgwick-Wilson: Brief answers are fine, Mrs. Martin. Is that your objection, Mr. Shaw?

Mr. Phillip Shaw: Thank-you, Mr. Sedgwick-Wilson.

Mr. Sedgwick-Wilson: To reiterate, Mrs. Martin, Mrs. Thompson told you that she had no idea what time her husband came home Sunday night? A yes or no will suffice.

Mrs. Martin: Yes, that's correct, she said she had no idea what time he came home.

Even after all these years, I could see the smile on her face, the one drawn by the Vancouver Sun illustrator, her hair perfectly coiffed, her mouth lipsticked and ready for her red carpet photo op.

The only thing she hadn't done, mercifully, was to tell the court or the media that I was known as Emily Taylor at school. Perhaps she hadn't considered it. But, oddly, after her testimony, after her picture appeared in the paper for several days, Elaine Martin suddenly disappeared from the stage. A one-hit wonder.

"What time *did* you come home, Langford?" Montgomery asked directly.

"I left the studio just after nine. Unfortunately for me, I made a really stupid decision to walk home. If I'd only taken a bus or a cab or the water taxi, someone would've seen me. But no, I still wanted to walk off my mood. I was feeling like such a shit. It was like a re-evaluation of my whole life; I was developing a whole new vision."

"You didn't know you'd need an alibi," Jacob said sympathetically.

Will smiled. "True. But I'd already let off enough steam. I'd already decided I was an asshole. I should've just gone straight home to Emily. But I wallowed in self-pity instead. I thought she'd never forgive me."

"How long would it have taken to walk home?" Monty asked, steering him back on track.

"About an hour. I wasn't going slowly, but I wasn't rushing either."

Monty scribbled in his notebook. "So you did get home about ten. Which means, if Emily's original statement is correct, she did have an inkling that you were with her around that time. Which also means you couldn't have been the guy who was seen through the windows or coming down the stairs from the art studio at ten or ten thirty. What about Linda Courtnell? What time did she come by?"

"She arrived about five to nine. I was packing up to leave. She said she saw my lights, decided to say hello, and pick up her portfolio."

"Did she say why she wanted her portfolio that late at night?"

Will lifted his head. "You know, I don't think anyone has ever asked me that question." He was silent for a moment, thinking. "She said she had to show it to someone. Something about proving a point."

"Interesting." Monty steepled his fingers again, a habit I noticed he adopted when he was deep in thought, or studying a new acquaintance. "Try to think about exactly what she said. Don't force it – the memory's there, it's just been buried for nearly thirty years."

The steward came by and refilled our drinks; we sipped silently for a moment.

"What about the testimony from Linda's friend, Wendy Collins? What did you think about her?"

Will didn't need to pause this time. "I thought she was a flake. I have no idea why Linda hung around with her. They'd been friends a long time and I think it was just habit. You see, Linda Courtnell was extremely gifted. She would have had a highly successful career as an artist. Wendy, on the other hand, was a spoiled little rich girl who really had very little talent."

"Wow," Monty breathed. "Harsh!"

Will laughed mirthlessly. "I've had a lot of time to think about it, as you can imagine. As a teacher, I tried to encourage any little spark, but Wendy was impossible to nurture, mostly because she was self-centred, expected everything to be handed over on a silver platter. Her parents were trying to teach her some responsibility by insisting she earn her own spending money, but they started too late to un-spoil her. She took the job on the reception desk at the Institute, but it was mostly for show. I think she spent all the money on nail polish."

The camera loved Wendy Collins. Her youthfulness burst out from the lens, her wide-eyed, innocent beauty magnified exponentially. Thus the newspapers, tabloids, and television programs spent hours filming her testimony. The headlines are gut wrenching even now. 'Everyone Knew Professor Was Having Affair' claims murder victim's best friend. Young Girl Prey to Older Man. Sexy Teacher Seduces Student. She Thought He Would Leave His Wife…

Mr. Sedgwick-Wilson: Ms Collins, please tell us how you knew the victim, Linda Courtnell

Ms Collins: She was my best friend.

Mr. Sedgwick-Wilson: Shall I give you a moment?

Ms Collins: No, no. I'm okay.

Mr. Sedgwick-Wilson: Can you give us a little more detail about how close you were to Linda, please?

Ms Collins: We've known each other since we were in Grade Seven. We went to high school and then Three Arts Institute together. We are - were roommates.

Mr. Sedgwick-Wilson: I guess you knew her very well then.

Ms Collins: Yes, I did.

Mr. Sedgwick-Wilson: Can you please tell me what happened on the night that Linda was murdered?

Ms Collins: We went out for dinner with a group of friends. There's a nice pub on Granville, very close to the school, and it's cheap but the food is good, so that's where we go pretty often. It's got a good view of...

Mr. Shaw: Objection! We're not here for a restaurant review.

Mr. Sedgwick-Wilson: Ms Collins, please tell us the details of that particular night only.

Ms. Collins: Of course, yes. Linda and I met her boyfriend Garrett and a couple of other friends at the pub around seven that night. We had a few beers and shared some nachos and stuff. Then Linda made an excuse to leave.

Mr. Sedgwick-Wilson: What time did she make this excuse to leave?

Ms. Collins: It was around eight-thirty or maybe a quarter to nine. Before nine, anyway. She told Garrett she had some work to do at the art studio. But I knew what she was really doing.

Mr. Shaw: Objection! Hearsay.

Mr. Justice Lent: Sustained.

Mr. Sedgwick-Wilson: I'll rephrase. Ms Collins, did you speak to Linda about her real reason for leaving the restaurant?

Ms Collins: Yes, I did. When we went to the washroom after she said she was leaving, I told her that I knew she was meeting Professor Thompson.

Mr. Sedgwick-Wilson: And what was her reply?

Ms Collins: She just laughed and said, Of course I am! And then she left. Everyone knew she was having an affair with him.

Mr. Shaw: Objection!

Mr. Justice Lent: Sustained. The jury will disregard.

"Her evidence wasn't exactly strong," Jacob said. "Linda could have meant anything by saying 'of course I am'."

"Yes, but nevertheless her testimony was damaging. Do you think Linda Courtnell had a crush on you?"

Will looked surprised. "Again, no one has ever asked me that particular question. No. She did not have a crush on me."

"How do you know?"

"Because she would have told me. Linda was straightforward and never afraid to speak her mind. She didn't give a damn about what anyone thought. I mean, she'd even defied her parents by going to art school. She would have marched right up to me and said, 'I like you and I want to take you to bed' and to hell with the consequences. Besides, you just know. With Wendy, I was very cautious. I would never have been alone with her for a minute. She kept looking at me with adoring eyes, just waiting for an opening, thinking she was being subtle. Linda and I had a good, healthy relationship - the kind of respect that often happens between a brilliant student and a teacher. I knew she was a genius and she knew I could help perfect her technique. There was absolutely no sexual vibe at all."

"What do you mean, she defied her parents?"

"According to her, Randall wanted all of his three kids to step into his various businesses. He insisted that they have business degrees. Linda's brother Harrison acquiesced, even though it made him miserable. She said he was also a talented artist, but was obedient to their father. Linda was determined not to do that. She didn't even care if he cut her out of the will. She told him that either he supported her wish to attend art school, or she'd turn her back on the family."

"Where did the talent come from? Their father was – and really still is – a giant in real estate and so on, but he showed no sign of an artistic bent from the research I've done," Jacob mused.

"Their mother," Will answered. "She was a quiet, dutiful wife, so she stood behind Randall in everything, taking on charity work and making sure their home was perfect. But if you ever saw the way Paula Courtnell dressed up a convention centre for a presentation or an auction or whatever, you'd know she was artistic. She volunteered a lot at the art school, loved helping to set up displays and so on."

"So Randall gave in to his daughter?"

"Yes. He did make her promise that if she wasn't successful, she'd come back into the fold."

"What would Randall Courtnell have defined as successful?"

"Ha. Probably making money from her art. Showings in Paris and Rome. That sort of thing. Which she was perfectly capable of doing, had her life not been taken away."

"What did Harrison Courtnell end up doing? You'd think he would have been really pissed off that his sister got to follow her dream and he didn't."

Jacob turned some pages in his thick file. "He took over the real estate end of Courtnell Holdings. Until the market plunged this year, he was making huge amounts of money for his father. But he's heavily involved in the Olympics, so the rentals and building projects have saved him big time. It doesn't appear that he did anything with his art, at least under his own name."

"What happened to the portfolio?"

We all stared at Monty for a moment, slightly confused.

"Linda Courtnell's portfolio, the one she came back for," he clarified. "Was it in the studio?"

Just like that, Montgomery Cardwell opened an uncharted path. I began to believe Simon's prediction that he would uncover information that no one else had, but hope, at least in this case, was something I had difficulty trusting.

Monty looked at his watch. "OK, the steward wants to serve us lunch soon, so let's keep going. We're making great progress." He shuffled some papers, made a few notes, highlighted a couple of sentences.

"Frank Jeffries was the Real Estate Agent and Manager of the factory-turned-market. He testified that he'd seen you and Linda together a lot and that he'd heard rumours. How the *hell* was this stuff allowed in that courtroom?" It was almost as if Montgomery were talking to himself, but if he'd asked, I could have told him that those same sentiments were as familiar to me as the beat of my heart.

Then he looked up at us with more alacrity. "Did you know that three of the people involved in your case were failed artists?"

"What do you mean, failed artists?" I asked.

"I mean they had entered the contests that Three Arts Institute ran, and for which Langford chaired the adjudication committee - and they lost. Some more than once."

Will shook his head. "I can't believe it. Why wouldn't someone have brought that up?"

Monty's big shoulders shrugged. "No one knew it, not even Simon. I just found out this week. It's amazing the information that has been posted on the Internet these days. All kinds of histories for the various schools, including Three Arts. They listed every contest that they've held over the years, all the entrants, and all the winners. By super genius deduction, I was able to name the losers."

We chuckled, though everyone was aware of the tension and our response was mostly in gratitude for Montgomery's attempt to lighten the mood.

"The writer of this history points out that many of the losers went on to become very well-known artists. Of the three involved in your case, two actually managed to gain a lot of respect in the art district - in Vancouver at least."

"Don't hold me in suspense any more; who were they?" Will leaned forward in his seat and I unconsciously did the same.

"They were – or I should say *are*, because they're all still with us – Sergeant Charles Haynes, Harrison Courtnell, and Ronald Stevens."

We gasped and made other noises of shock and disbelief.

"The police officer who investigated the case was a failed contestant and no one brought that forward?" Jacob was incredulous.

"Minimally, Haynes should have declared a conflict of interest," Monty said. "But obviously the bastard wanted to be part of that homicide investigation no matter what. But how could he have kept his entry a secret from everyone, Will?"

"The names of the contestants weren't released unless they won. Certainly the Judges never knew their names. We tried to keep everything anonymous to ensure fairness. You couldn't vote for someone's painting just because you liked them, or vice versa of course. All correspondence went through the office; informing them that they won or lost, inviting them to the presentation and reception, giving feedback if they asked for it. Some of them would come up to me at the reception and tell me who they were, say they hadn't won, but appreciated the direction and so on. Some wouldn't speak to the Judges at all, which was their right. Harrison Courtnell attended with his family, but I thought that was because of Linda's win. I had no idea he had entered the contest himself. I certainly don't remember ever seeing or speaking with Sergeant Haynes or Ronald Stevens - until Linda's murder and the trial of course."

"They probably didn't attend the celebration, especially if they were pissed off. Or maybe the murderer did go, and you didn't notice him in the crowd. That might've been a severe snub in his mind." Monty held up his long fingers and counted. "Okay, one, you have a disgruntled police officer wannabe artist who, right from beginning, pins you as the suspect, which could've been his plan all along. Two, you have the brother of the winner, who could've been just as angry with his sister as he was with you, making her murder in your studio a fitting revenge. Three, you have another wannabe who happens to walk by your studio on the night of the murder and testifies that he saw you walking out of the building at ten o'clock."

"The defense could have made such a dent in their testimonies with that information!" Jacob's voice was almost hoarse with the injustice.

"You're right, Jacob. The defense should have done some research on all the players," Montgomery conceded. "As they say, though, hindsight is 20-20. The contest might not have entered their minds as a motive."

"Every entrant signed a release form, stating that their names could be used by the Three Arts for promotion purposes, which was extremely vague. The names could've been used if they won another contest or if they became famous later on. Exactly what they are now doing on their website, I guess," Will added. "But at that time, the non-winners wouldn't really have been listed anywhere public. Now and then, they might win some other award and would mention Three Arts or something."

"There were so many things that first defense team didn't think about," I said, unable to keep the bitterness from my voice.

"Even Simon didn't find this stuff, Emily. The Internet has opened up the whole world," my husband said.

I gulped down the sudden spurt of anger that leapt up from my stomach, feeling my face turn red with the effort. Will put his hand on mine, I felt angry toward him, too, wondering why he was always so patient and calm. I couldn't figure out how he could give Mr. Shaw and his legal team any excuses at all for their incompetence. Once again, vital information that "our" team should have discovered years ago had been uncovered so effortlessly by Montgomery Cardwell. Information that might have saved us so much pain, humiliation, and despair. Yes, the Internet had opened avenues that they didn't have thirty years ago, but all that meant was they should have worked harder. Even Simon's team obviously had flaws. My disappointment and resentment grew exponentially, becoming a rage that had no place to go but into twisted knots of frustration.

To distract myself, I looked out the window of the small jet. The sun glinted off the silver wings and straight below us, a shadow of ourselves glided over the brown fields of the prairies. A shadow of what might have been or what was going to be?

"The homeless woman. The one who testified that she saw you and that you spoke to her as you came down the stairs," Monty prompted.

"Shirley Johnson." Will looked as though he were back in the unfinished marketplace, the woman's wrinkled brown face gazing at him as he came and went. "She was a very tragic case in lots of ways. She'd lost her husband and two sons, who were practically babies, in a car accident, then became addicted to pain pills. Most of the time she just sniffed glue or drank cheap wine. But she wasn't disruptive or smelly, so the islanders tolerated her. A lot of us would buy her gift certificates for a meal, stuff like that. I talked to her every day when I was at the studio."

"She's the witness that Simon eventually discredited, right?"

Will nodded his head, almost sorrowfully. "Yes. He found her in a rehab, where she recanted. She said the very nice police officer prodded her to remember that she saw me on that specific night at that specific time."

"But in reality, she couldn't distinguish one night from another and couldn't possibly have known the time."

"Exactly."

"Getting her to recant went a long way toward the positive result at the Supreme Court," Jacob said. "Also, proving that Linda Courtnell could have died anywhere from 10 p.m. to 8 a.m. was brilliant. The medical examiner insisted at the first trial that she died just after 9 p.m., but the temperature of the wall would have sped up rigor. Then they opened up the whole debate about the tattoo needle being used to draw on the body; Langford had never used a tattoo needle in his life and the weapon was never found. When Simon's medical witness provided evidence that Langford could not have been the suspect who left that drop of semen, they had a very good case for dismissal."

"Simon did a very good job with the tools he had," Monty said. "He really did prove that Langford is not guilty."

"The only reason the Supreme Court did not state 'innocent of all charges', in my opinion, had to be political. They didn't like to admit the justice system was flawed. Not until David Milgaard and Stephen Truscott and victims like them, did we start to admit that a completely innocent person could be convicted. We have all the ammunition we need to get the Minister to declare William Thompson an innocent man." In the fierce way Jacob said it, we could all read his determination.

"You're right, Jacob, but I disagree that we have all the ammunition we need. There isn't any DNA evidence, so the Minister won't necessarily be one hundred per cent convinced. In the majority of cases like Langford's, the clincher was the DNA evidence. Look at how much trouble Truscott had proving his innocence, mainly because they couldn't use DNA. In Langford's situation, we've only got the semen droplet, which was shown to be from a secretor. And even though Langford is a non-secretor, the judges bought the premise that Linda could have had sex with someone else before the rape. They were persuaded that Linda was sexually promiscuous and therefore the drop didn't necessarily belong to the killer. They were convinced that the murderer was far too careful and organized not to have worn a condom.

"Simon believes that we have to amass a little more proof before we go to the Minister. The legal team agrees with him. They don't want to blow the last chance to have a complete exoneration. And it really is the last chance. Realistically, there won't be another viable route for you to take if you don't get your innocence proclaimed through this appeal. You'll have done pretty much all you can."

We all nodded, understanding the gravity of pursuing the truth, knowing this was the last shot. We'd been through every other level of appeal available to us. Short of finding the real murderer, Bill's innocence would always be doubted. A cloud of gloom settled over my heart. I thought of naïve, younger Emily to whom the term "secretor" had been a foreign concept, but one with which I became entirely familiar. I'd read and reread the story of David Milgaard, appalled and fascinated at the parallels with my husband's own tragedy.

The steward interrupted my reverie with lunch. We decided to continue talking, making the most of our time, as we ate shrimp appetizers and steaks, roasted potatoes and salad. I would scarcely have believed we were on an airplane except that I could see white clouds circling around us in the sky.

"Ronald Stevens, the other witness, held onto his story forever. He still claims he could see you in the studio window, lit up by the lights, staring outward. And since he didn't finish his shift at Micon until ten o'clock, it had to have been about 10:15 when he walked past." Monty chewed thoughtfully on his food. "I think we find Mr. Stevens and see if he's changed his mind yet."

I thought of the number of times someone had said something similar in the past. I found my throat closing as I tried to swallow a piece of the succulent steak. When I began to cough, my eyes watered and I let the tears stream down my face. I croaked out some reassurance to the group and went into the washroom.

The cubicle was luxuriant by normal airplane standards, but I still felt hemmed in. My face was red and blotchy, all four of the mirrors reflecting panic. The tears hadn't finished but I knew they weren't from choking. I sat down on the toilet lid and buried my face in my hands. I hadn't wanted to come on this trip. I didn't want to look the past in the eye. I missed our girls, our house, our dog. All the negativity swirled around inside me; I felt angry and self-pitying. I tried hard to think of Agnes Lake's allegory. This was my seventh fire. This was the time for me to stride with strength and determination to change our lives for the better. But I didn't know if I could go through one more test. Hadn't it been enough that I'd been denied my husband for nearly twenty years? That I'd almost died in a car accident and lost the ability to have children? That my parents had not survived their crash? Surely I'd been through enough.

I heard the tap at the door just as I was building up for a long weep.

"Emily, are you okay?" Will asked.

"I'm okay," I answered in a voice clearly filled with anguish.

"Let me in."

I unlocked the door and Will stepped into the cubicle. He wrapped his arms around me while I cried. Complete acceptance and understanding vibrated from his body to mine, soothing me instantly.

"I know this is horrible," Will whispered into my ear. "We'll call the girls every morning and night."

For the first time in a very long time, I realized that William Thompson had missed the point, at least as far as I was concerned. It didn't occur to him that, while I was certainly lonely for home, it was this journey that was most excruciating for me. He hadn't been aware that I had lost my resolve over the years. Except at the time when my parents died, I hadn't let him know that I just didn't want to fight any more. I wanted it to go away, yes, but I wasn't sure I had the strength to do it personally. I wanted the lawyers, the BCAWC and Montgomery to take the case and just do it.

"No, Will, it's only partly that. I'm just so mixed up. I thought that I wanted this done, but now that we're going over the whole thing, I'm having so many doubts. I don't know if I can do it." As soon as the words left my mouth, I was ashamed of my lack of courage. After all, I had been free all those years while Will had suffered the indignity and horror of prison.

He took a step back and held my chin in his hand. "Emily, I know how you feel. Every once in a while, I get a twinge of abject fear. I'm not sure how I'm going to feel when I set foot on Vancouver ground again. But this appeal is the right thing to do."

I looked into his eyes and saw the fear there, the agony, all backlit by a fierce determination and love. Will was just as scared as I was, but he had amassed so much strength of character that he was willing to face anything to prove his innocence. Whereas I had hidden away and harboured nothing but anger. Inwardly, I gave myself a good shake. How could I let my husband down, this man who was my soul mate, whom I loved more than anyone in the world? I gave him a fierce hug.

"You're right, my darling, of course you are. I'll be okay, I swear. I just need to wrestle these demons now and then."

"Hey, we'll wrestle them together."

After a couple of snide remarks about the Mile High Club, said mostly to dispel the tension and ignore the tear traces on my cheeks, the group resumed our analysis of the case.

"Were there any other players? What about Greg Hughes? Did he have anything to do with Linda or the other students?" Montgomery asked, pushing away his plate.

Will dabbed at his mouth with the kind of cloth serviette you might expect in a fancy restaurant. "Greg is gay. In 1980, most of the profs who were homosexual stayed in the closet, even though Vancouver was a free spirited town then. There was a fairly big movement toward gay rights, which we flowed from the west coast of the U.S., but most teachers didn't do anything overt."

"Did most people know about Greg anyway?" Jacob asked. "Would the students have known?"

"I think most of them did. Greg didn't teach art, by the way. He taught music. The Three Arts Institute included visual arts, music and literature, remember. So most of his students weren't the same as mine."

"So his studio was a music studio?"

"No. He didn't give music lessons there. He was renting the studio for his own uses. He wrote music as well as dabbled in visual art. He used all kinds of media – oil, metal, sculpture, you name it."

"Did the research show where Greg Hughes ended up?" Monty asked Jacob.

Jacob literally licked his fingers before he scrolled through his computer files. "Yes. Apparently he still has a studio in the Marketplace. He has also gained quite a following for his art, which, as Langford just pointed out, is very eclectic. He's also had a few songs published and performed. In addition, he belongs to a band called..." Jacob scrolled a bit further and looked up with a grin on his face. "...The Gay Wags."

We couldn't help laughing, Will most of all.

"I can just picture Greg coming up with that name. I really liked him. He was a bit odd, a little over the top in his mannerisms, but witty and very talented. Once you got to know him, he was a pleasant kind of guy."

"Okay. Let's move on to some other players. What about your boss, Rachel Ouellet?"

"She was a great person. She really tried to help us," I offered. "Rachel believed that Langford was innocent. She appeared as a character witness."

"How about these other girls, who corroborated Wendy's story that 'all the kids knew' you were having an affair with Linda? Silvia Parsons? Sharon Michaels?"

"All of their testimony was thrown out by the Supreme Court," Jacob reported. "The judges agreed that it was hearsay. The witnesses may have all *believed* Linda was having an affair with someone, but they hadn't actually heard the name of the man, and Linda had never confirmed an affair at all."

Montgomery shook his head. "Unbelievable. Again, proof that the original police officers formed an opinion and then built a case around that belief. Rumours like the ones those girls were spreading suddenly became fact."

"Thank goodness there are better checks and balances these days," Jacob said, "and better training. What's your proposal, Montgomery? What's the plan of attack?"

Sipping on a cup of coffee with a side of Bailey's, Monty looked relaxed, but his eyes were alight with enthusiasm. "You, Emily and Langford are expected at the lawyers' offices tomorrow morning, as you know. They have a myriad of details to go over with you. In the meantime, I am going to pay a visit to a police officer who, I hope, has a very guilty conscience."

Chapter Sixteen
March, 2009
The Artist

The arrivals area of the terminal was jammed with reporters, curiosity-seekers and friends. He watched as the Thompsons came down the escalator, looking like two performers who were descending from the heights of the circus tent into the applauding arms of their fans. A ripple went through the crowd, a release of tension, as everyone made an audible sound at the sight of the two recluses. He was certain that his sigh was one of the loudest.

Ex-Professor William Thompson was still handsome. Despite being over fifty, with nearly twenty years in prison behind him, he was striking: brown hair sprinkled with grey, body lean and tall, straight shoulders, exactly the right number of wrinkles that simply made him appear distinguished; brown eyes direct and bright. The Wife (as he still named her) was even more eye-catching. Slim, blond, her oval face unlined from this distance, skin clear with an attractive pink dusting her cheeks, eyes wide and blue. Their hands were entwined; their bodies leaned in for an intimate touch. King and Queen. Notorious, infamous, respected, renowned. Righteous, deserving.

Thompson was now a famous artist. Critics and aficionados all praised his work. Langford Taylor. Langford, of course! The village where they'd met. Such sentiment, so touching. Emily Taylor. How had he not been able to find them?

She was such a clever bitch. She hadn't died in the car accident after all. And everyone had conspired to protect her, hide her. They thought she was such a little angel. He shivered with hatred, his face reddening with his own embarrassment. If only that car had not appeared above the ridge, he would have checked to make sure she was dead, or finished her off when he found her still taking a breath.

Nineteen years and three months he had watched William Thompson languish in the prison. Thin and haggard and haunted. Then suddenly, the man had disappeared. No more news. No more appeals. Just gone.

How had The Artist not been aware that The Wife was living in Abbotsford the entire time her husband was in prison? How had he not known that she was a regular visitor at Kent? She had cuckolded him. He wanted to wrap his hands around her skinny neck and choke her until the veins in her eyes exploded, until her face was red and blotched with the arrival of death. He shook his head, slid through the automatic exit doors and gulped in the fresh air. He waited while the trembling abated.

He had only himself to blame. He'd been far too satisfied with his accomplishment, Thompson jailed, The Wife killed. He'd been content to keep tabs on Thompson's failed efforts to gain release, ignoring all else. No mention had ever been made that his wife was still around, goddamn it. What the hell was the matter with those BC bloodhound reporters? They were obviously incompetent. The RCMP had their man! That was the end of it for the media, other than the glorification of Linda Courtnell year after nauseous year.

He had been relegated to low-lifes again. Tattoos. But he had, now and then, added some very lovely pictures. Bodies hidden in acid, buried in cement, bricked into walls, never to be found. Absolutely no one had missed those losers. Who could love the emaciated, drugged-out, useless excuses for human beings that made up his victim list? Of course, that also meant no news, no thrills, no ecstatic rides. Nothing had ever given him the pleasure that the Thompson case had. He had learned the art of rape, however, which had been the gift from the Thompsons that had kept on giving. Although he laughed at his own joke, only his eyes betrayed the flutter of mirth.

As he watched people scurrying through the arrivals doors or outside into the blustery day, heading toward buses and taxis, shouting to each other, arguing or embracing hello, The Artist felt only pity. They had no idea what it was like to be taken to a higher plane by the Creative Force.

He was now very close to his goal of one hundred souls who had been led to the Spring. Souls who would merely have spent their lives in misery, creating nothing but havoc and sorrow. In their last few hours, under his guidance, his technique of pain and slow death, those people achieved a greatness that they would otherwise never have known. They experienced a magnificent transformation in his hands: from groveling, malodorous freaks to works of art in a matter of hours or days. Pure, creative energy. As each of the subjects took his or her last breath, he could see the light in their eyes, the knowledge that they were about to die setting them free. The Artist knew something that other "artists" did not. The only way to achieve perfection, complete creative perfection, was by suffering and dying. It was only at the point of death that creation exploded in your head, making you and Art one, taking you to a place of utter beauty. The Artist could not wait for his own death, but as long as there had been souls needing redemption, he was destined to be the Creative Force, The True Artist.

It was paradoxical that the death that had given him the most thrill was the only one born from hatred. The Artist knew that he had provided Linda Courtnell with a perfect creative experience, but his initial intention had not been at all pure. How odd that he should have felt the highest rush from this particular act. Perhaps, and here again he felt a flutter of amusement, the rest was work while Linda had been strictly for himself. Settling of scores, self-preservation, and most of all, pleasure.

He straightened his shoulders. He knew that he was taking a huge new step. In the last three months, ever since the whisper about Langford and Emily Taylor's new existence, he'd experienced a dramatic shift. His days as the Creative Force were coming to a climactic end. Soon it would be his turn to experience perfection.

Calm now, he waited while the glow of his reveries passed from his face. He knew what he had to do. He walked confidently back toward the throng of supporters and curious bystanders, a face from the old days come to witness the Thompsons' return to Vancouver.

Chapter Seventeen
March, 2009

Charlie watched the tall black man stride purposefully toward his front door. Here was a confident man, Charlie thought, someone who was at ease in his body, comfortable with himself. Charlie had once been comfortable too. He'd believed in his view of the world. Policing people who had squandered their lives, destroyed their bodies, and even made their own children suffer, meant exacting justice. Tit for tat, eye for an eye. No matter what you had to do or say to accomplish it, they had to be punished. In recent years, Charlie had lost his certainty; nothing was uncomplicated any more, all grey, no black and white. He thought it was ironic that, as a person aged, the rights and wrongs became less clear. Weren't the elders supposed to be wise? Or did wisdom mean embracing the notion that nothing in life is straightforward?

From the moment Tom called, Charlie knew what he had to do. In fact, he'd known for several years that he should confess. But time had somehow marched inexorably on and the Thompsons had disappeared. Charlie had convinced himself that they must have found happiness, that they no longer cared about the difference between "you are innocent" and "we're letting you go because we screwed up and didn't properly prove your guilt". Charlie had carefully studied all the cases of wrongful conviction over the years – the famous ones and the ones that passed under the public radar. He was well aware that the majority of people who were victims of an over-zealous or incompetent investigation did not normally rest until proven innocent. He certainly didn't blame them. Perhaps he'd known deep down that the Thompsons would be back, for he was not in the least startled by their private investigator's request for an interview. He'd hoped that they would go to the Minister with the evidence they already had, but he wasn't surprised that they were being meticulous. In the same circumstances, he would be damn thorough, too.

Montgomery Cardwell showed Charlie his identification and then perched gracefully on a flowered chair in the sunroom.

Joan, fluttering about nervously, her voice thin and high as a result, tried to act as if the private investigator were a typical guest. She brought them freshly baked banana bread and coffee. She almost begged to hang around, but Charlie dismissed her with his famous condescending nod, to which Joan bristled but obeyed.

Once the two men had stirred their coffees and taken a bite of the moist cake, Montgomery dispensed with the niceties.

"Sergeant Haynes, I think you have some information about the Thompson case that you've never revealed."

He spoke gently, coaxingly, his eyes kind yet penetrating. The PI reminded Charlie a great deal of himself, the velvet hammer, a man who could intimidate yet cajole. Just the suggestion of menace rippling under the surface, with an offer of taking the friendly route instead.

As Charlie hesitated, Monty looked up, scanning the room, shifting his focus from the old man in the easy chair. He caught his breath.

The paintings covering the walls were shocking. Amid the flowers in vases and the lace curtains, the comfortable furniture, the art was, at first glance, nondescript. Monty had initially caught only a flash of colour and had ignored the detail. When he took that second look, he realized with horror what the drawings depicted. Faces twisted in pain. Bodies surrounded by garbage. Blood, saliva and vomit speckling the decayed cityscape.

Despite the gore, one redeeming factor, hidden within each of the cityscapes, begged the viewer to look again. It was, ironically, the flash of colour that Monty had noticed first when he merely glanced at the paintings. A startling yellow flower poking through cracked pavement; a bright pink stuffed bunny held out to a tearful child; a wrinkled old hand clutched by a youthful one. Once the positive feature became evident, it also became the most prominent. It drew the eye toward hope.

Awestruck, Montgomery audibly released his breath and looked more closely at the old man. Charles Haynes still had his round face, though creases and age spots now dominated. His eyes were a deep blue, even more striking within his crumpled visage, almost like one of his paintings.

When he smiled, you could almost believe he would tell you the truth every time.

The old man followed the younger man's eyes as he studied the paintings.

"These are the originals," Charlie told him. "I sell the prints. I've made an extraordinary amount of money trying to portray the dichotomy between dejection and possibility. It's as if I am apologizing to the drunks and whores and druggies that I kicked while they were down, while I was in a position of trust and should have shown some kindness. As though by showing to my viewers, my fans, that these down-and-outs are victims, human beings, I can make up for being so self-righteous. Encourage others to be different from me. Demonstrate that a little bit of kindness can raise the poor and mentally disturbed from despair to hope. Just making that statement probably proves my continued arrogance, however. Nothing of course is that simple."

Montgomery was startled by the man's speech, the nuanced vocabulary and the self-effacing manner. As Charlie paused, the PI suddenly realized that Sergeant Haynes had delivered exactly that: a speech. He'd rehearsed those well-chosen words; probably spoken them many times at openings and presentations. A wave of mistrust, along with a surge of dislike, kept Monty even more alert.

"I do have information," Charlie finally said in a soft whisper that his guest had to lean over to hear.

Which of course was the retired officer's intent, Monty thought. Throw you just a little off balance.

"But first, please call me Charlie. I'm no longer a Sergeant."

Montgomery had the feeling that the last sentence was as much a self-condemnation as a statement of fact, but whether or not it was sincere was debatable. He took another sip of the excellent coffee and contented himself with eating the banana bread as he waited.

"I decided that William Thompson was guilty the minute I saw the girl, the way she was desecrated, in his studio. The way the monster used his talent to debase her body, and, hell, to contaminate art while he was at it. Thompson always had an air of entitlement. Like he deserved everything he ever got. Gorgeous wife, huge talent, lots of money..."

Montgomery couldn't help but interrupt. "But they didn't have any money at all."

Charlie smiled thinly. "Oh, but you could tell that they would. He might have been on the bottom rung, but he was climbing up that ladder as fast as he could. He and his wife were willing to sacrifice in order to get there. Unlike the choices I made. I chose safety and stability in exchange for my art."

Lots of people did that, Montgomery thought angrily, but they didn't go around laying judgments on everyone else. He held his tongue, though, because he sensed that this time, he was getting the truth, as harsh or self-incriminating as it may be.

As though reading his mind, Charlie continued, "That was my underlying bitterness, my Achilles heal. I hated the police force. I hated most of the people I had to deal with. I thought they were pathetic losers." He waved his hand around the room, acknowledging both the power and the irony of his art. "Now I draw them and give most of the proceeds to charity. My whole retirement has been an apology."

Charlie gave a rueful snigger and sipped on the coffee. "I don't mean to sound as though my life was ruined or that I have been unhappy. Far from it. I have been exceptionally fortunate, both in love and careers. I performed police work with the fierce belief that I was enforcing what was right. Though I didn't much like it, I did the job well. Plus I had friends, I socialized, I even had fun sometimes, and that got me through. When I was assigned to the better parts of Vancouver, especially Granville Island, I was almost happy in the situation. Then along came Linda Courtnell. There was something about the Thompson case that awakened all the dormant bitterness, all the regret, the anger. I can't fully explain it. But I have spent a lot of years thinking about it and, in my own way, trying to make up for it."

"You paid for Shirley Johnson's rehab, didn't you?"

Charlie gazed into Montgomery's fierce brown eyes. "You *are* just like me," he said. When the PI couldn't erase the flash of anger, Charlie laughed heartily. "I don't mean in the bad ways, Montgomery Cardwell. I mean in the intuitive, deductive way your mind works. Yes, I paid for Shirley Johnson's rehab, sort of. I made up the difference between what the government would give and the cost of a good institution. Ironically, she made such great progress that she pretty much outed me. When she was finally off the pills, she could think straight and she recanted her testimony. She realized that she had been duped into telling a specific story in exchange for booze and drugs."

Montgomery put up his hand to stop the man. "Charlie...you are aware that I will have to pass this information on to the Court?"

The old man nodded his head slowly. "I'm very well aware, Mr. Cardwell. I am long overdue in the telling. But don't for a minute think that I am being heroic. I've considered confessing my sins for a long time, especially since my doctor told me that I am dying." He coughed. "I *am* eighty, which might seem old to you, but I have developed lymphoma and the prognosis isn't good. So I shall die a lot sooner than I planned.

"When I heard the Thompsons were back and had decided to go ahead with their appeal to the Minister, I knew what I had to do. I don't want to die with the Thompsons on my conscience. I realize that I may be charged with obstruction of justice, or even worse." He paused, gathering his breath. "I am prepared to come forward officially, even if it means huge disappointment from my wife and daughters, my friends. I can only beg for their forgiveness."

Montgomery's suspicion began to subside a little. No wonder Haynes had rehearsed every word. He was changing the course of his life with this speech.

"I am hoping that we can come to an agreement on something, Mr. Cardwell. And all I will require is your handshake. If, after you hear about everything that I did in the past, you don't think my story will prove William Thompson's innocence, you will agree not to use it. I can guarantee that I will confirm a lot of hunches and accusations about the incompetent way we handled the case. The Supreme Court has already acknowledged that, however. I can also guarantee that I will be revealing quite a lot of new information. Obviously, I must leave it to you to put the pieces together. I have personally become convinced that William Thompson is not the murderer. But you might find that there isn't enough concrete proof in what I am going to tell you. In that case, I am asking, please don't destroy my family for nothing."

Montgomery looked thoughtfully at the old man over his coffee cup. Then he stood up and shook Charlie's hand.

"I promise you, sir, that I will take your information, follow the leads you give me, and put the pieces together. If I don't need to bring you into the case in order to prove my client's innocence, I won't." He looked deeply into the older man's worried blue eyes.

"But I also must warn you, Mr. Haynes, that I *will* prove my client's innocence. I will win a declaration to that effect from the Minister of Justice. And if I need to use your testimony, I will use it. Even if it means destroying your family's good name."

Charlie stared back, his eyes once again sharp and clear. "I destroyed my family's name some time ago, Mr. Cardwell. They just don't know it. Of course, I am hoping they never will."

As the PI sat down again, Charlie asked, "Are you going to take notes?"

For an answer, Montgomery pulled out a small voice recorder and pressed the button.

Chapter Eighteen
September, 1980

Blood oozed from the wound. Plop, plop, plop, on the wooden floor, louder and louder, each drop an explosion in the silent room. The girl was slumped over a ladder on one side, while the man hammered the nail into her wrist on the other. When the camera operator entered the room, they both looked around at him, but their faces did not register surprise. Instead they smiled, hers a bloodless grin, his a wide-mouthed welcome.

"Glad you showed up, Officer," he said pleasantly. "You can help me get this bitch up on the wall. She's a lot heavier than you might think."

The camera edged toward the two people, following closely as someone else began to lift up her dead white arm on the other side. The dead girl turned her head toward him, her face morphing into an old, brown, toothless crone whose breath spewed the stink of stale beer into his face. He howled, but his cry was muted. Heat surged into his face. His heart pounded with fury. She fell to the ground at his feet, laughing, a deep guttural sound, and he began to kick at her face. Blood spurted up from the crevices as her head caved in. A gelatinous mass began to gush toward his feet. He kept kicking, up and down, furiously...

"Charlie, Charlie, wake up." Joan's voice was frantic and pissed off at the same time. "You're kicking me for Christ's sake."

Joan never swore, so the epithet startled him awake more than anything. She was leaning over him in the semi-darkness of their bedroom, her face shadowed and frowning.

"You were dreaming and you started kicking your legs up and down. You even hit me a couple of times. What the heck were you dreaming?"

Charlie struggled to a sitting position, sweat at his temples and his upper lip. Suddenly he had to pee. "I can't really remember," he lied, trying to sound stupefied. "I'm so sorry, Joan. I have to go to the bathroom."

"Maybe you should sleep in the spare room tonight," she groused at him, settling down under the blankets once more.

Charlie straightened his side of the bed and went to sit on the toilet. A full moon shone through the beveled glass and lit up his hairy belly. He felt as though he were just recovering from a long illness, shaky and disoriented. A cloud of anger and frustration moved over him.

"Bloody hell," he murmured, standing to flush the toilet and wash his hands. He returned to the bedroom, grabbed his robe, and listened to Joan's soft snoring for a moment. Then he went downstairs to the sunroom. He poured a healthy shot of Irish whiskey into a mug and settled in his favorite chair.

This case was giving him the nastiest nightmares he'd ever experienced. He wasn't sure why; he'd certainly handled worse killings on the Hastings beat. But Charlie didn't bother to psychoanalyze himself. He just wanted to solve the case. He knew the identity of the murderer, but proving it was not going to be easy. With little forensic evidence and a lot of circumstantial, with witnesses who were not very reliable, the situation was not looking good. Ronald Stevens had turned out to be an exception.

The man showed up at headquarters the day after the plea went out via the media for any relevant information. Although Tom suggested that Stevens was only interested in a reward – of which there was none at the time – Charlie thought his motive was more complicated than that.

"I saw Professor Thompson, the owner of that studio, on the night of the Courtnell girl's murder," he announced to the two police officers, sitting upright on the stiff chair in the interview room. "In the studio."

Charlie went into gentle mode. "It's great that you have come forward, Mr. Stevens. Not many people like to get involved in these things, so I admire your courage."

"Of course, of course. I want to be a good citizen." Tall, skeletally thin and balding, his face a light shade of red from either blushing or recent sun contact, Ronald Stevens looked like a pink crane. He nodded his head up and down as he spoke as though pecking at the words. His voice was high-pitched, singsong.

"Please state your name and address for Officer Fairburn."

The man did so, his voice taking on a pompous quality, as Tom scribbled furiously.

"Where do you work, Mr. Stevens?"

"At Micon Industries on Granville Island," he answered, obviously fully aware that this was an important fact. "Right near the scene of the crime," he added, just in case the police officers missed the point. "Every Monday to Thursday night I pass that studio where the murder happened. The walkway to the bus stop goes that way. I work the noon to 10 p.m. shift four days a week and then I have three off."

"Can you please tell us what you meant when you stated that you specifically saw the studio owner on the night of the murder? Take us through your movements step by step, please."

Stevens blossomed at the use of television cop speak. His words began to flow quickly. "I was walking past the studio as usual and I saw him – Professor Thompson - standing in the window. He was just staring out. I've met the professor before, so I knew right away who it was. Then when I heard about the murder, I figured I'd better come and tell you." He cleared his throat. "Have they got a reward posted yet?"

Tom's eyes narrowed, sent a message of 'I told you so'. "Not yet," he said vaguely. "But you never know."

"Well, if there ever is one, you know, I wouldn't take it all myself, I mean I would give some to the art school maybe or…"

"Let's not get ahead of ourselves," Charlie interrupted, still gentle but adamant. "Are you certain that you saw the owner at the window on that particular night? You said you pass that studio after work every night, right? How do you know you didn't see Professor Thompson on some other night?"

Continuing to nod, Stevens answered, "I do pass that way regularly, but I know I saw him on the night of the murder because I had attended a lecture of his that very morning. Just out of interest, you know? I'm an artist." If he'd had feathers, Charlie thought, he would have preened. "That's why I looked up at the studio. I'd just seen him that morning. So I know the exact date and I know the guy."

Charlie felt a pulse of excitement. "So you would easily have recognized Mr. Thompson?"

"Yes, absolutely. I know Professor Thompson quite well. I went to the lecture because I wanted to see what he had to offer art students."

"And were you impressed, Mr. Stevens?" Tom asked.

After a slight hesitation, the man said smoothly, "Oh yes, really impressed. He's a very talented man."

"Describe exactly what you saw in the window of the studio," Charlie prompted.

"Professor Thompson was standing staring out at the night. Or the creek or whatever. Just standing there. I watched as I walked along, past the market building, and he never moved. I waved, but I guess he couldn't see me. I was in the dark."

"Was there a light on inside the studio?"

"Yes, but not much. It looked like a lamp was on or one of the banks of lights or something. Not the whole set."

Charlie wondered, "How do you know so much about the lighting in the studio?"

"Oh I don't, really. But some nights the place is lit up like a movie shoot and sometimes there's just a desk lamp or something. And sometimes it looks like half the room is lit, as though there are rows of lights. You know what I mean – the kind of switch where you can light up half…"

"Yes, of course, I know what you mean," Charlie said, afraid he'd get sidetracked on a discourse about electricity. "You did tell us you walk that pathway every night, so I guess you'd be quite familiar with what the studio looks like under various kinds of lighting."

"Exactly." As proud as if he'd found the murder weapon. "I've also been in there."

Charlie was quiet for a moment. "Inside the studio?"

"Yes. I'm something of an art aficionado in addition to being an artist myself. I've entered contests and such, plus I bought one of the Professor's paintings for my wife. I'm sure that…"

Charlie cut him off, irritated. Everyone thinks they're an artist, he thought. "Well, that isn't really relevant to this case, Mr. Stevens. Let's move on to something that *is* crucial. I want you to think about this very carefully. What exact time did you see the Professor in the window?" He waited a beat, then added, "You see, Ms Courtnell was murdered around nine at night. So if it was earlier..." Charlie let the sentence dangle, ignoring Tom as his partner raised the pen from his page, giving him a quizzical look.

"It was precisely 10:15 p.m.," Ronald Stevens answered primly.

"And how do you know that?"

"Because I was finished work and I have to catch my bus at 10:30. And I do tend to dawdle. I like the sights and sounds of the Island. It's the subject of a lot of my paintings."

"But you said it was *exactly* 10:15 when you looked up at the window," Charlie prodded. "How can you be so precise?"

"Oh." Ronald raised a thin, steady arm, pushing his sleeve back to reveal an enormous watch almost hidden in the mass of black hair on his wrist. "I look at my watch every five minutes, until I get on the bus. It keeps me moving."

Charlie smiled. "You like to be precise."

"Oh, my wife doesn't like to be kept waiting," Ronald Stevens said gravely.

"So you look at your watch every five minutes. And you are sure you looked at your watch that night at exactly 10:15."

"Absolutely sure."

"Is there anything that caught your attention at that exact moment? Maybe you looked up at the windows, a little startled to see Professor Thompson, and then you looked down at your watch right away? Sort of by habit, but prompted by seeing him in the window?"

"Exactly. That's exactly what happened. I was very surprised to see him standing right there above me. Then he suddenly closed up the windows and disappeared. And I was surprised again and that made me look down at my watch. Which is what I do often. Look down at my watch, I mean. So I don't miss the bus."

"Well, Mr. Stevens, I'm giving you this paper to write up your statement and our secretary will type it up for you to sign. Is that okay?"

Stevens nodded enthusiastically.

"It'll only take a few minutes. Would you be willing to testify in court if it come to that?"

"Oh, absolutely. My wife told me I would probably have to and I'm fine with that. I saw what I saw. And if a reward comes up, I'm sure you'll let me know."

"I certainly will, Mr. Stevens. Now, can I get you a coffee or a tea while you're waiting?"

"That would be great. Tea, please, with milk only. And if you happen to have some cookies, I'm a bit peckish."

"We're not saying Professor Thompson is guilty of anything, though, Mr. Stevens. You realize that, right? You won't spread any of this around but keep it confidential unless you are asked to testify in a court of law. Right?" Tom asked.

"Oh of course, of course." Ronald Stevens crossed his legs, picked up the pen Charlie handed to him, and primly began to write.

The Sergeant went into the squad room and began to fill a mug with thick black tea. Tom followed his partner.

"Lead much, Charlie?" Tom hissed in his ear.

Charlie almost dropped the milk container. He gave as nonchalant a shrug as he could manage. "He saw what he saw, Tom," he said, giving his friend a wide grin.

Tom's eyes narrowed as he stared for a moment into Charlie's. "I'm not sure I like the way this case is going. First you talk Ted into the time of death, now you shamelessly lead this idiot. I dunno, Charlie. Are you that sure?"

Charlie turned to face his friend. "Tom, I am so sure of this case that I would do *anything* to convict that son-of-a-bitch." His eyes were blazing, his face set and confident. "Anything, you get it? You know my track record better than anyone. I've never been as certain as this. And I've never convicted anyone who didn't deserve it."

That you know of, Tom felt like saying, but he simply gazed back at Charlie for a few long moments. Finally, he made a decision.

"Okay, buddy, I trust your instincts. Let's go for it." And with those words, Tom began to aid and abet his Sergeant, his friend, his hero, with every ounce of exploitation and righteousness that he could muster.

Chapter Nineteen
March, 2009

"I knew Tom was doing it for me," Charlie told Montgomery Caldwell. "I talked him into it. For a very long time, I was absolutely certain that we had our man. I'd watched Thompson for a long time, saw how he dealt with people, especially other artists. I thought he was a cruel, manipulative individual. I deliberately convinced Dr. Sato to narrow the timeframe for the murder so that it fit William Thompson perfectly. I never mentioned the tattoo needle and neither did Tom or Ted, especially since we'd discovered absolutely no connection between tattoos and the Professor. In those days, the rules about sharing evidence with the defense were very loose. If they didn't ask, you didn't tell. Can't be done nowadays."

"Nowadays we have to catch the culprits with proof," Monty said.

Charlie laughed in response and immediately began to cough loudly. Montgomery leapt to his feet but stood there helplessly as Charlie's face reddened and the coughing became a silent wheeze. Joan reentered the room, ministering to her husband with quick, practiced strokes. As soon as he could speak, Charlie gently waved her away.

"My heart isn't pumping very well," he told Monty. "So I lose my breath a lot. Joan knows how to massage me back to life, eh, honey? Okay, okay, woman, I'm fine now."

Joan, her thin face etched with worry, gave Montgomery an accusatory glance.

"It's all right, he promises not to make me laugh again," Charlie said.

"Don't keep him long," Joan said, peering up at Monty with such ferocity from her tiny frame that he almost stepped back.

"Stop worrying, Joan," her husband interjected. "We'll take as long as we need."

Charlie accepted another coffee from Montgomery, who had wordlessly refilled their cups and plates.

"I never involved my family in the police work," Charlie explained. "Just let me know in plenty of time if you have to make all of this public." He shrugged philosophically and continued his tale.

"There was only one other person who could back up what Ronald Stevens claimed about seeing Thompson on the premises. Shirley Johnson was practically a resident of the old factory. I knew, though, that she wouldn't make a good witness," Charlie said, "so I decided to clean her up. It wasn't that different from what a lot of prosecutors did in those days. They still do, actually - clean up your client, your defendant, your witness – make them look less sleazy, dress them up in the clothes of the innocent."

"But why did you feel so guilty that you paid for her rehab?" Montgomery inquired.

Charlie looked up at him, his eyes filming over. Illness? Tears of regret? Monty refused to give him a break by averting his gaze.

"I found her huddled under a blanket behind the stairwell in the market building," Charlie began, ignoring the question. "She was next to her rusted-out grocery cart as usual. I pretended I was just doing a routine search of the whole building. Nothing out of the ordinary. I had seen Shirley there many times before. Any of us who regularly visited the island knew Shirley."

Her brown face is a mass of folds, like a withered old teddy bear whose fur has been handled by too many hands. Her hair is still jet-black and falls in twisted, filthy ringlets. She smells so badly that the odor propels people away from her involuntarily, even the do-gooders. She wanders all over the island, sometimes pushing her cart, other times with an old backpack or a ripped shopping bag, always talking to herself. She picks up rocks, garbage, fallen flowers or nuts, even dead birds. Her hands skip through the air with palsy as though she plays an invisible keyboard.

When he finds her under the filthy blankets, he tries to bring her to consciousness, but she is limp and unresponsive. He kicks her viciously, rolls her over and shoves her upright against the wall. She looks up at him, her eyes a deep sun-speckled brown, clouded by grief and distress. He immediately feels ashamed.

"The shop owners gave her stuff – coffee, sandwiches – and the rest of us gave her gift certificates to get the coffee or sandwiches. Some people gave her money, but she just spent it on booze, so we encouraged the certificates instead."

"She went around the island begging?"

"Actually, no. She never begged. That was the funny thing. Shirley didn't seem to care if she ate or drank, even. She was always searching."

"Searching?"

"Yah. She would ask people if they'd seen her husband and her kids."

"Right. Mr. Thompson mentioned something about Shirley's loss of her husband and kids in an accident."

Charlie nodded. "He was one of the most generous toward Shirley, I have to admit. I saw them interact on numerous occasions. The old factory was one of her favourite hiding spots, even as they started to renovate it into the Market Place. Shirley hid behind various pillars and later, when the renovations began, she'd tuck in beside the machines or the concrete they'd unearthed. I knew she watched for the Professor. On my night patrols, she'd be there at the bottom of the stairs, waiting for him. He'd listen to her, and even more, she listened to him."

Charlie hesitated, as though embarrassed to continue. "I decided almost immediately that she would have seen the Professor that night. She just wasn't aware of times and dates. In my mind, her not knowing didn't mean it wasn't true. I got Captain Webster's permission to pursue her testimony by whatever means. When I first put her in the rehab, my intent was only to clean her up. Get her in shape for the Court. Then I would let her back out onto the street if that's what she wanted." Charlie held his hand up, as though to shield himself from Monty's disgust. "I know, I know. It was despicable. I want you to understand just how far we were prepared to go to convict Bill Thompson. As far as the entire department was concerned, including Captain Webster, Thompson was a monster.

"Anyway, the strategy worked. Shirley got cleaned up and she testified. She did a damn good job of it, too. She was off the booze fairly quickly, though it took a long time before she could function without being zoned out on various meds. When she testified, she was completely dependent upon me and still only half aware. All I needed to do was make a few suggestions. The prosecutor used her well, too. He told me to release her, but she wanted to stay in the rehab centre. She loved it there and by then they loved her too. So I made sure she was able to stay by topping up what her welfare payments covered. I'd spent many hours with her at that point. I never stopped going to see her. Even after she recanted. Even after she left the rehab. I think I was a little in love with Shirley Johnson."

He lumbers along the polished tile in the hallway, feeling awkward and big, an overweight puppy far too eager for her attention. A hulk of masculinity in a sea of females. Sunlight glitters through the stained glass, throwing a patchwork of colour over the floor. He thinks it is art.

Shirley smiles at him from the chair by the window, her teeth still grey and jagged, but her face alight with health. Her hair is no longer visible, hidden by the old-fashioned garb that she insists upon wearing, but he pictures the thick, black strands as they used to be, long and wavy over her shoulders. Her eyes, as always, are captivating, but even more so now that there are no clouds. She reaches out her hand and grasps his firmly, her papery soft skin a gift of silk.

"Probably no one else knew that Shirley was a well-respected nurse before she became mentally ill. She and her family had lived in Kamloops. Shirley won a few awards as nurse of the year and that sort of thing. She was brilliant and caring and kind. When her husband and two boys were killed in a car accident, she could not forgive herself for surviving."

"Was she in the car with them?" Montgomery knew they were straying a little off course, but he was curious.

"Worse than that. She was driving. It was raining hard and it was dark. Her husband and the boys had fallen asleep. The road was one of those winding mountain trails and there'd been a rockslide. She swerved around the rocks and went over the side. Shirley was thrown free, landed on a clump of bushes that cushioned her fall, but her kids and Larry were trapped in the car. She tried to pull them out, but she couldn't. By the time she scrambled up the hill and flagged down a passerby, by the time the emergency crews finally got there, all three of them were dead. Here she was, a nurse who'd saved many strangers' lives, and she had been unable to save her own babies and the man she loved. Shirley could not come to terms with that. She'd injured her back, was given pain pills, and over time, graduated from those to booze and illegal drugs. Somehow she drifted onto Granville Island and was lost in her own mind for years."

"You saved her," Montgomery observed.

"Yes, but almost at the cost of her dignity. When her mind cleared, Shirley realized that her testimony was a lie." Charlie was silent for a moment. "It was Simon Callas who prodded her memory and got her to see that she couldn't possibly have known the day or the time or even whether or not the man she saw coming down the stairs was Bill Thompson. But she never blamed me. She blamed the pills and the booze and the mental illness. And, God help me, I never corrected her."

"What happened to Shirley?"

Charlie smiled. "That's the one good thing that came out of all this. She became a nun, believe it or not. I visited her often in the convent, too. Then suddenly she went off to India to work with the Missionaries of Charity. Shirley gave a lot to people and she wouldn't have accomplished that if she'd stayed on Granville Island. I have to say, her transformation did make me feel better about my actions for a time." He fell silent, then added, "She died in Calcutta in 2000."

Montgomery sat for a few moments in thought, basking in the sunlight streaming through the large windows. It was a comfortable room, an artistic place, almost as though the old man's creativity permeated the chairs and carpet. In spite of the fact that Charles Haynes had committed some very grave errors, Montgomery felt somehow that this sin, at least, had been atoned. Perhaps never in the Thompsons' eyes, or hearts.

Cardwell knew that many law enforcement officials had made the same kinds of mistakes. Rushing to judgment, conducting an investigation that made the facts fit the theory. Just because others had done it, didn't mean Charlie got a pass. But Monty thought of Shirley Johnson, of the paintings in this room, of the charities that had benefited, and somehow his animosity toward Haynes abated. Not complete forgiveness, perhaps, but a definite softening of Montgomery's assessment of this man.

The PI spoke into the silence. "Ronald Stevens will not recant his testimony. Even when Simon Callas pointed out the near impossibility of his claim by demonstrating how a person would look as they stood inside the lit studio. There were – and still are – a lot of streetlamps along the pathway, which cast quite a bit of light. Not only that, the studio was on the second floor. The figure in the window would have had to be pressing his face against the pane in order to be seen clearly. Why on earth would someone who'd just murdered, raped and mutilated a young girl have his face pressed against the window? I'm sure you know all of this, Charlie."

"I do. Stevens claimed he was standing far enough back from the pathway to see straight up to the second storey and that the streetlamps were not always lit. If Simon Callas couldn't shake him, no one will."

At that moment, a dark cloud passed over the sun and Montgomery shivered. He felt an unexpected premonition of disaster and turned off the voice recorder. Despite Charlie's regurgitation of his sins, the case was still not completely solid.

The Supreme Court had already reviewed Shirley Johnson's revised testimony.

The original jury had heard about the tiny spot of semen that could not possibly have been left by William Thompson, because the owner of that fluid was a non-secretor. In fact, a very large percentage of males are secretors, just like Thompson. Compelling evidence that ought to have exonerated the accused. Somehow, the jury was persuaded that the victim could have had sex with someone else before she came to the studio. Linda Courtnell was supposed to be having an affair with Thompson, plus she had a nice, clean-cut boyfriend who admitted they were intimate. He, too, was among the majority secretors. Ludicrously, the jury bought the premise that Linda first had sex with an unknown man, then went out to whoop it up with her boyfriend, and finally, decided to drop in to see if the Professor was in the mood. Linda Courtnell, a motivated, gifted artist whose focus appeared to be solely on her burgeoning career, was portrayed as a wild party girl. How had Langford's defense attorney not been able to demolish that scenario?

By the time Simon Callas was presenting the case before the Supreme Court in 1999, the semen sample was gone. Once a verdict was entered, and an appeal denied, keeping the evidence was not a requirement in 1980. Simon had been nearly apoplectic when he considered what DNA testing could have done for his client. The Judges did, however, agree that the odds were against William Thompson being the rapist, and therefore, the murderer.

Wendy Collins and Frank Jeffries eventually admitted that their testimony was based on rumours. Linda had never told anyone that she was having an affair. By all accounts, Emily and Langford were in love and happily married.

Elaine Martin's testimony was dismissed as hearsay, as were the accounts of Linda's friends.

The use of the tattoo needles was revealed. No evidence was ever uncovered that William Thompson knew how to use one – or for that matter, did not know how to use one.

There was absolutely no forensic evidence that tied William Thompson to the murder.

But that also meant there was nothing to confirm his innocence, either, within the strict word of the law.

Monty began to tick off the possibilities in his mind. There was the chance that Ronald Stevens could be persuaded to rethink his stance, with a well-placed word or two about his own personal motive. He had been, after all, a failed artist at the time, a loser in a contest operated by Professor Thompson. Maybe it was Linda Courtnell in the window that night. Could Montgomery suggest to Ronald that the police had come to suspect that he had committed the murder? Or would that kind of manipulation be just like the methods used in the past by Sergeant Haynes?

Perhaps Harrison Courtnell would have something more to say than he did all those years ago. Monty was suspicious of the young man's visage in all the photos of the family from 1980. Did Harrison look guilty? Did he have information that his parents would not allow him to speak about?

And then there was the man sitting in front of him. Did Charlie Haynes have another motive for being so forthright other than a wish to die without a guilty conscience? Montgomery didn't really think the man in front of him was a murderer, but he had learned in a very personal way that appearances can be deceiving.

William Thompson had been wrongly convicted by a series of very bad judgments and flimsy evidence. The public reaction, the high, positive profile of the victim and her family, along with the emotional reaction of the police officers involved, had all combined to create a case out of nothing. Eyewitness testimony was the least reliable element in an investigation, Monty knew, but in this situation, it had been the key to conviction. How could they satisfy the court's demand for absolute proof of innocence when there appeared to be no evidence at all, one way or the other?

As Montgomery ruminated, a drizzle of rain began to tap against the window. Charlie was fumbling around in a large art portfolio that was propped against the side of his chair. He pulled a stack of thick, square canvasses from among the papers.

"These are small oil paintings, but you will see that they are very unique," he explained, as Montgomery focused his attention once more on the old man. "I must apologize for the time you have spent here, for you will see that I used you. I needed to confess my sins, and you happened to call before my priest did."

Charlie's shoulders shook in an embarrassed laugh at his own joke, but Montgomery was not smiling. Had the old man tricked him? Lost his mind? What the hell was this?

"I have the evidence you need. Getting Stevens to recant is a good idea, but you don't have to. In fact, you don't have to use any of the old evidence, except perhaps the point about the tattoo marks. Remember, you agreed that you wouldn't ruin my reputation if you didn't need to – we shook on that." He paused for a moment while Monty tried to decide whether the old man had lost his mind or not. "I can prove, without a whisper of a doubt, that William Thompson is innocent."

With that, he laid the first photograph on the table between them. "These began arriving three months ago."

Montgomery Cardwell, hardened PI, almost vomited.

Chapter Twenty
March, 2009

When the call came through, Will and I were relaxing under the silky sheets of the king sized bed in our hotel room. The suite was huge, exquisitely furnished, and incredibly comfortable. Not to mention the view of the mountains and the ocean. I had to admit that money could provide the creature comforts, but having just made love to my husband, I knew there were certain things that were not for sale.

Last night, there had been a celebration of sorts in a downtown restaurant close to our hotel. During the party, we experienced several reunions, some awkward, some welcome. Today, we had spent the entire morning and much of the afternoon with the lawyers, while Montgomery visited some witnesses. Fortunately, Jacob had taken control of the legal issues, because Will and I were somewhat overwhelmed. The enthusiasm and determination of the group that Simon Callas had gathered were infectious, however, and we had left the meetings feeling optimistic.

The newspapers were filled with the sensational story once more. Old photos of both William and Linda plastered the front pages. The entire saga was reiterated in all its sordid detail. Unable to help ourselves, we had bought up a bunch of the tabloids, which were now spread around the floor by the bed. Overall, to our surprise, we had gotten the sense that public opinion had moved slightly over to "our side". We didn't bother to analyze the results, however; we'd gone straight to bed, both tired and amorous.

Sated, a cold glass of lemony water propped on my lap, along with a bowl of salty cashews, I discovered that the knot of anger had loosened just a little.

"I couldn't believe all the people there last night," I said.

Will murmured and turned on his side toward me, propped up on his elbow. His eyes held that shine left over from sex, infused with love, which always sent a shiver down to my toes. "It was quite extraordinary," he agreed. "Patsy and Gary haven't changed a bit. Still The Owl and The Pigeon."

I laughed, thinking of the couple's attire, black leather and silver chains, Patsy's grey hair in its perpetual braid, her face still lean and pointy. Gary was completely bald now, more round than ever, his eyes blinking delightedly from behind his owlish glasses.

"They actually had two kids," Will added, his voice infused with disbelief.

"They adopted them," I said. "A sister and a brother. They were found in some tenement with the body of their mother. She'd overdosed and no one knew for two days."

Will sat up straighter. "Oh my god. That's as sad as Cate and Carly's story."

"It really is. We'll have to tell the girls that bad things happen everywhere. We just have to overcome them. But it's just like Patsy and Gary to take on a couple of kids who probably have even more problems than our daughters do. Patricia told me they've had some issues, but overall the kids are amazingly resilient."

"Just like ours," Will said. "Can we call them yet?"

I laughed down at him and popped a cashew into his mouth. "Not yet. They'll be in school. It's only a half-day, though; they've got an early release. So one more hour."

"We don't have anything planned for tonight, do we?"

"Absolutely not. I'm too hung over." I lifted my glass of water in salute.

"I couldn't believe the nerve of some of the people who came either to the airport or even to the party last night," Will said, sitting up. "Officer Fairburn, for instance. What the hell was he doing there?"

"According to Jacob, who was the only one to speak to him, he was in Vancouver on some business and wanted to stop by and apologize. When Jacob asked him what he was apologizing for, he said 'Just tell them I'm sorry for what happened to them' and left."

"Weird. Almost as weird as Ronald Stevens showing his face at the airport."

"It was good to see Teresa and Joseph again, though. They've got three kids and all of them seem to be doing well."

"Yah, they've always been supportive. I kind of felt bad that we didn't keep in touch with some of those people."

"We couldn't. I mean, if you go into hiding, you've got to hide from them all, the good, the bad *and* the ugly."

William laughed. "I know. But before that. I wouldn't let anyone see me in prison, so most of them drifted away long before we left the west coast." We were silent for a moment, then Will cleared his throat, choking down the bad memories and moving into the present. "I really enjoyed talking to Rachel and Greg. Can you believe that Rachel is still Dean of Three Arts? She's almost seventy and has the same energy she had all those years ago."

I pictured the tall, willowy woman with her black and grey hair tucked behind her eyes, dark eyes clear, body strong and graceful.

"I know. She's amazing. I can only hope to look like her when I'm seventy, which isn't that far off."

Will stroked my naked leg. "You're still young, my dear," he said in a wicked voice, "and eminently fuckable." His hand slid all the way up to my thigh. "And always will be."

"How romantic." I popped another cashew in his mouth to distract him. "How is Greg? I noticed you had a long conversation with him. I didn't get to do anything but say hi. Monty's report was really positive about how he's doing these days."

I pictured Greg Hughes, as tall as William, perhaps a little thicker in the chest, his ruggedly handsome face at odds with the flamboyant checkered suit and bright red scarf at his neck.

"He seems to be doing really well. Still teaching music at the college, still painting. Monty was right; he's got quite a following for his landscapes and he plays with his band every weekend at the Merriam Pub. I don't think he has a partner, but he's certainly come out of the closet."

I laughed. "That's for sure. His outfit was so trite, it's almost as though he was shouting 'I'm gay and I want everyone to know it'."

Will got up and padded over to the bar on the far side of the suite. "I'm going to have some hair of the dog. A Caesar. Want anything?"

"Oh yah, a Caesar would be perfect."

When we were settled with our drinks, pillows stuffed in behind us, Will continued. "Greg is a different kind of guy. I agree that he's overstating his sexual preference. I think he does that because he's just soo atypical...I mean, he's tall and rugged looking, the opposite of what most people think when they think 'gay guy'."

"You must have been amazed at the number of students who showed up," I said, sipping my excellent drink, perfectly spiced and salty.

"I was. Gratified too, because they all told me I'd been a good teacher. Missing that career is one of my biggest regrets, as you well know."

We fell silent for a few minutes and I felt that knot once more, a blaze of such fury that my face flushed red with the intensity. Returning to Vancouver, however hopeful we might be for a positive conclusion, was bringing back all those feelings of frustration, despair, hatred and resentment. The emotions were almost uncontrollable because there was no one to take it out on: I couldn't rail at anyone because we still had no idea who'd taken Linda Courtnell's life and ours while he was at it. I tried to shift my focus, for my husband's sake.

"I was really surprised to see Dennis Maloney and his wife. And Terry Somers. I'm glad his company has done so well, almost like payment for saving my life."

"Trust me, there could never be enough payment for that," Will said, squeezing my hand.

"Will, I almost forgot!" How could I have forgotten? Was the bad overcoming the good in my mind the way I'd allowed it to in the past? I figuratively shook my head and focused on my news. "Did you notice the tall young man standing with two women near the door?"

Will thought for a moment. "Not really, honey. I guess you were surrounded and I was surrounded and..."

"True," I said, warming now to the happy memory. "It was Justin! And Laura and Fiona had brought him."

Will looked quizzical.

"Remember the little autistic boy in my class – the last one I ever taught in Vancouver? Before the accident?" Was everything always going to be 'before and after Vancouver', I wondered briefly, and then pushed the thought away. "Laura and Fiona were such wonderful little girls. They took very good care of Justin. He was sweet and smart and funny. Now they're all adults of course. Both Laura and Fiona are married with children of their own and Justin is amazing. He can make eye contact and was appropriately social. It's almost a miracle. Laura told me that they'd all remained friends over the years and that they'd never forgotten Miss Taylor. It was incredibly sweet." My eyes filled with tears. Will grabbed my hand and I just let them roll down my cheeks. "Oh, Will, this is so hard."

"I know, darling, I know." He laid his head on top of mine and kissed my nose, while his other hand wiped away my tears.

Suddenly I looked at the clock as though it were a life raft. "We can call the girls now," I said, joy suffusing my limbs. "But we better get dressed first!"

Face washed, tears whisked away by a dash of powder, I looked far more normal than I had thought I would. Both of us, dressed once more, went into the separate office area to start up the computer. We sat side-by-side in front of the laptop at the desk. The Skype image was clear and interference-free. Cate's beautiful freckled face, her long hair tied into a ponytail, grinned happily over the screen.

"Hi, Mem!" Cate's voice was joyful and enthusiastic. "Hi, Daddy!"

Will's face lit up. The girls had had no trouble with the word "Daddy" – they'd had no previous experience with that word. In their former household, Carl Sanderson had demanded Sir or, once in a while, Father.

"I'm here, sweetie." He leaned in to make sure his image was in the camera, our faces cheek to cheek. "Is Carly there?"

A chorus of voices sounded in the background. Cate picked up the laptop and swung around to her sister, waving from her wheelchair, her red hair with its lustrous strands of white forming a cloud of curls around her head. One by one, each of the siblings waved or danced a hello. Even May did a two-step for us.

"We're all here, see? Except for Alain. He's taking Angel for a walk."

For the next twenty minutes, we talked and laughed with Cate, Carly, Trevor, Benjaman and Meghan in turn, then had a good conversation with May. In the interim, Alain came home and held our little dog up to the eye of the computer. Everything was going well, though the girls missed us. We told them we missed them too, gave kisses and hugs, lips to lips through cyberspace. We both felt reenergized when we ended the call.

Almost as though it was deliberately timed, the telephone in the suite rang shrilly the second the laptop's screen saver appeared.

"Hey, Monty," I heard William say. "Sure, of course. Yes, absolutely. That's fine. Do you want any dinner? Okay, yah, sure. I'll take care of it."

My husband turned to face me, his face puzzled.

"Montgomery and Jacob want to meet in our room. After all, we have the office." He waved his hand around the enormous suite. "Monty sounded odd. I wonder what this is all about. I told him I'd order room service."

We wandered around anxiously, busying ourselves with orders, setting up the office for four. When the room service arrived, we arranged food and drink for easy reach and waited. To distract myself, I played with my email and paid a couple of bills online. At last, the knock at the door resounded through the suite. Will let Jacob and Montgomery in and ushered them to seats in the office. The PI carried a large black portfolio puffed out at the sides with hidden contents. He placed it carefully on the floor beside his chair.

"You guys look like you could use a drink," Will said carefully, scanning their eyes. They both looked nervous, yet tinged with an edge of excitement, almost shock.

"Absolutely," Montgomery answered, his handsome dark face crinkling in a wide smile. "Scotch if you have it. On the rocks, please."

Jacob looked up from the depths of the armchair in which he sat. His deep blue eyes and wavy black hair gave him movie star looks, although he looked a little tired just now. "I'd love a beer, Langford," he said gratefully.

When Will had poured the drinks and refreshed our Caesars, we sat expectantly staring at Montgomery. He took a long, satisfied sip and placed his glass on the side table. Once again, he took his favourite stance: the steepled fingers, elbows resting on his knees, his face intent.

"I went to visit former Sergeant Charles Haynes today. He's now a full-time artist, a very successful one I might add, and his work is, to say the least, unusual. He told me all about what he termed 'sins' that he committed when he was investigating your case, Langford. He manipulated Ronald Stevens into being definite about the time in his story. He used poor Shirley Johnson. He made sure the tattoo issue was passed over and he convinced his friend Dr. Sato to narrow the time of death to fit you."

"None of that is much of a surprise, we know," Jacob interjected, when he saw the disappointment cross our faces. "But then Charles Haynes gave us something explosive. Monty's just setting the context."

Montgomery nodded. "Haynes is dying of lymphoma, and he admitted to me that his imminent death was what prompted the confession."

"I hope he doesn't expect forgiveness," I interrupted, giving more force and anger to the words than I meant to.

"Nope, not at all. Doesn't expect it and didn't ask for it. He just wanted to get it all off his chest before he dies. Then he showed me what he really wanted me to see in the first place. At first he wasn't sure what to do with it, he says. Take it to the police? That would've been my choice, I told him. But he says it's more appropriate in the hands of the defense and he didn't know whom to trust at the police department. Former Captain Webster still wields a lot of power. Personally, I think that's a load of crap. He just wants to be left out of the equation as much as possible. But I'll tell you his requests later."

Montgomery took a breath. "This evidence is going to completely exonerate you, Langford. Inside this portfolio is the real killer's complete, detailed confession."

The silence was so deep in response that I could hear the clock ticking, the laptop humming, someone talking loudly as they hurried along the hallway outside our door, my heart hammering. The air in the room was suddenly stifling. If I'd been able to take a breath, I wasn't sure I would feel refreshed. My thoughts ground to a halt.

"Who?" my husband croaked and a hundred faces flashed through my mind.

Monty stood up, unable to contain his agitation. "That's the only thing we don't know. But the killer has told us in his own words why and how. He has also revealed that there were many other victims. It's horrific, absolutely horrific." He crossed over to squat in front of us, placing his hands gently on ours, trying to soften the blow. "He has provided us with paintings and photographs. Dates, times, and places of burial for the others besides Linda." He stood up, and, returning to his seat, took another long gulp of his scotch as Will and I tried to digest his words.

"Of course, we will be bringing everything to the police. First we have to consider whether or not you should look at the evidence or be content to hear it from me, and Jacob, who has seen it too. Secondly we must consider whether or not we expose Charles Haynes."

"Expose him?" I asked.

"Yes, expose him for tampering with witnesses, withholding evidence, and any number of relatively minor crimes. Relative at least to being a rapist or a murderer, which he is not."

I was having difficulty understanding anything at the moment. I was also fighting to keep the anger from bursting through the dam. Why the hell wouldn't we expose him? Those 'relatively minor crimes' had contributed to a major offense against my husband and our families.

"Can I make a suggestion about how to proceed?" Jacob asked, sounding weary.

My husband looked at me, searching my eyes. Then we both nodded, still too numb to speak.

"To be perfectly honest," Jacob continued at our assent, "I am starving. I feel a little lightheaded as a matter of fact. Do you think we could eat? And while we eat, as nasty as this sounds, we could outline the new evidence and what it's going to do for your case. Afterward, you can decide whether or not you want to look at the paintings and pictures."

Thus we found ourselves incongruously munching on sandwiches and crisp vegetables and French fries as we listened to a horrific tale.

"Three months ago," Montgomery related between mouthfuls, "a series of deliveries began arriving at Charlie Haynes's business address. His company is called Haynes &

Hands Inc. and is primarily an online order and delivery operation. His daughter does book showings of her father's work in various galleries, but they don't run a studio of their own. He keeps the inventory at his house, so they don't need storage. The office is rented out by one of those virtual centres – basically, you pay for a large post box and an address. Grace Haynes works from home, picks up paintings, gets them framed if they need it, and ships them from a local postal depot. Charlie gets his art supplies delivered to his home and does all his painting there too. As a result, they don't go to the virtual office very often. Mostly, Grace checks the box for orders that have been sent by snail mail, as Charlie called it. Once in a while, he also receives fan mail or advertisements and so on.

"After Christmas, Grace went on an extended holiday with her family and didn't come back until the middle of January. Charlie was very ill by this time and hadn't been doing much painting anyway, so business was very slow. When she finally went to the office, there were two large brown envelopes addressed to Charlie. One had been delivered at the first of January and the other at the beginning of February. A third one arrived at the beginning of this month, March. So there are three sets altogether."

"Do you think there are more to come?" Will asked.

Montgomery shook his head. "No. The sender claims these were all he had."

Jacob took up the tale. "Inside the envelopes, there were several small canvasses, or what appeared to be canvasses, I should say. There were also photographs. Accompanying each delivery was a letter, which rants on and on while giving details about his crimes."

Montgomery reached into the portfolio and withdrew a long white envelope, on which someone had written, 'Sergeant Charles Haynes'. "This is the first one," Monty explained. "He writes that he killed Linda Courtnell for revenge. He won't say what her transgression was, but apparently she humiliated him. He admits that he was a failed artist and that killing Linda in Langford's studio was a way to get back at both of them. He claims that he never thought the police would arrest the Professor and convict him of murder, but he says…" Monty looked down at the letter. "'It was the feather in my cap'."

"He writes a lot of arrogant, cruel things," Jacob added. "He's clearly insane."

"Or wants us to think so," Monty said.

"Back up to the failed artist thing. Could the writer be Ronald Stevens? Or Charlie Haynes?"

"Or Harrison Courtnell," I inserted, remembering the third person Montgomery had mentioned on the plane.

"We'll show you that it couldn't have been Charlie," Monty said. "But yes, Ronald Stevens and Harrison Courtnell are definitely on the list as suspects."

"The important thing to remember right now, though, is that these envelopes and their disgusting contents are proof of your innocence, Langford. We can't focus on the 'who'. We have to let the police do that."

"For now, at any rate," Montgomery agreed. The tone of his voice suggested there would be retribution in the future and I found myself wanting to egg him on.

"How do the pictures and photos prove Langford's innocence?" I prodded, anxious to move forward in some way.

"Each of the envelopes is dated." Montgomery put a typed list out in front of him. January 1, February 1, and March 1, all clearly postmarked. They were all delivered from Langford, B.C."

Will and I looked at each, gasping.

"I did check. You were not anywhere near the town of Langford on those dates. The police may want to verify my findings and perhaps question the postal workers to see if anyone was mailing them for you, but once they see these photos and letters, I don't think they'll go any further." Montgomery hesitated. "There was something that you never admitted to, something the police kept questioning you about. Of course you couldn't admit it – you were innocent. But do you remember any odd question that stood out?"

William closed his eyes, trying to slide back thirty years in memory. Finally, he shook his head. "I'm sorry, Monty, I really can't."

"They might have asked you something about The Artist…"

Suddenly Charlie's wheedling, condescending voice echoed in Langford's ear. *"Were you jealous of her, Professor? Do you think of yourself as THE Artist? Was this upstart little girl going to surpass you?"*

"Yes!" Will interrupted. "Now I remember. Haynes kept asking me if I thought I was *the* Artist, better than anyone, certainly better than 'that little upstart', as he called Linda."

"There was a signature on her body," Montgomery said carefully, putting down his plate and sipping once again on the scotch. "On the inside of her thigh. In cursive writing, just like a regular autograph: The – capital T – Artist, capital A. They searched all of your paintings and sketches and found no such signature. They tried to get you to brag about your work, maybe admit that you thought of yourself as *the* Artist. But you never faltered. So all of a sudden, the signature was forgotten, dismissed as unimportant."

Jacob continued, as though to halt the locomotive of our dismay. "The murderer killed many other people, as Monty has said. He painted and signed their bodies, which he then photographed. In each of the pictures that he sent to Haynes, the sender made sure we spotted his signature, which exactly matches the one found on Linda's body. At least the crime scene cops had taken their pictures properly, if nothing else. This afternoon, buried in an evidence box, we found one crime scene photo that, if you look carefully, shows the autograph. Unless you knew what you were searching for, it was easily missed, since it ran along a rivulet that he had painted."

Involuntarily, I shivered at the image.

"Each of the photographs that the suspect sent is dated," Monty continued. "The murders took place before *and* after Linda's death. Some of them long after you were incarcerated, Langford. You can't possibly be the culprit."

"Could the pictures have been staged? I mean, how do we know they are authentic?"

"He used one of those old instamatic cameras," Montgomery said. "It's very doubtful that they could have been PhotoShopped in any way. However, the police will have to follow the trail the killer has left to check out his claims. According to the letters, some of the bodies are buried in specific places, while the rest he dissolved in sulfuric acid."

"My god!" I murmured. "This is absolutely horrid. How could such a man not have been caught?"

"He says that, with the exception of Linda Courtnell, he murdered people he termed 'low-lifes', prostitutes and druggies. No one missed them. Even if they were reported missing, it was assumed they had disappeared on purpose."

"Jesus. Just like that pig farmer's victims," Will commented, thinking of the Port Coquitlam murders.

"Yes, very similar," Jacob said, his voice thick with sadness and disgust. "This killer believed he was taking souls out of their lives of drudgery and futility into a higher plane. They became true art, experienced the perfection of art, through their suffering and dying. He was their conduit to a union with something he called the Creative Spring."

"He was nuts," Monty barked. "*Is* nuts, I should say. He developed a perverted philosophy out of his desire to kill. Made it a mission instead of a crime. We will get this man, I promise you. Even if I have to join the RCMP to do it."

"Monty, I believe you'll get this guy locked up, and soon. I think he confessed because he wants to be caught and you are the man to do it. In the meantime, once the police have the evidence, the legal team and I will be shouting to the courts, the Minister, hell, the whole world," Jacob stated intensely. "William Thompson will once and for all be declared innocent."

We were stunned into silence once more by the ferocity of Jacob's determination, by the hope that surged through the room. Will reached for my hand and I turned to see that tears were flowing down his cheeks. I threw myself out of my chair and into his arms.

"Everything is going to be all right, Em," he said, stroking my hair.

Those words echoed in my ears, down the lines of memory, through the years of agony, past the time of being someone else, and collided into the present. Flash of Will's arms around me, our baby still alive and tucked safely in my womb. Flash of a dreadful bang from behind as piercing headlights forced me down a lonely, mist-enshrouded embankment. Flash of my mother's face drenched in tears. Flash of William, pale and quiet, behind a glass panel.

Had someone truly orchestrated the terrible events that had thwarted our lives? Had someone tried to kill me? Had someone deliberately framed my husband? Would everything really ever be normal or were we forever doomed to be the targets of a madman who could try to make art out of gruesome tragedy?

Chapter Twenty-One
March, 2009
The Artist

A thrill of excitement started in his chest and spread downwards until even his toes felt a tingle. Never had he imagined that he would be given such a gift. It had not occurred to him that he, too, could experience perfect art. The fact that he was The Artist had seemed to preclude him from the encounter. Whenever he had imagined his death, it was a simpering, dull kind of end: in bed melting from the inside through cancer or hit by a car in the street or keeling over from a heart attack. Mundane, just like most ordinary people.

Shortly after he'd heard the news about the Taylor-Thompsons, he had been struck by the number one hundred. He saw and heard it everywhere. It was a shock when he realized that the number of people who had been transported to the Creative Spring was in the nineties. Of course – the sudden appearance of one-zero-zero on television, radio, and print was a message. He was supposed to stop at one hundred. He was astonished at the simplicity, the purity, and wondered why the goal hadn't been revealed to him before. Perhaps he would have rushed and made a mistake. Got caught before he reached the one hundred.

Even more astonishing, a voice began whispering in his ear. He would turn around in the middle of a room, or a street, or a bus, but no one would be there. At last he realized that his own personal Creative Spring was speaking to him and him alone. A Creative Spring that had evolved to an even higher plane than he had. But he was special, the voice told him. He would conduct the one hundredth death and his work would be complete. He assumed the Voice meant that he, too, would die after completion of the perfect one-zero-zero.

Through the guidance of his Spring, The Artist began to realize that he himself had been somewhat of a fool. He'd allowed emotion to cloud his judgments at times. He'd felt jealousy, acted out of revenge. Now he knew that the only thing that mattered was arranging the proper death. He had given this gift to ninety-nine people by mid-March and lo and behold, the Thompsons came to town. Now he knew on whom to bestow the one-zero-zero mantle.

In the meantime, he prepared the altar, the place where one-zero-zero would be led into the Spring through pain and a slow ebbing of life energy. He could barely contain his joy.

Even people whom he saw every day had remarked on the happiness that glowed from his face. "Hey, you sure look happy", some had said, or "Wow, you look ten years younger. What's happened?" another had remarked. He felt like jumping up and down, sharing with all of these poor deluded people that the ultimate knowledge was open to all of them. They had only to allow it to happen. But of course no one did. They wandered around in their pathetic bodies in this wretched world of things. Things like paintings by Langford Taylor, whose style The Artist had copied and mastered so easily so long ago. What absurd creatures humans were!

Everything was ready. The paint, the tattoo needle, the ropes, the acid.

Chapter Twenty-Two
March, 2009

Once Will and I had regained our composure, Montgomery went right back to business. He held up a packet of thin white examination gloves. "I want us to read some of the letters, on the assumption that once the evidence is deposited with the police department, we won't get this chance again. I didn't want to make copies – too risky – hence the gloves."

We peeled off two each and guided them onto our hands.

"Although I agree with Jacob that our prime task is to acquire your declaration of innocence, I can't help but be angry enough to want to punish this son-of-a-bitch." Monty once again was almost breathless. His obvious effort to contain his wrath was almost as great as my own. He waved his gloved hand in Jacob's direction, his eyes flashing, as though he were a mime saying one thing with his hands and another with his expression. "I know, Jacob, I swear I can read your mind. I promise you I won't interfere with the police investigation. But I really want Emily and Langford to hear the voice in these letters."

Jacob said nothing, but he gave a nod, granting permission without saying yes out loud.

Monty continued, satisfied. "Notice anything that sounds familiar. A phrase, a particular word, a saying. People often have a distinctive quality to their speech that also comes out in their writing. Maybe this guy has revealed himself in some way."

He carefully removed the letters from inside the envelopes; three long diatribes of several pages in length. Then Montgomery paused, looking at us directly and honestly, as though trying to temper his own impulsiveness.

"You don't have to do this. As you know, Jacob doesn't think it's a good idea. Plus, it's going to be difficult. All you really need to do is tell me to take the evidence to the police, acquire your declaration, and let the law do the rest. And if that's what you want me to do, I will of course honor your wishes."

For an answer, both Will and I reached out to grasp a packet of letters in our latexed hands.

Charlie, my dear boy…

The Creative Spring is the energy that we all came from and that we all desperately want to return to. Haven't you read anything, *my dear Charles?*

You know how we're born in liquid, Charlie my lad. That's the Spring. We go back to the Spring when we die. It's like immersing yourself in perfect beauty, like soft warm water, like a spring pumping life, energy.

If a person wants perfection, they need to experience the perfect death. They have to be one with Creativity. Inside each of us, we have this creative urge, my dear boy. You have it. I have it. We use it. Some people do not. They have to be led toward it.

People have it all wrong, dear Charlie. It's not life that's precious. It's death. It's dying. Slowly and painfully. You should see their eyes, my boy, when they know that death is upon them. The world suddenly spins to a halt and they see the light dancing on the stream.

The best way to experience True Art, Original Creativity, Charles my lad, is to suffer. We suffered when we were born. We were born in pain. We must die in pain. The greater the pain, the more the suffering, the more perfect the death.

I have brought all of these people to the Spring. When you look at them, be happy for them. See how I have painted mountains and rivers and skies for them. Their skins became art, their souls became free.

I struggled through each of the three letters, the knot of anger twisting inside me. Most of the time the writer repeated himself. Often he went into disgusting detail about each of his murders, describing the reactions of his victims. At times I would gasp out loud, shake my head; once I even stomped my feet. I couldn't withhold the emotions roiling inside me: disgust, fear, shock, and yes, hatred. I despised this monster who was attempting to explain his killing spree with a twisted thesis on creativity. How dare he! He had crushed the life from the helpless, the misguided, the most vulnerable members of society.

Will was the first to finish reading, but he waited for me, and then spoke tremulously.

"I have never encountered anyone quite this insane," he said. "Even in prison. The psychotic inmates were mostly zoned out with meds or transferred to an asylum. This guy...how is he wandering around? How do people not see that he is crazy?"

Montgomery shook his head.

Jacob said, "At the risk of sounding like a television shrink, I do believe this guy is disintegrating very quickly. He may have been walking around unnoticed up until now. He's been able to maintain some kind of façade to hide his murderous side. But I don't think that's going to be possible much longer. The trigger had to have been hearing about your return."

"The first of these letters arrived at the beginning of January. He must have heard that we were still alive. We just told everyone in Burchill in December."

"The letters were posted from Langford," Will said. "Why Langford? It has to be someone who knew that I was born there."

"Or someone who heard your new name. I think he was taunting you," Jacob said.

"So he was presuming that Charlie would give us the letters," I added.

"Do you notice any patterns in the letters, Langford? Anything that triggered a memory?"

Will looked up at Montgomery, his face lined with thought. "I wish I did. I was practically willing myself to find something. But nothing in these letters triggers any memories or connections."

The PI tried very hard not to look disappointed, but by now we were used to his expressions and we could see that he was frustrated. We had the proof of William's innocence, but not a clue as to the identity of the real killer. "Okay. What about the photographs?"

"The images will haunt you forever," Jacob cautioned us. "I've never seen anything like these pictures. Monty, even you were shocked by them and you've seen some pretty bad stuff in real life for godssake."

Monty sighed. I was beginning to get irritated that they were talking as though we weren't in the room. "Jacob is probably right. But I think you can certainly handle the paintings."

"The paintings are not as graphic because they're an artistic rendering," Jacob agreed quickly, "but I still think you should by-pass them. I don't know if trying to trigger your memory is a good enough reason for having them on your minds for the rest of your lives. And I'm not just talking about the actual images."

"They aren't painted on real canvas, are they?" I asked.

William looked at me with a puzzled expression, but I could see that I was right by the shock on the faces of the other two men.

"They're painted on skin, aren't they?"

"Yes," Montgomery said, in one word opening a world of horror, a collective memory of human torture and revulsion, a reminder of the depths to which some people can plunge.

Will stood up and paced. "I have to ask again. How has this creature been able to walk around in the guise of a normal human being?"

"We'd have to acquire the services of a forensic psychologist to give us a real answer," Montgomery said, "but it has mostly do with his victims, I think. He picked on people who wouldn't be missed, or if they were missed, there were other, plausible reasons for their disappearance."

I tried to imagine living a life that would not be missed by anyone. No students, colleagues – no family, no Cate or Carly or siblings – no friends, no May or Alain or Agnes or Edgar or Frances...tears formed in my eyes, an ache for all those people in the world who died without love. I knew that May had a strong desire to share her largesse. I longed to talk to her about what we could do for people like these. Victims whose actual skin had been used as an implement; victims exploited for the purposes of fear and contempt.

Jacob brought me back to the present. "He must be a very clever person, too," he said quietly. "A fiend who can pretend to be ordinary. A predator who can form relationships, at least enough of them to appear to be an average person. Either that or he is naturally different in some way, such as being in a position of authority that few would question. He has to be someone you know, Langford. And perhaps who knows you too, Emily. I've always thought your car accident was not an accident – I believe this monster was the cause of that, too. He'd ruined Langford's life. For some reason, he decided to take yours away completely."

"If it weren't for Terry Somers, he'd have succeeded." I shivered, then straightened my shoulders and sucked in the air of determination. "We have to look at the paintings, Will. If there is any chance that we will recognize the person through their so-called art, we have to take it. We didn't come all this way *not* to be courageous. We certainly have overcome some horrible nightmares in the past – viewing these atrocities will simply have to be one of them."

I stood up. "I want to be standing when I look at them," I said. "I don't know why, but I think I'll feel less vulnerable. Can you hold them up for me, Monty?"

"Of course." Montgomery, still wearing his gloves, lifted the small paintings out of the portfolio.

They were nearly perfect squares of canvas, six of them altogether, a pale covering attached to each of the four corners. Skin. Dried and stretched. Pale where it folded around the edges of the canvas, vivid with colour where it did not. Montgomery laid them out around the room, propped against chair and desk legs.

As Monty prepared the grotesque display, Jacob refilled our drinks. I took long sips as I stepped closer to the canvasses that the PI held aloft. Will joined me and we stood, shoulders touching, silently studying the art. I thought of a definition of art that I had once read: "Human effort to imitate, supplement, alter or counteract the work of nature". That final meaning fit this abomination – the artist was indeed counteracting the work of nature; abusing the outer protection of these poor, defenseless souls.

One by one, Montgomery held the pictures up for us to scrutinize. At first glance, the pictures looked like typical country landscapes. There were trees, streams, ponds, hills, and flowers. Gradually, the eye became aware that the underlying difference was the base upon which the painting had been accomplished: the pale, stark canvas of human skin. Every bump, freckle, scar or other imperfection had been used as scenery props. The nuances of colour, whether brown or white or black, blended with the oil to give a shimmering quality. Over time, some of the colour had faded, seeped into the decaying cells, rescued through the drying process. They were reminiscent of the animal skins that some people used for clothing or decoration.

"He used Eddie Pink," Will said suddenly, holding his gloved finger just millimeters away from one of the pictures, tracing one of the backgrounds. "Just like he did when he...when he painted Linda."

Monty looked confused. "What's Eddie Pink?"

"It's a special mixture of oil paints that I developed," Will answered. "I never shared the formula with anyone. Before I went to jail I used it often to depict the sky just at that moment of dawn or dusk where the sun meets polluted air." He paused. "It was never meant as an environmental statement, though some people have attributed that sentiment to me. I just liked the colour."

"Why 'Eddie Pink'?"

"I named it after my father." Will smiled. "He was a colourful guy and I always thought of him when the sky lit up. He might not have liked the title, but he wasn't around by then to be insulted."

"Didn't someone testify at your first trial that the painting on Linda Courtnell's body resembled your style?" Jacob asked.

"You're right," Will responded. "It was Rachel Ouellet. Poor Rachel. She was practically browbeaten into admitting that the colours were a special mix. I don't think she ever forgave herself, even though I kept telling her it wasn't her fault."

"Couldn't someone have copied your formula by studying your paintings? Or would they have had to steal the recipe?" Monty asked.

Will thought for a moment. "I suppose someone very clever at copying other artists' paintings could achieve the same colour mix. I always assumed the formula had been stolen. I kept a record in my studio."

Jacob flipped through the transcript for the section he wanted. "The prosecution went so far as to state that the killer used a particular colour that no one else could duplicate. Yes, here it is. The prosecution asserted that the painter of Linda's body applied certain techniques that only William Thompson could have used. Crown Counsel Sedgwick-Wilson makes the case here that certain colours are, and I quote, 'as distinctive as a signature'."

Montgomery placed the squares of death tenderly back into the bulging portfolio, then straightened up to sip from his drink once again. He was lost in thought for a moment. "Okay. We have the evidence that Langford couldn't have murdered Linda Courtnell. We confirmed that this killer used Eddie Pink on several other victims, none of whom you could have killed. Somehow, this murderer got access to your formula."

As I thought about signatures, an image abruptly floated into my mind. "Monty, can I see that third painting again? The one that has a stream running right through the middle..."

Montgomery had obviously studied the paintings well, for he knew exactly which one I meant. I had to lean in very close to see the object that my brain had flashed on.

"Right here. Is this the signature?"

Monty nodded. "Yes, Emily. That's it. Good eye. In fact, in every one of the paintings, there is either the entire signature or at least a part of one. As I told you, he made sure the signature was included in all the photos, but in the paintings, they are more obscure. Maybe because they are just pieces of..." Monty trailed off, the horror of what he was saying settling like a cloud in the room.

William bent toward the painting, a stance that artists often take, looking at every drop of oil and its unique contribution towards the whole. "I see it now," he said, his voice trembling with astonishment. "It's very cleverly disguised as part of the rivulet, here..." Once again, his gloved finger brushed the canvas lightly.

I wondered if my husband was unconsciously trying to connect directly to the other victims. We were the only targets (that we knew of) who had suffered a different kind of fate. The only ones alive. If, in fact, 'The Artist' was responsible for my accident, I was alive only through sheer luck and the courage of Terry Somers. For William, the killer had designed a different scenario, a type of lifelong torture that also cost Linda Courtnell's life.

As Will continued to hover near the painting, I kept probing into the edge of my recall. Something peripheral, heretofore relegated to a file in my brain marked 'unimportant information', was misting in and out. I had seen that signature somewhere before, I was sure of it. But the memory would not surface. Suddenly I was exhausted. I felt as though I could easily say goodnight, gentlemen, and crawl under the soft blankets. The emotional roller coasters were taking their toll.

In fact, this was the way it happened: Will, Montgomery and Jacob stayed in the office, talking, getting well and properly drunk. I, on the other hand, did exactly what I thought about doing earlier in the evening: said goodnight, gentlemen, closed the bedroom door, and crawled under the soft blankets. Some time later, Montgomery took a taxi home, while Jacob went to his own suite.

Will awakened me as he slipped into bed beside me.

"Sorry I woke you, honey," he whispered in my ear. I turned over to face him and he cradled me in his arms. "I'm so excited I don't know if I'll be able to sleep."

"I'm afraid to stay awake and think positively," I confessed sleepily, looking up at him. "As though I might destroy the good Karma."

He smiled at me, his deep brown eyes sparkling with a fire that had almost been extinguished years ago. I thought about how very much I loved him, admired him, and would never again let him go. I felt a shiver of anticipation, tinged with fear.

"Hey! I think I know a way to put us to sleep," he said, giving a sexy chuckle. His soft warm lips sent my body and my heart to a soothing place of ecstasy.

As it turned out, our lovemaking gave me the strength I needed to deal with the terror that the next day would bring.

Chapter Twenty-Three
March, 2009

That morning, Vancouver was doing her utmost to remind me of better times and convince me that the best was yet to come. The weather was perfect; clean, salt-scented air, warm sunshine, the cloudless sky a deep blue. All around, the mountains were encouraging spires, pointing toward hope and possibility. I no longer felt hemmed in. In fact, I felt a tremor of freedom.

What would it be like to no longer hide my married name? Would we write about our past some day? Wouldn't it be wonderful for Will to travel everywhere with his art, unafraid of discovery?

As soon as William saw the sun glinting through the windows, he became fully conscious despite the lack of sleep. This was the day he would prove his innocence and he was full of energy. Jacob, William and I splurged and took a limo to our lawyers' offices, driver in cap and all. It wasn't entirely selfish. Jacob and Monty were worried for our safety and wanted us to be accompanied by the driver all day. Once the news got out, which might happen despite our vigilance, we would have to be on guard.

It seemed to me that every time we crossed through an intersection over one of the long, sloping streets, I caught a hint of the harbor, winking at me. I imagined the waves splashing against the shore in noisy celebration. If I wasn't careful, I thought, I just might begin to hope.

At the door of the tall glass-eyed building, sun sparkling off the tinted windows, we met Montgomery, portfolio in hand. The smiles we shared were profound and intimate; we knew a momentous change was about to take place.

The visit to our lawyers was indeed a joyful coup. Our team summoned members of the Vancouver Police Department, along with some forensic advisors from the Royal Canadian Mounted Police, to act as witnesses. Before we shared the information, Jacob convinced the appropriate officials to sign a written agreement that Charles Haynes would not be charged with obstruction of justice. Jacob was articulate and, although he was not completely honest, he was able to argue that Charlie's age and illness were extenuating circumstances.

I wasn't surprised that it was my husband who had insisted upon the agreement, hammered out during the conversations of the night before. Although I didn't completely concur with William, I could certainly respect his desire to absolve the man who would now be responsible for his exoneration. Luckily for Charles Haynes, the decision was not mine to make, nor my pardon to give.

It was a tedious morning. The initial exhilaration became somewhat buried under a mass of paperwork, ceaseless questions and endless streams of bureaucratic personnel. The only sector deliberately left out of the negotiations was the media. Our team had decided immediately that it would be premature to make any announcements until the Minister of Justice had agreed to view the evidence, or appointed a Judge to handle the matter. Later in the morning we received a call that the Honorable Claudia Belle would be acting for the Minister, which was an astonishing development. A meeting in the Judge's chambers was arranged for two days hence. In effect, she was agreeing to read and view everything in an unprecedented forty-eight hours. Our lawyers decided that a press conference could only wait until the next morning at the latest.

"We don't want to take the chance that the news will leak out," Jacob told us. "We want to be able to exert some control. And Emily, Langford...this will surely be the end of your privacy until the next big news item comes along and takes your case off the front pages. I know you had a touch of the attention when you arrived at the airport here. But after tomorrow morning, your case will be publicized through every kind of news media all over the world. They're likely to flash your pictures; old photos if they can't snap new ones. The sensational news about a serial killer is going to open a huge Pandora's box, but at least it will eventually deflect the spotlight from you to the real killer."

"I went through that years ago, so I know how bad it can be. Do you think it's safe for us to go ahead with our plans for today?" Will asked.

That lump of anger, the one directed at the "unknown subject", the one that had nowhere to go and no one to blame, still sat inside my stomach. It began to outweigh the touch of fear I'd felt last night. Instead, I started to feel incensed, bitter that, despite this morning's triumph, we were still victims.

Montgomery's words did nothing to dampen my burgeoning desire to scream or stamp my feet. "I was going to talk to you about your safety," he answered. "To be blunt, no, I don't think you're safe. Even though the killer delivered a confession, he made certain not to identify himself. We're still focusing on Harrison Courtnell and Ronald Stevens. If Charles Haynes had anything to do with the murders, he isn't any danger to you now. But remember, you have until tomorrow morning before the culprit knows we have the evidence."

Jacob agreed. "The murderer might believe that Charlie, to avoid trouble, decided not to show the proof to anyone. Our monster didn't demand that he turn it over to the police. He just wanted to make a confession to someone."

"The forensic psychologist from the RCMP has been really helpful," Monty added. "She thinks Jacob is right – the culprit is disintegrating and perhaps quickly. He wanted to confess and maybe get caught. But he is conflicted about that, too, so he pretty much left the decision in Charlie's hands. But she is also of the opinion that the killer might have some other plan in mind, just in case Charlie didn't tell."

"In other words, we have one afternoon and evening left in anonymity," I said, biting back my anger. "Then you think this asshole might be coming after Langford."

Our two friends nodded, but Montgomery added, "Emily, you might consider Jacob's theory that your car accident was deliberate. The killer could also come after you."

"Precisely. I do wish you'd stick around the hotel. The killer might not know about Charlie's decision. On the other hand, if he has some alternative plan, we don't know what that might be," Jacob warned. "What if you are both targets?"

"If you do insist on going out, make sure you are in public places. Don't be alone with anyone. Even very good friends," Monty said, noticing our dismayed looks.

Will and I had some loose ends to tie up and people to see 'before we slept'. Plans had already been made. We gazed at each other, assessing the advice. Clearly, Will was more concerned than I, but he was also determined to end our time in Vancouver without stones unturned.

"This monster has had control over our lives for more than twenty years," I said. "Surely we can keep this quiet and have one day to enjoy the city that we lost."

Monty and Jacob did not look convinced.

"Okay," my husband said finally. "Let's compromise. Emily wants to meet with some friends at noon for lunch in the False Creek Pub on Granville Island. I want to speak with Rachel Ouellet, who was my mentor and friend while I was at Three Arts. I'll be meeting her at the school. There are a few former students who are coming by, too. So both of us will be in very public places."

"As long as you take the limo to the Island," Jacob responded. "You know May had you promise to spare no expense where safety and success were concerned, so the driver has been hired to go wherever you go."

I smiled at the mention of my smart, funny, beautiful best friend, wishing that she were here at this very moment.

"We'll take the limo, Jacob," I agreed readily. "Will, I'm pretty sure you'll take longer talking to Rachel and the kids...adults now, I should say...than I will with my friends at lunch. I'll get someone to walk me over to Three Arts and then we'll both take the limo back to the hotel. Okay, everybody?"

"Okay," Montgomery said, "sounds like a good plan."

"I'll make sure the limo driver stays on the Island waiting for you," Jacob confirmed. "Can you give him an approximate time so we can coordinate everything?"

"No problem. That'll keep Rachel on track, too. The woman is a ball of fire and can talk all day," Will said. "Do you want to meet us back at the hotel for dinner?"

"I have something even better in mind. How about dinner at the Bluewater Café?" Jacob suggested. "It's in Yaletown on Hamilton Street, and I've heard it's just about the best place in the city."

Will and I laughed. "We've heard of it, Jacob," I told him. "But we've never been there!"

"Somehow we never had the time," Will said, provoking a laugh from all four of us. I could scarcely believe we were joking about twenty years in jail.

"I'll get us reservations," Montgomery offered. "How's six o'clock?"

"Can you bring your wife?" I asked.

"Sure, thanks, Emily, I know she'd love that. I'll give her a call so we can arrange a sitter."

"Our last day of anonymity for a few weeks," Will said, grabbing my hand. "Let's go, sweetheart, we'll be saying good-bye to Vancouver once again, but on a happier note."

Little did we know, Charlie Haynes had already received two telephone calls. He had spoken quite candidly to both men, whom he'd known for a very long time.

The limo driver, whose name was Patrick Ferris, cheerfully drove us through the sunny streets, taking the long way around at Will's request. We held hands in the back seat, watching the world go by through tinted glass. William smiled at me and I felt the knots begin to loosen. Maybe he was right; everything was going to be wonderful.

We drove down Robson, away from the shops and offices, and hit Lagoon Drive. Stanley Park was in early bloom, trees majestic and green, towering over our heads, sentinels of happiness. People were out enjoying the air, the way they do every day in Vancouver; walking, jogging, biking, babies on shoulders or in carriages or flying along in a carrier behind their parents' bicycles. Stanley Park Drive took us to Beach Avenue, where the inlet was early spring wild, a strong breeze kicking the water onto the rocky shores, tossing sand in the air.

When we reached Bidwell, Will asked Patrick to turn. Bidwell Public School looked the same, a classic style with a wide-open paved playground and green yard. Children were racing back and forth, screaming and laughing, freeing the energy they held back in the classroom.

Next we drove up Davie Street. Wordlessly, we passed the apartment building where we used to live. It still looked tidy and comfortable, a place in which young couples might feel at home. For some reason, that made us both smile again.

We turned onto Granville Street and over the bridge to the Island. Despite the newness of the season, False Creek was dotted with sailboats, Aqua buses, ferries and small outboards. The water was calm here, a slate grey-blue with streaks of gold from the sunshine. It looked alive and filled with energy. Suddenly, in front of us on Railspur Avenue, was The Three Arts Institute. Across the way on Johnston, the new Emily Carr Institute looked stately and modern, while Three Arts had remained what it had been: a former factory, red bricked and ornate, but aged.

"I'll be in the coffee shop just off Cartwright," Patrick said. "It's all one-way streets around here, so I'll be parking a little way off, but that'll make it easier for me to come back and pick you up. Just call my cell when you're ready."

We got out of the car and stood hand-in-hand in front of the doors, almost afraid to move. Just beyond the school, we could see the pathway that led to the Marketplace and the studio. Then out of the corner of my eye, I caught a movement.

Dennis Maloney, accompanied by an entourage of young men and women – could I really have taught these adults when they were so young? – came happily toward us, arms and hands offering hugs and shakes, everyone speaking at once. I'd had no idea all of these people could be rounded up at such short notice. I allowed the wave of people to start carrying me along as soon as I saw Rachel Ouellet on the stairs of Three Arts, she too accompanied by a group of men and women who were once young students.

"Looks like I might be longer than I thought," I said to my husband, unable to keep the grin off my face. "If you're finished before me, come join us. Otherwise, I'll see you here in a couple of hours."

Will and I parted after a long look of joy and satisfaction. If only we had known.

The False Creek Pub was the same as it always had been – a big, wooden structure with wide oak flooring and weathered tables. It was warm enough to gather on the huge porch overlooking the restaurant's namesake – False Creek – although there were some upright heaters strategically placed just in case. As I lifted a large frothy glass of beer in a toast, I was almost overwhelmed by the emotion of this reunion.

The conversation was loud and boisterous. Justin hadn't been able to come, but Laura and Fiona were there, both accompanied by their husbands. A large contingent of students and teachers from Bidwell Public School came and went, some just for a hug or shake of the hand, others to sit for lunch. I was overwhelmed by the gathering, a result of Dennis's efforts to welcome me back. There were some staff and former students from Abbotsford, too, many of whom had retired or moved to Vancouver for work.

I felt wonderful. The presence of these amazing people made me realize that, despite the ongoing hell of Will's situation, I had managed to have friends and a satisfying career. I had cared a great deal about the children, and seeing them as adults, functioning and happy, was extremely uplifting. I imagined that Will was feeling much the same way at that same moment.

Remembering that I had an important dinner date, I started to drink mineral water after the first beer. Besides, I had to keep my wits about me as the conversations bounced from topic to topic, from one particular period in my life to another, completely different time and place. Adjusting to the faces of my students from young children to adults was disconcerting, too. In Burchill, I had the privilege of watching them grow and change every day.

One surprise was, at first, awkward and unpleasant. I noticed the hush in the room before I noticed the presence of a woman at the steps leading onto the deck. Elaine Martin still looked the same, though her red hair was streaked with grey. Those familiar green eyes were filled with tears, her face abject and filled with a tinge of fear. She expected me to reject her, I realized, and I also knew that this is exactly what I intended to do. The instant I saw Natalie, though, standing next to her mother, grown up and beautiful, a complete mixture of her parents, I changed my mind. There was no reason to hold onto the anger any more. The only person to whom I could allow myself to direct rage and even hatred, was the real murderer of Linda Courtnell, and I might never know who that was.

So I got to my feet, walked slowly toward Elaine, and pulled her close in a hug. She sobbed on my shoulder, clinging and shaking, whispering over and over again, "Please forgive me."

I hugged Natalie too, then led them over to a spot at the picnic table. Elaine was still unable to staunch the tears. I grabbed her hand.

"Elaine, it's okay," I told her, realizing that this was actually true. "I do forgive you."

"I don't know why I did it," she sniffed. "I got caught up in the drama. I don't even know if I thought it was real."

"It's all right. I'm sure you know we're here to file the appeal and I have every reason to believe that William will be exonerated. You have to live your life, Elaine. You can't feel guilty any more."

Natalie squeezed my hand, tears beginning to slide down her face, too. "Mrs. Thompson, thank-you. My mother has never been able to forget her mistake. She needed your forgiveness. Thank-you for being so kind."

I'm not very kind, I thought. I only forgave her because you are here, so sweet and supportive of your mom. And because Elaine never did let the press find Emily Taylor.

Chapter Twenty-Four
March, 2009

Margaret Thompson had not been wrong about her son when she warned her future daughter-in-law about his bad temper. She had just been wrong about how it manifested itself.

Emily had witnessed Will's temper only twice. On a visit to Langford Island, their favourite, private place for exploring their physical attraction to one another, they'd had a ferocious argument over sex. Ironically, it was Emily who wanted to consummate their relationship; Will was arguing that they should wait. Young and somewhat overcome by her emotions, Emily had yanked Will's school ring off her finger and tossed it in the air, fully expecting her boyfriend to catch it, beg her forgiveness, and carry her off into the bushes. Instead, the ring disappeared forever until it surfaced in a Langford Taylor painting.

On that occasion, Emily had been taken aback by the fury in his eyes and etched on his face; he had literally transformed. William was normally a quiet, attentive person whose sensitive brown eyes were legendary among women. When he lost his temper, his eyes blackened into deep holes of anger and red spots appeared on his cheeks. He then lapsed into a lecturing mode, ranting and raving about the ills of the world and the sins of the offender in particular.

The second occasion was when Emily announced her unplanned pregnancy. That time, she had again been astounded by the change in his countenance, and had been subjected to a harangue that lasted two whole days.

Will had lost his temper with his mother far more often, mostly because she was a bitter, disagreeable person who knew exactly how to push his buttons. Margaret always believed, when she observed the alteration of Easy-Going William to You've-Gone-Too-Far William, that he harbored a latent violent streak. She was convinced that he refrained from hitting her only because she was his mother. But Margaret Thompson was wrong.

As a child, William lived in a house where the tension was always a living, breathing entity that sat over the three occupants like a possessive cat. When he was young, Will had no idea why his mother was always unhappy. He spent a great deal of time trying to cheer her up, ignoring her negativity, keeping the peace. When he grew up, he realized that his gregarious, generous father had been just as free with his love outside his home as he was inside it. Only two mysteries ever existed for Will once he discovered his father's numerous infidelities and the source of his mother's bitterness: why they stayed together and why Edward never got caught. After Edward died, Will had been far less patient with his mother, especially as she attempted to transfer her lifelong disappointments from her philandering husband to her son.

However, William Edward Thompson was neither violent, as his mother thought, nor like his father, as most other people thought. He kept a very tight control on his darker emotions. On the whole he was a positive, optimistic person who took delight in life. Art was his outlet, his pride, and his joy, until Emily came along.

Bright, cheerful, and smart, Emily was his complement, his soul mate, and his best friend. She kept him anchored, because she loved him so completely, and because she was the polar opposite of his mother. Together, they were, for the most part, extremely happy and satisfied.

When he was accused and convicted of Linda Courtnell's murder, Will's dark side emerged. He was enraged, frustrated, and scared. Society, in the form of the legal system he had to depend upon, abandoned him. He lost his wife, his child, his reputation, and his freedom. Margaret's philosophy that the world was a negative place began to overtake his inner self.

Once imprisoned, inmate Bill Thompson spent most of his time in solitary confinement. The other prisoners followed the newspapers just like everyone else and had been stirred up by Linda Courtnell's horrific death. The girl was a student, little more than a child. She was the bonafide Princess of Vancouver – the city from which most of the prisoners came – with a blossoming talent that promised she would be the city's Queen before long. The sensational murder kept the prisoners just as enthralled as the general population. Therefore, threats against the convicted murderer's life were continually issuing forth from inside the institution. Truth be known, there were several guards who probably would have looked the other way had anyone made a serious attempt. Hence, William Thompson languished for nearly twenty years with little company but his own.

In the rare circumstance when he did encounter the other prisoners, in the laundry room or courtyard or library, Bill was accosted and taunted. Most inmates, however, only hit him once. Unarmed, on the receiving end of the most vicious of his transformations, the aggressor quickly backed off and left Thompson alone again. It didn't take long before the entire population of Kent Institute declared hands-off. However, William never actually struck anyone; it was the suggestion of an underlying rage, a terrifying potential, which kept even the most hardened criminals at bay.

As it turned out, solitary confinement was Will's savior. If he'd been able to consort with the other prisoners without being killed, he might have become the violent person his mother envisioned. Surrounded by aggression and hatred, William would probably not have been able to survive intact. His innate optimism would surely have been crushed. As it was, he spent hours reading, writing, painting, and, whenever possible, talking to his wife. He read philosophy, religion, and art history, as well as legal texts that pertained to his case. He even made friends with a couple of the guards, who admired his artistic talent and came to appreciate Will's wise ability to listen and support. Through the long, oppressive years, especially after Emily had fully recovered, William developed his own solid values and outlook on life. At his essential core, he believed in people. He decided that he would give them his trust and affection unless they demonstrated their unworthiness. He appreciated life, in all its struggles and wonder, and had complete faith in Emily's love. He came to believe that positive energy could overcome all battles and that an individual could achieve any goal with deep commitment and hard work.

When he and Emily moved to Burchill, he became Langford Taylor in every way. For every minute of every day, he savored his freedom, particularly being able to touch and make love to his wife. Although they'd had some harrowing experiences in the little town, they had also developed a group of friends and supporters that was unparalleled. Cate and

Carly were a gift that added indescribable joy to his life. Langford Taylor was inordinately happy.

All he needed was for the justice system, which had so deeply wounded him, to declare his innocence, give him back his name and his reputation.

He wasn't aware of another need until he heard the voice on the telephone.

William and Rachel spent an hour or so with the former students who'd come to see him. He caught up on many of their lives, talked frankly about what prison had him taught about life, and boldly hinted that they might want to be listening to the news tomorrow morning. When he and Rachel said their good-byes and retreated to her office, Will was feeling almost deliriously happy.

They sat down at her sumptuous Dean's desk, a huge old wooden structure carved with ammeters and voltmeters and other symbols of higher learning. Will had just stretched his legs out in front of him, settling into the soft leather chair for a long and pleasant chinwag, when the telephone shrilled.

Rachel apologized and picked up the receiver. "Oh, yes, of course," she said. "I didn't forget. The papers are in your mailbox." She listened for a moment, nodding as though the caller could see her. "By the way, I have a visitor in my office that you might like to talk to. Bill Thompson."

Even Will could hear the enthusiasm in the response.

"Sure, here he is."

Rachel pulled the telephone cord taut and handed the receiver to William.

"Bill, my dear boy," said the voice on the other end.

It was at that moment that William Thompson realized the other thing he needed. He needed the real murderer to be stopped.

Chapter Twenty-Five
March, 2009

It was almost four o'clock before I looked at my watch again. "Holy shit," I said in a ladylike fashion. "I promised my husband that we'd have time to change before our dinner date."

"Where are you going for dinner?" Dennis asked.

"The Bluewater Café."

There were only a few people gathered round the table now. They all raised their glasses when I lifted my mineral water for a toast. "We're celebrating our return to this city that we loved. I'm so thankful to all of you who came here today. Once the appeal is successful – which I'm confident it will be – we'll be back." We clinked our glasses.

By the time I said final farewells, thank-yous and see-you-agains, it was close to four-thirty. Dennis walked me over to Three Arts, which was mostly deserted. The big front doors, however, stood open and welcoming, both digesting and divesting themselves of a few straggling students. By now, the early spring sun was beginning to hug the mountaintops and slide through the valleys. I hugged Dennis again, thanked him profusely for the wonderful reunion, and headed up the stairs toward Rachel's office.

As I passed the huge mural that graced the wall of the stairwell landing, I thought of how many times I had passed this picture without appreciating it. As beautiful this painting was, it served only as background to the sweeping staircase. The landscape, now that I looked at it carefully, was both familiar and intriguing.

Rachel was not at her desk, though the door was wide open. I stopped an impossibly young professor as he walked past me in the hallway.

"Excuse me. Have you see Dean Ouellet?"

He smiled, a friendly Preppie smile. "Yes, as a matter of fact. She left a few minutes ago to go to a meeting. I was with her when she got called to discuss a student matter with another professor." He sounded proud that he had been with the Dean and not been the caller.

"Was a man with her? My husband was visiting her and I was supposed to meet him here."

"Oh, you mean Professor Thompson!" he cried delightedly. "I used to be one of his students. It's nice to meet you."

We shook hands, although I was pretty distracted by that point and wanted him to answer the question.

"That means you met with him too?"

"Yes...but that was before I met with Dean Ouellet."

Now I was totally confused and must have shown the bewilderment through my expression.

"A bunch of former students, including me, met downstairs in the faculty lounge with the Professor and the Dean," he explained in that same proud tone. "Then the Professor came upstairs to the Dean's office..." He pointed as though I wasn't aware that the open door led to Rachel's domain. "I saw him leave about half an hour later."

"Half an hour?" I asked, incredulous.

"Yes. About one thirty, or quarter to two."

"Are you sure?"

"Absolutely! I stuck my head in the Dean's door and asked if we could meet. She said the Professor was headed next door and might be back, but I could meet with her in the meantime. He never did come back, so..."

"Thanks," I rudely interrupted.

The young man shrugged, but gave me another of those smiles, and walked away.

William had left Rachel's office at one thirty or so, but never joined me in the pub. So what had he meant by 'going next door'? Why on earth would he go anywhere else when we'd promised to meet here? I went down the massive staircase slowly, while I made two calls. The first was to Will's cell phone, which told me that the 'customer was unavailable'. Next, I talked to Patrick Ferris, who said William had not returned to the limo. He also told me to take as long as we wanted; the reservations had been moved to seven. Had Will found out about the delay in dinner plans and decided to visit some old haunts? It seemed so unlikely. We'd promised to follow the plan exactly as we'd laid it out for Jacob and Montgomery.

I stopped on the landing to think. As I did so, I turned and looked once again at the mural. There was something so recognizable about it, not just from my distant memories, but a technique, a method, a flow of the brush that made me hold my breath. Trees, streams, ponds, hills, and flowers, ordinary scenes, and yet…

Suddenly the peripheral thought that had floated through my mind last night snapped into place. I leaned closer to the painting and read the two words. The signature. The Artist. I straightened up quickly. Someone had stood on this landing, probably for days, likely on scaffolding or ladders as he reached to the top of stairway. Someone who had murdered Linda Courtnell as well as many others, someone who must be well known at The Three Arts Institute.

The silence in the huge entranceway was deafening. Two things instantly occurred to me as I stood there, my heart pounding. It was as though my eyes had been shut; now they were forced open wide. Another memory that had tugged at me last night appeared as two words: my boy, said in a singsong, unnatural tone. I knew who had killed Linda Courtnell and nearly one hundred other people. My first impulse, one that cut through every caution and concern for my own safety, was to warn my husband.

I raced down the remaining stairs and through the doorways into a waning sun. When I got to the pathway, I remembered exactly what was next door, in the opposite direction to the pub. A place in which William had vowed he would never again set foot. I cut across the lawn and sprinted toward the Marketplace. Already the lights on the pathway were flickering as they came alive in the settling dusk. Lots of people strolled up and down the sidewalk, laughing or arm-in-arm, or speeding toward the Aqua Bus. I nearly ran into a bicyclist, who swore at me and disappeared.

I was out of breath. It took me a few seconds to realize that I was at the Marketplace. It looked completely different. Instead of a pile of concrete and pillars, a modern facility with wide clear windows and flowerbeds beamed beckoningly. I ran along the outside, then stopped in the doorway. The place buzzed with people. No staircase. How were the studios accessed these days?

I ran back outside and noticed a recess in the wall. The staircase had been enclosed, creating an exit straight to the outside. I yanked it open and hurried up the tiled steps to the landing. The door into the second floor was also closed but unlocked. I threw myself into the hallway.

Carpeted and hushed, subdued lighting adorning its walls, the entrance to the studios was certainly posh thirty years later. I slowed up and gasped back my breath as I neared the studio William had rented. I hadn't set foot in this building since Linda Courtnell's death. Suddenly, I was in front of the door that had led to my husband's hell.

It was so quiet that I began to wonder if Will had gone somewhere else. Had he really come next door to his former studio? Was my instinct wrong? Had we merely missed each other in transit? Then I heard voices, a low, murmuring sound from inside the room. I knocked and turned the doorknob. The door opened effortlessly so I stepped over the threshold without asking.

At first I couldn't see anything but a floor-to-ceiling partition to the left that cut the room into two sections. A soft, orange light glowed from the opening by the far wall. A jumble of furniture and easels to the right was shrouded in darkness.

Suddenly a face appeared in the entryway of the partition, grinning at me, looking incongruous beside the Japanese motif of the partition. A tall, broad-shouldered man, very like William in stature and body type, this man could certainly have stood in a back-lit window and been mistaken for Professor Thompson.

Greg Hughes waved with a royal flutter of his long fingers and crooked his finger for me to approach, then disappeared inside. A handsome man, his affectations were at odds with his basketball player height and rugged face. He was dressed in a flamboyant, checkered suit, a blood red scarf at this neck. Hair slicked back, a hint of make-up and lipstick, he looked like a character from a 1940's film. He looked exactly as he had at the airport two nights ago.

I walked across the room, unsettled and puzzled. "Greg!" I called after him. "Have you seen...?" Now I was close enough to see through the doorway of the partition. That was when I saw my husband.

William stood on a wide bench that was anchored to the floor. From the ceiling above it, a series of pulleys dangled. I thought immediately of the block and tackle assembly in

Alain's old garage. He used it to raise engines up from inside the cars. Presumably, the studio was outfitted to lift heavy art objects in a similar way. In this case, though, the object was human.

A thick rope wound around William's neck. Hands tied behind his back, he was red faced and gasping. I realized that he was standing on the tip of his toes. The noose, hooked up to the block and tackle chain, was tight around his throat. I could see a crank on the wall, immediately next to Hughes. As though to demonstrate, Greg turned it lightly. It made a clicking sound as it pulled Will forward and upward, inching him closer to the edge of the bench.

"Mrs. Thompson, my dear girl. How nice of you to join us! I did think that you might drop in. I am trying to make a bargain with your husband and he just isn't being very nice." His voice was pretentiously high-pitched, a whispery imitation of a female tone.

Suddenly my hearing and sight went into overdrive. I could feel a huge wave of energy bursting through every cell. My thoughts were rapid and photographic. To my left, a small table piled with paraphernalia: small open cans of paint; a large pail of thick, translucent liquid; brushes; a long, silver instrument; needles. To Greg's right, another small table: an enormous black gun; a shiny hunting knife. Ahead of me, the Monster I detested; a rope, the instrument of death, dangling near his elbow. A small distance to the Monster's left, my husband, my William, eyes bulging, gasping desperately for oxygen.

"So you are The Artist," I said, inching forward, my heart pounding.

"I am indeed," Greg answered proudly.

"You painted the mural in the hall." Another quarter step forward.

He laughed, a grating sound like fingernails on a chalkboard. "My dear Mrs. Thompson, why would you mention *that* of all things? Yes, I painted that beautiful work of art. Not that anyone ever noticed. They walked by it every single day, never appreciating its significance."

I noticed that Greg's voice was climbing slightly higher, as though he too were running out of air.

"But you raped her," I said.

Thrown off guard by this statement, he stared at me for a moment, then laughed again as understanding dawned. "Aha. The gay thing." He fluttered his right hand exaggeratedly. He spread his fingers out in the air, crunched them into a fist, and pulled slightly on the rope with his left. Suddenly his voice was deep and booming. No trace of the affectations, the act. Just the Monster.

"It was the best disguise ever. People expected me to be different. The prejudice against homosexuality is still quite alive, my dear, despite some appearance of openness. Back then it was rampant, especially among the police. No one ever thought of me as a suspect, especially in the Linda Courtnell case, because she was raped. They erroneously thought rape is about sexual attraction and that, as a gay man, I couldn't possibly have done it. Isn't that stupid and disgusting?"

"Yes." Closer. "You're saying that people are generally stupid and disgusting. Is that why you kill them?"

"Oh, my, no, not at all. My dear Mrs. Thompson, didn't they let you read my letters? Didn't you learn about The Spring? I was doing my victims a favour. I wish I had time to teach you. There would be so much for you to experience. You too could have died into perfect creativity. Maybe they thought you were too refined, too delicate to bother with such matters. You should demand to read the letters, dear."

"I read them all right. *They* were stupid and disgusting."

His eyes flashed and I regretted my show of temper. The crank clicked loudly in my ears. Now William's face showed a tinge of blue around his neck and eyes. He was straining to stay on his toes and I could tell he was close to falling off the edge of the bench. I had to be careful.

"Maybe I just don't understand, Professor Hughes," I offered in a calm, reasonable voice.

"That is probably true, you poor thing. The only way to really achieve perfection is to suffer and die. It's only at the point of death that you and Art, you and The Spring of all creativity and utter, flawless beauty, are one. I killed people to give them the greatest gift they could ever receive. Even Linda. I did kill her because she was going to out me, not to mention the fact that she kept winning the contests *I* deserved to win. And I did love the revenge on the Professor here. But at the end, even Linda had that look. The look of knowledge and of gratitude that I was the one who led her to that higher place."

"What do you mean, Linda was going to 'out' you? Was she going to tell everyone you weren't gay?"

Greg laughed. "No, no. It was far simpler. It was her portfolio. She had a painting that I had copied. You see, I'm extremely good at copying. In fact, I've made a good deal of money pretending to be other painters. How do you think I was able to copy your husband's sorry attempts at art? I've sold Monets and Morrisseaus and all kinds of other masterpieces besides my very own. I had a pseudonym, too. Rangel Guzman. Isn't that clever? It's a mix of two Mexican artists. I used it to enter your husband's stupid contests, which I never won, as I might have mentioned.

"I came close to winning a Seattle contest with one of Linda's paintings. She found out about it. She was going to tell everyone what I'd done. That night, the cunt actually came down the hall to my office from *his*..." Greg's face turned purple with anger. His hand, waving in the air, landed on the pulley. William made a soft moaning sound, but he stayed on his feet. "...to show me her painting in her portfolio, the one that I had entered in the Seattle contest. She said she could prove that I had committed art fraud, and why did I do it? As if Linda Courtnell's paintings were worth hundreds of thousands or something! Art fraud. Fuck. I have no idea how she found out, the little bitch. She must have researched all the art contests in the world. Naturally, I was stupid enough to use my own name and somehow, she saw it, along with her goddamn painting. Must've been in one of those local newspapers or art mags or...never mind. Suffice it to say, I had to get rid of her."

His face suddenly transformed into deep sadness. He tapped the gun and the knife. "One-zero-zero, Emily. And he will not cooperate. I had to resort to the use of these cowardly instruments. And still he won't do as I say." He gave another small *click* on the pulley.

"And here I was such a fan of his. I got a studio in the same building. I even made my own key so I could come in after he left just to admire his work. And he shunned me and my genius!" Greg turned his back to me now, facing William instead. "I had to pay you back, you must understand that, my dear boy."

I moved silently. I was very near to the table at my left. So close to the Monster that I could smell the sweat of his insanity mingled with the aftershave of his facade.

"Maybe I can help persuade him," I said, keeping my voice steady.

Greg didn't appear to notice my proximity. He turned and gave me a look of pure gratitude. "You would do that for me?" He turned away from William and took several steps toward me. Now we were only a small distance apart.

Clearly, the RCMP psychologist had been right. Greg was disseminating before me. His eyes welled up with tears and he was now pleading. From flamboyant actor to cruel killer and rapist to philosophy teacher to begging little boy in a matter of minutes. I could touch the table now.

William made a choking sound as his toes gave way under the strain. For a second, he dangled on the rope before he was able to scramble back to a semi-standing position on the edge of the bench. His eyes clouded over; he was going to die if he stayed that way much longer.

The knot of anger burst through its restraints. Pictures flash-bulbed through my mind. Linda Courtnell, tortured, painted and mutilated. My baby, draining from my body in pieces. My husband, pale and withdrawn behind a prison enclosure, unable to touch me. My mother, leaning over to gently brush my hair from my damp forehead. The skin canvases. William, trussed up, deprived of oxygen, next on the Monster's list.

With a roar scarcely recognizable as human, I picked up the cans of paint one by one and flung their contents at Greg Hughes. He crossed his arms in front of his face, standing in one spot, whimpering, sniveling. I kept hammering the paint at him, red, yellow, blue; catching him on the side of his head, through his fingers, into his eyes. The Artist dripped with oily colour.

"You bastard. Did you give any of those poor souls a choice? Did you *ask* them if they preferred death?"

I grabbed the needles and flung them like darts; they bounced off his legs. He moaned and wept, but didn't budge. "You're no god. You're a sick, worthless monster who likes to torture and kill people. Did you think they looked at you with gratitude when they died? You're an asshole, an idiot, a fucking low life. They looked at you with pity because you are nothing but a loser."

When one of the needles lodged itself in his foot, he removed his arms from his face and stared at me, tears streaming down his ugly, demented, disgusting cheeks.

"You're a fucking pervert."

I dipped a large paintbrush into the pail of nondescript liquid and flicked it at his face. I was howling like a wolf, a bear, an animal cornered and attacked.

Keep the air flowing outward; don't breathe in.

He stood there, arms outstretched in a crucifix, his head bent forward.

"You think you're dying a martyr, don't you? You aren't going to die, you bastard. You are going to live and suffer."

I kept dipping the brush and flinging the liquid at him. A hiss and spurts of gas emanated from his skin.

He opened his mouth and said, "I am the Creative Force...The Artist..."

I flipped the liquid at his face. A huge blob landed in his mouth, just as he inhaled to continue his rant. His eyes bulged as he took a breath and swallowed. Instantly, his legs folded. He dropped to the ground, spittle and dust flying into the air. I felt several stings, as though I had put my hands and arms in a wasps' nest. I looked down and saw little red blisters bursting from my skin. *Don't breathe it in.*

Greg Hughes was vomiting on the floor, writhing uncontrollably. I sidestepped him and reached over to release the pulley. Jolted free, William almost fell, but I was there. I blocked his fall with my body. Pushing him back to sit on the bench, I yanked with all my might at the knot around his neck. Within seconds, the rope was curled on the ground like a snake. Will wasn't exactly breathing, but then again, neither was I.

Limping and dragging, I pulled him around the partition, through the darkened room, and into the deserted hallway. We both took a ragged breath and Will immediately passed out. My hands trembling from both shock and the pain, I pulled out my cell phone and dialed 911.

Inside the studio, I could hear the Monster choking and coughing. Once again, I held my breath and rapidly crossed over to the injured man. My mind was a red-hot mass of anger: all I could see were his victims, tortured and trussed, the pain indescribable before their humiliating deaths. I lifted the pail of liquid off the table, holding my breath, dragging it close to his head. I put the paintbrush, now withered and corroding, into the colourless liquid. Upending the pail very close to Hughes, I watched for a moment as it snaked its way along the floor toward him. *According to the letters, some of the bodies are buried in specific places, while the rest he dissolved in sulfuric acid.*

Back in the hallway, I collapsed against my husband. I shut my ears to the grotesque sounds from within the studio, the thrashing, gasping and sizzling. I closed my eyes to the blisters bubbling on my skin. I focused on two things only: Will's steady breathing and the solid thump of his heart.

Chapter Twenty-Six
March, 2009

The late morning sun was speckling the hospital windows with dust. I opened my eyes and examined my arms, plastered white with bandages. In the other bed, very close to mine, William was sound asleep, a mild snore rumbling from his nasal passages.

Jacob looked up from the chair next to me and gave me a weak smile. "Hi, Em," he said, his deep blue eyes filling with tears. "How are you?"

"I'm okay, Jacob." I saw doubt flash across his face. "Really. A bit sore, but they must've given me some good pain meds because this..." I nodded at my covered wounds "...doesn't hurt. Plus I feel like I just woke up from a terrible nightmare."

"You did," he said. "I'm still in shock, so I can't imagine what you are going through."

"How's Will?"

"He's going to be fine. He'll have a sore throat for a while and some blisters on his neck, but he actually fared better than you did."

"I answered their questions eventually, didn't I? I think I kept going in and out of consciousness last night."

Jacob chuckled. "I can't believe you demanded to have me with you before you would talk to them. You have a lot of chutzpah, girl."

"Thanks. But after what we've been through with the legal system, I am never taking any chances."

"The way that bastard kept coming at you. Unbelievable. Good thing you had some stuff to throw at him in defense. Unlucky for him that he knocked that pail of sulfuric acid off the table. It must've splashed all over the place. I'm glad it only splattered on your arms. He got a dose of it right in the face, it sounds like."

I will not think about it.

"He did have his mouth wide open when the pail fell off the table," I said. "It seemed like such a small spray, but he just dropped to the ground. He's still alive, right?"

"Yes, but barely. Apparently, even if you swallow a small amount, sulfuric acid cuts off your breathing."

I nodded as though I had never taught Science, never memorized the properties of acids and bases. *Sulfuric acid is highly corrosive. Swallowing can cause severe burns of the mouth, throat, and stomach, leading to death. Can cause vomiting, diarrhea, circulatory collapse...*

"Then of course, he collapsed right into the puddle on the floor," Jacob continued, repeating the story I'd told. "He's in horrific pain. They can't even give him enough morphine. They've got him on all kinds of fluids and have performed some surgery. I know we shouldn't wish these things, but it doesn't look like he'll survive much longer. The doctors are surprised he's still alive."

I know we shouldn't wish these things…

"I didn't even really try to save him," I said.

"Good thing you didn't, Emily. Just making an attempt to drag him was enough. Besides, once he knocked over the pail and fell, he was literally covered with acid. Even if you'd had the strength to pull him away, you would've been burned far worse than you were."

I looked at Jacob's kind face and tears stung my eyes.

Just then, Will struggled to a sitting position. At the same time, Montgomery opened the door and went straight to his side, helping my husband swing his legs over the bed. Before I knew it, Will was lying beside me, his arms around me, the sobs shaking his chest because he couldn't allow the sorrow to touch his throat. I could feel a wave of sympathy from Jacob and Monty. The two men surrounded the bed, hovering protectively until Will was calm.

A few minutes later, we sat together on my bed. Jacob and Montgomery pulled their chairs in close. We all sipped juice and talked. Montgomery did most of the speaking, filling in the blanks, astounding us with the information that had been gathered in the last twelve hours.

Greg Hughes had taken over William's studio shortly after Linda Courtnell's murder. No one else would rent it, but Professor Hughes said that he would do it "to honour his friend Bill". Last night, the police discovered a mountain of evidence in that studio. Whether he had always kept it there, or whether he had moved it recently during his disintegration phase, no one knew. More paintings, more pictures, more letters. Forensic evidence on the tattoo needles and clothing.

Linda Courtnell's old portfolio, which had provided a nice surprise for her family, as it contained some hitherto unpublished paintings. Although Greg Hughes could no longer speak, in fact was literally clinging to life by a thread, his confession was loud and clear.

Professor Hughes had actually helped with the 1980 investigation. Ingratiating himself with Charles Haynes, he learned a great deal more about the case than he should have. After listening to the description of the body's landscape painting, he suggested a similarity between William's style and the killer's. Perhaps Charlie should mention this to the prosecutor? Rachel Ouellet would make a good expert witness. What if she testifies for the defense? Show her a picture of the body's landscape and she might be forced to comment on the similarities...such as the use of a certain colour? Her testimony would be a gift to the prosecution.

Afterward, he stayed in touch with Haynes, even teaming for art shows. Charlie and Joan had attended several of the Gay Wags' appearances. When the former Sergeant became ill, Greg often visited or called. It was during one such call that Charlie told him about Emily and Langford Taylor and, later, advised him of their return to Vancouver. Friendly, innocent conversation between two acquaintances.

Greg Hughes had played the part of eccentric homosexual extremely well. However, he had told me the truth: he was not gay. The prostitutes on Hastings recognized his picture and confirmed that he often hung around, paying for sex, particularly with younger women or girls. He was closer to a pedophile than a heterosexual.

Some of his band members, the Gay Wags, confessed to wondering about Greg's sexual orientation. His affectations were often exaggerated and more Gemini-worthy than natural. They had also never seen him with a man, but then again, they hadn't seen him with a partner of either gender. Whenever they thought about Greg's sex life, which apparently wasn't often, they assumed he was somewhat asexual.

Charles Haynes gave every appearance of deep shock when they awoke him - and Joan - in the middle of the night to question and inform him. But there was no question, in Montgomery's opinion, that Charlie had to have recognized his friend's 'voice' in those letters. He must have realized that Greg Hughes was the killer, yet he did nothing to assist the investigation other than hand over the evidence. Who knows how many people Hughes had tortured and murdered in the months before Charlie met with Monty? And would he have actually come forward if the PI hadn't called for an interview? If any of the allegations about obstruction of justice were proven, Haynes could be facing a prison sentence in his waning months. The agreement with the Vancouver Police Department not to prosecute was null and void. In any case, his family was no longer unaware of his 'sins'.

Greg's victims were numerous and largely unknown. There was no way to predict how many or where their remains might be found. He'd used sulfuric acid in his metallurgy, so the presence of the substance in his studio didn't raise any flags. However, in reality he stored a large amount of an illegal, highly concentrated form.

William, his voice still rough and low, abruptly interrupted Montgomery. "I know how many."

We all stared at Will. Suddenly, I remembered. *One-zero-zero, Emily. And he will not cooperate.*

"Ninety-nine," I said. "Greg must have had ninety-nine victims. He told me that William was supposed to be his one-zero-zero, his one hundredth."

My husband began shaking his head. He took a long sip of water and then spoke softly once more. "No. I wasn't supposed to be his one-zero-zero. *He* was. He wanted me to kill him and paint his body."

We all sat stunned, trying to digest this revelation.

"I didn't really believe him at first. Once I'd refused him, though, he threatened to shoot me if I didn't get up on the table and put the noose over my head. I figured I had a better chance on a rope than with a gun..." Will swallowed more water. The rest of us waited patiently, knowing he had to talk it through, even though his words were slow and difficult to hear. "I thought I could stay alive long enough to be missed. I kept hoping someone would come along and rescue me." He grinned, his eyes looking deeply into mine. "I just didn't expect it to be a cute little blond. Not that I remember much about your heroic efforts, my love, I was unconscious most of the time."

Montgomery and Jacob chuckled at the image of little me being the rescuer, but I could only force a slight smile. Inevitably, I would be giving Greg Hughes what he wanted, but at least I'd ensured it would be a long, painful death. All night, I had expected the guilt to overtake me, but it never happened. I just kept telling myself that *I was not going to think about that*.

"Don't ever do my job for me again, Emily," Monty said, putting his massive hand gently on my shoulder.

"Don't worry, I won't. I think I'll have some scars to remind me about going where I shouldn't go." I lifted my arms off the tray.

"As for you," Monty continued, turning to my husband, who had been nodding while I was 'scolded'. "Why in hell did you go racing off to that studio instead of calling me?"

Will raised his shoulders in an 'I-don't-know' shrug. "The only thing on my mind was to make absolutely certain that I was right. Greg had said 'Bill my boy,' on the telephone and I suddenly remembered how often he used that phrase when we worked together. The exact same phrase that was repeated in the letters. I just reacted. I went over there to confirm my suspicion. It was really stupid."

"Yes, it was, but thank god you're both safe." Montgomery was letting us both know his true priority.

"Why was he so twisted?" Will whispered, his face reflecting the shock that a man he'd known and worked with could be such a monster.

"Apparently his mother took off on the family when he was a small boy," Montgomery said. "She ended up on the streets of Vancouver, drug-addicted and tricking for her habit. Greg's father used to drag his son around Hastings at night, supposedly looking for the mother, but it seems he was just emphasizing the contempt he felt for his former wife by showing Greg what scum she and they all were. As far as anyone knows, Mrs. Hughes was long gone before Greg was very old, either dead or taken off. But his father kept taking him to the worst parts of the city, always teaching some kind of lesson. He died when Greg was in his late teens."

We shook our heads, overwhelmed by the horror that can be inflicted upon children, some of whom grow up to be even greater monsters than their parents.

"The legal team is going to hold a press conference this afternoon," Jacob said, thankfully changing the subject. "There is a huge group of reporters hanging around the hospital, which poor Montgomery had to wade through. Lucky for me, they have no idea who I am. Judge Belle called earlier to say that the Minister of Justice is going to be directly involved again, given the new developments. Of course they have to go through the wads of evidence first, but I'm sure it'll be quick. You might even hear the words this afternoon. *William Edward Thompson is innocent of all charges.*"

Will tightened his arms around my shoulders. He was silent, maybe because he'd talked too much, but more likely he was overcome with the emotions that Jacob's last statement evoked.

Jacob talked a while longer about the legal processes and the press conference. Greg Hughes's family, who were few in number, had been informed; his students had been told. It was a testament to his acting skills that the reactions were mostly of disbelief. I thought of the number of times we'd read in a newspaper, "neighbors said he/she was a quiet person." Were we so easily fooled or were we just not paying attention?

Endless thoughts swirled around my head. What about me? Did my actions last night make me a bad person? Why didn't I feel one iota of guilt? Was there something wrong with me?

I held it together until I saw her in the doorway. Round, light brown face, eyes deep and shining with love and sorrow, arms wide open to embrace me. My best friend, who accepted me for the person that I am, failings and talents, good and bad.

"Emily, Langford...I've come to bring you home."

"May!" I cried and burst into tears as we hugged.

As I lay there on my bed, unable to give my friend an equal hold because of my wounds, I let everything go. I cried for the missing years of loving my husband wholly, the lost babies, the death of my parents. I sobbed for Greg's tortured victims, the vulnerable, addicted, mentally ill people on whom he inflicted his hatred. I wept for Linda Courtnell and all her never realized potential. I shed tears for my husband, whose near death experience would haunt him forever. I cried for myself. I had been pushed into committing an act that had taken a little piece of my soul with it.

When I was a little calmer again, May took me for a spin in a wheelchair, out onto a balcony overlooking the courtyard of the hospital. She sat in the sun with me, holding my hand, not speaking, knowing instinctively that I had to work it out for myself.

I thought of the Ojibwa Seventh Fire legend and of Agnes's tale. In that fierce seventh test, as the world shifted, there was no one to guide our way. Even my own morals, the way I tried to live my life, had not been enough to keep the anger from bursting through. I'd held it, nurtured it, far too long.

"The young Anishinaabe will turn to the elders for direction to the traditional ways but many elders will have lost the spirit in the suffering of the past. The persistence of these eager youth in the meditative silence brought about through the drum beat will be rewarded as they come to hear the spirit of the forefathers in their heart. With the knowledge of the forefathers re-awakened they will once again be as they once were many moons before. In this time a new people will emerge." I thought of listening to the beat of my husband's heart in that studio of death, as he drew his life back again.

I recalled some words I had read about the Eighth Fire. "There will come a time when more and more people will be reborn in the ways of the ancients. These rekindled spirits will once again flow in harmony with the Eternal Spirit of the Grandfather and of Mother Earth. This Eternal Fire is the Eighth and Final Fire. Not everyone will find healing through its radiating warmth."

As I sat in the radiating warmth of the sunshine, with my friend's hand solid and supportive in mine, with the future ahead with my family, I was determined to forgive myself. I decided that I would find healing.

Chapter Twenty-Seven
June, 2010

The old Burchill Courthouse is not used as a seat of justice any more. In the past, the late Victorian brick structure had been the town jail as well as the community hall and courthouse. Nowadays, it is normally the venue for our village's amateur theatre. However, on this very warm day in June, its former significance is being resurrected.

Her Honor Claudia Belle flew all the way from Vancouver to be present, while Justice of the Peace Mary Jo Samuels will represent Ontario's jurisdiction and Renae Ogemah will represent the Children's Aid Society. Chief Dan Mahdahbee will add an Ojibwa blessing. All the legal presence is simply for pomp and circumstance, because the papers have all been signed and sealed beforehand, but we are overjoyed with the formalities of the ceremony.

Media swarms the big stone steps at the front, but they are not permitted entrance. On his microphone, turned to face his cameraman, one newspaper reporter hints that the presence of a famous private investigator, by the name of Montgomery Cardwell, demonstrates "a paranoid level of defense". However, it isn't true; Monty, with his wife and their two children, are invited guests, not a security measure. Someone else has been hired for that job, which is mainly because of the intense media interest. Although the curiosity about our story has waned in the last few months, this ceremony is drawing the attention back again.

Every seat in the stately old building is filled with friends and family. Friends from Vancouver and of course, many, many people from Burchill are here.

Cate walks up the aisle of the stately old building first. Her long red hair is piled high on top of her head. She chose a soft green dress with frilly sleeves, and she looks very feminine, very grown-up. Carly follows behind, walking steadily and skillfully with her artificial limbs, only the cane belying her difference. She decided to dye her hair back to its original colour, so the white no longer glares. Instead, the braids that fall gracefully down her back shine red and gold in the sunlight from the high transom windows. Trevor, dressed in a grey suit, tall and smiling, walks behind his sisters with more confidence than I thought possible. Benjaman, bouncing after his brother, waves and shakes hands with people as he passes by. May and I think he's hilarious. Meghan brings the line of children to a close, looking happy and calm, her hair cut short to show off her beautiful eyes.

Next, May and Alain Reneaux walk hand in hand, once in a while catching one another's eyes as close couples do. They look ecstatic, delighted to be able to celebrate this life-changing event with the community that nurtured and supported all of us. Later, the entire congregation is going to the Reneaux country home for barbeque, games, and lots of 'beverages of a social nature' for the adults.

I take my husband's hand and we, too, start down the aisle. Unsuccessfully, I fight the tears stinging my eyes as I smile at the people surrounding us.

There's my brother Sean, his wife Susan, and their three sons all the way from Ireland. I grasp their hands as I pass, so grateful for their presence.

In the last year and a half, many things have changed and many, by choice, have remained the same. William Edward Thompson received not only a complete exoneration but also an apology in the form of six million dollars from the British Columbia government. Charles Haynes died at age eighty-one from cancer. Charges against him had indeed been dropped for humanitarian reasons. Gregory Hughes died three days after his tragic accident.

The Linda Courtnell Centre for The Destitute was financed by contributions from the Thompson, Reneaux and Courtnell families. There is now a database for missing persons and those who are living on the streets, which is as accurate as possible. Caravans from LCC traverse cities every day, all over Canada, to provide sleeping bags, food, and hope.

The Anishinaabe Schools of Art opened in Vancouver and Toronto simultaneously to provide opportunities for students with potential but no means for paying college tuitions. Within the next few months, another two Anishinaabe Schools of Art will open in Nunavut; the delay is due to the fact that the buildings have to be constructed.

The Sanderson children are doing very well. Counseling continues, and perhaps always will, but Cate,

Carly and Trevor have begun making presentations in our area, speaking to other children about grief. There are still nightmares, some lingering insecurity, and a secret or two stashed away, but we have moved in the direction of forgiveness, optimism and happiness. Even I have begun to forgive myself.

Today is one more step in that process. The children wanted to make the event a community celebration to demonstrate to others how persistence and love can win over adversity. Their parents were more than happy to oblige.

When we arrive at the end of the aisle, we stand bathed in sunlight from the huge stained glass gracing the back wall. Chief Mahdahbee, Her Honor Belle, Justice Samuels, and Ms Ogemah, stand erect on the dais before us. They take turns speaking the words that publicly seal our decisions.

Her Honor Claudia Belle states, "The government of Canada, through the province of British Columbia, presents William Thompson with this formal apology."

"From this day forward," Renae Ogemah says, her spiky hair and flashing eyes at odds with the formality of her words, "this order of adoption shall be in effect."

Justice of the Peace Mary Jo Samuels pronounces, "From this day forward, these name changes shall be law."

Chief Dan Mahdahbee intones, "The People recognize these changes and endorse them."

Trevor, Benjaman and Meghan Taylor Reneaux.

Catherine and Carly Reneaux Taylor.

Thus the children have been adopted, yet remain siblings by name as well as nurture. We have ensured, legally, that should something happen to May and Alain or to William and me, the other couple will be their guardians. Never again will these beloved children be left alone.

My husband chose not to revert to William Thompson. That name had been used in vain for too long. He had become famous as an artist using my name. So he added William to Langford Taylor and we began a matriarchal tradition.

It is an unusual extended family. We had unusual beginnings. We are rich, infamous, famous and talented. We are definitely odd.

But what we share with everyone here today, as we stand and pledge our love and commitment, is the desire for happiness, the belief that the world can be a better place if only we choose well. Having exited the Seventh Fire, we have chosen the path of truth as we know it; we listen to the spirits of our forefathers. We prevailed through hardship, as many people have before us. Despite our wealth, we try to find joy in simple things and we are generous. Despite our past, we are thankful. The rewards have been, and will continue to be, boundless.

About The Author

****

Catherine Astolfo retired in 2002, after a very successful 34 years in education, in order to pursue her true passion - writing. Her short stories and poems have been published in a number of small Canadian presses. Her novel series, the Emily Taylor Mysteries, The Bridgeman, Victim, and Legacy, has received wide acclaim, including a Brampton Arts Award. Catherine has been involved with Sisbro & Co. Inc., a film production company, since its inception and remains as a silent partner. Her books have been optioned by Sisbro. She is a member of Crime Writers of Canada and Sisters in Crime. She lives in Brampton, Ontario with her husband and two cats.

5841396R0

Made in the USA
Charleston, SC
10 August 2010